19/4/18   GI   03|17

Return this item by the last date shown.
Items may be renewed by telephone or at
www.ercultureandleisure.org/libraries

east renfrewshire
CULTURE
and LEISURE

Barrhead:	0141 577 3518	Mearns:	0141 577 4979
Busby:	0141 577 4971	Neilston:	0141 577 4981
Clarkston:	0141 577 4972	Netherlee:	0141 637 5102
Eaglesham:	0141 577 3932	Thornliebank:	0141 577 4983
Giffnock:	0141 577 4976	Uplawmoor:	01505 850564

The Daughter of
Lady Macbeth

Ajay Close

SANDSTONEPRESS
HIGHLAND | SCOTLAND

First published in Great Britain
Sandstone Press Ltd
Dochcarty Road
Dingwall
Ross-shire
IV15 9UG
Scotland

www.sandstonepress.com

The publisher acknowledges subsidy from Creative Scotland towards
publication of this volume.

ISBN: 978-1-910985-42-7
ISBNe: 978-1-910985-43-4

Cover design by Brill Design
Typeset by Iolaire Typography Ltd, Newtonmore
Printed and bound by CPI Group (UK) Ltd, Croydon, CR0 4YY

For Michael Lynch

There is the land, and the sky. Squares of red earth broken by the plough, bleached fields of winter grass and, from horizon to horizon, the milky blue. The Romans laid this road. For a few miles here it serves as a farm track, before cutting through the hills on its way south towards England. The odd hiker can be seen as late as November, but by now the strath is deserted. This is the slack time in farming, calving and lambing both months away. The rat holes in the grainstore have been patched, the fences mended, the beech hedges cut down to boxes of black twigs whose ruthless planes, up close, are mostly air. A fitful wind rattles the last rusty leaves, which are sapless and brittle but still brilliant with life, like the rest of this landscape, at once muted and vivid in the cold sunshine.

He breaks the shotgun and takes two cartridges from his coat pocket, his face gaining the narrowed look it wears when he is absorbed in any task. Each cartridge slots into its chamber, the gun snaps together. A familiar excitement stirs within her, not exactly pleasure, not quite unease.

The baby kicks in her belly. She presses a hand to the spot. He notices, the way he notices everything, not remarking on it, salting the knowledge away. A wind-stunted blackthorn has grown out of the drystone wall. The lichen on its branches is the same diluted shade of green as the dress she bought to wear at her wedding. Antique silk crêpe de Chine, reeking of mothballs even after a week hung in front of an open window. She takes a deep breath to clear her nostrils of the memory. A hint of leaf mould carries from the coppice wood the locals call the *deil's grun*. Sun reflects white from the metalled road, a faint warmth on her face snatched away by the wind.

She follows him into the field, treading carefully. It will be weeks before the ground thaws. When he offers her the gun she laughs, but it's part of the game to pretend she might take it. Their eyes lock. He has this way of stopping the world, so her breathing slows and the blood runs backwards in her veins. He looks up at the sky and she feels her own face lift as if an invisible cord stretched between them.

'I'm not going to shoot a buzzard,' she says.

'I'm not asking you to.'

'What then?'

He nods down the slope.

A fox trots along the bottom of the field. Only the second she has seen in the flesh, and the first was a shadow slinking across the road, the discs of its eyes caught in a car's headlights. The same resistant glitter she sees in him sometimes. Aren't foxes supposed to be red? This one is a startling cinnamon against the wind-silvered grass. She tells herself the farm is part of its territory, he knew it would be here, and still she half believes he has conjured it out of thin air.

He is watching her with those blue eyes that at anything further than kissing distance seem jet black. The wind worries at the hair not covered by his cap. He hasn't bathed since yesterday, or shaved. Stubble covers his neck and cheeks, scratching at her across the air. Though he's well-wrapped against the cold, with a couple of jumpers under his army surplus greatcoat, she can trace the outline of his body. She

2

knows how the tendon twists over his forearm, the play of muscle under his sleeve. He leans towards her, or perhaps she moves. The power shifts. For a moment she leaves her own body and inhabits his suspense, feels the sensual weight of whatever she is about to do next.

The shotgun seems heavier than when she was aiming at the clays.

'What if I miss?'

'You won't.'

He smiles as he always smiles when she submits to his will, and she feels, as she always feels at this smile, simultaneously titillated and detached. Only playing. She lifts the gun to her shoulder the way he has taught her, nestling into the cheek plate, lining up the sights, noting the movement of the barrels between her inward and outward breaths. Silently she urges the animal to run. Not that it'll make any difference, she'll hit it anyway. It's like perfect pitch, a knack so innate it doesn't feel like a skill. And to think she might have lived her whole life never guessing it was inside her. Her quarry changes course, moving uphill. She slides her finger off the trigger and looks at him, so accustomed to the tension between them that the instant it slackens she knows something is wrong.

He takes back the gun. She turns to see a figure coming down off the ridge. His flannel trousers are streaked with mud. His camel cashmere coat, so smart on the streets of Edinburgh, looks ridiculous here. Fantasy has been her companion through these idle months but she has never let herself imagine this most predictable of encounters and now it is upon her, she feels – what? Dread in the pit of her stomach, a fizz of excitement in her blood. A steely thread of triumph. She closes her eyes. When she opens them again he is near enough to be heard should he choose to speak, moving towards them with a rapid, determined stride. And yet she knows: all things being equal, he would rather not. She has left him no choice. Now that she has seen him it is impossible

3

to look away, but her senses remain attuned to the boy at her side, the loose-limbed insult of his stance, the loaded gun balanced in his hand. What is he doing? He has told her countless times, always point the barrel at the ground.

How *old* her old lover looks to her now. He stops a few feet away, far enough uphill to cancel the boy's superior height. His ragged jawline is new, and those circles under his eyes. Very little in his face recalls the man she first met: so charming and attentive and impressively well-connected, half his circle moneyed, the other half with land. As her friends said, *quite a catch*. Not that she was looking for a husband particularly, but she would have been mad to pass up the chance. All at once her flesh remembers him, the smile in his eyes when she undressed, his hoarse whisper in bed. The next moment she knows: he's here because he once owned her. He's the type to defend his property even if he no longer wants it.

'If you'd told me you were coming,' she says, 'I'd have put on some lipstick.'

He ignores her, his eyes on the boy. In that clipped but ringing voice that still lifts the hairs on her neck, he says, 'I want a word with you.'

'Don't,' she breathes.

Sunlight catches the reddish glints in his hair and the granular skin that has always reminded her of sandstone. She thought of him, and by extension all men, as mineral. Until the boy, who is so unignorably animal.

'You like pregnant girls, do you? Knowing somebody else has already done the business? Sounds a bit bloody queer to me.'

'*Please*, Brod.' But she is to be allowed no say in this. There is no avoiding what is going to happen. It will follow its own course. That is part of her punishment.

The boy's hand tightens around the gun. The twitch of his lips is almost a smirk. 'If you're wanting a square go, I'm a wee bit busy the now.'

4

'You think this is a joke?'

His sandy neck is flushed, a bad sign. She has never seen anyone look at him with the challenge that glitters in the boy's eyes. The hostility between them feels oddly intimate. Strangers as they are, they share an understanding. She is at once the pretext for this confrontation and entirely beside the point.

When the wind drops, the distance between the three of them seems to shrink. She can smell his aftershave and hear the faint rasp in his breath. The boy does not seem to be breathing at all. Every muscle in his body is tensed. Unnoticed, the fox slips under the hedge on the far side of the field.

Moving to put herself between them, she stumbles on the frozen ground. The boy reaches out to steady her, and the aggression in Brod's face gives way to something like pain. At last he looks at her. 'Was it mine?' he says, as if the child she carries is dead, or dead to him. She was so certain he loved her, as certain as she has been for the past few months that he feels nothing. Once she would have risen to the challenge, licked her lips, sparkled her eyes, and won him back. She could still do it, even eight-and-a-half months gone – and what then: he loves her, until he's sure of her again? A wave of revulsion washes through her. It seems to come from her belly, as if kicked up by the child in outrage at his question. *Was it mine?*

'If you can ask that, you never knew me.'

'And he knows you, does he, your farm boy?'

She will never understand why she says it: 'With him I'm my real self.'

Later she will tell the police no one could have anticipated what happened next, but just beforehand she has a sort of presentiment. A blind lowers over her brain and, when it lifts again, though their surroundings are unchanged, the world is inside out. Everything that follows is already foretold. That crow flapping into flight. The sparkle of a car windscreen on the far side of the strath. The rabbit trapped by a stoat in the wood, its screams spreading like a stain through the air. The noise goes on and on. It's the boy who breaks the spell, wrapping his free arm around her and pulling her towards him so the soft bulk of her bumps against his bone and sinew. His body heat always makes her shiver, with or without clothes. Brod makes a grab for the gun. It happens with the terrible slowness of all irreversible events, yet there is no time at all between the shiver and the struggle and her scream and the flash and the shotgun's deafening blast.

PART I

I have given suck, and know
How tender 'tis to love the babe that milks me:

Macbeth, William Shakespeare

Cheese

Frankie split the bulb of garlic and I heard the papery skin strip from the clove, the creaking victory of the crusher, the percussive spitting of hot oil. A clatter as the lid settled on the pan. I was zesting lemons, a job I hate: trying to separate peel from pith when really it's all one. The grater made its grating noise. His knife sawed back and forth over the wooden board. The rosemary twigs splintered. The syboes, shorn of their whiskers, bled a little colourless juice. That complaining floorboard as he crossed to the stove. I don't use a lemon-squeezer, having a strong grip. A twisting column of bitterness splashed from my hand to the bowl. The saucepan lid clattered again, his spoon clanking as he drove it around the pan. I found the carton of cream pushed to the back of the fridge, a rubber *thunk* as the door slammed shut. The university clock struck noon, making it nearly an hour since we had last spoken.

'Did you get the pecorino?' I asked.

He didn't look up.

We used to enjoy cooking together. The gentle hysteria of would-it-be-ready? Grumbling affectionately about our guests.

'I said...'

'I thought you were getting it.'

'It was on your list.'

'You were in the offie. You only had to go next door.'

'And then we'd have two lots, if you'd done what you were supposed to.'

From simple enquiry to sniper fire in seventeen seconds. I didn't want to. I didn't think he wanted to, not really. And yet somehow we couldn't resist. When had we become this sort of couple? Ten years before we'd never had these conversations. We prepared elaborate meals for two to music, and slow-danced around the kitchen, the windows fogging with the steam of dishes we didn't always get round to eating before one of us dragged the other into bed. We argued, if we argued at all, about Dave Eggers versus Zadie Smith, the Arctic Monkeys versus the Strokes, Lindt versus Green & Blacks, not how many months had passed since he last squirted bleach down the loo, or why I rode the clutch in the BMW.

I scooped up the car keys. 'I'll go.'

'What d'you need the car for? They sell it in the corner shop.'

I stared at him for a moment, then put the keys in my pocket. 'Did you get everything else?'

'Aye.'

'Rocket? Sour cream?'

'Back off, Freya.'

The supermarket was clogged with families buying twice what they needed to get another fifty per cent free. Suitcase-sized cartons of cereal, jeroboams of milk, cellophane pillow-cases stuffed with crisps. When I got home our neighbour's new Barbarian was double-parked outside. She found it trickier than the Merc to get into tight spaces. The wind had changed direction. Mostly our corner of Glasgow reeked of diesel and fresh paint, but that day I could smell the farmers muck-spreading the Renfrewshire fields.

Inside, the house was pungent with garlic and rosemary. Frankie was sitting at the kitchen table. I dropped the bag on the newspaper he was reading.

'Pasteurised pecorino.'

He pushed the cheese to one side and turned the page.

10

'Are you all done then?' I asked. The worktop was buried in potato peelings, cauliflower leaves, capsicum seeds, torn cellophane.

'I'm taking five minutes.'

'You know those kids get cranky if they eat too late.'

'I told you, back off.'

Back off was a code phrase, a way of pushing the red button. Too often I exploded, allowing him to start the war while seeming to want to avoid one. (All our rows were fought as if adjudicated by a fair, yet foolable third party.) But there wasn't time for a fight that day: Kenny and Ruth were coming to lunch. It would be a relief to feign harmony for a couple of hours. There was even a chance that, by the time they left, we'd have forgotten why we were fighting and could laugh about our friends' latest foibles over the clearing-up. We tended to notice the same things. He knew the paths my thoughts would take, just as I had a feel for the chain of memory and association in his head. For years this had been a source of jokes, but recently we had been exploring the darker side of marital telepathy.

He cocked his head. 'Was that the door?'

'They won't be here till one.'

'You said the back of twelve.'

'Ruth rang to say could we make it later.'

'And you didn't bother to tell me?'

I switched on the electric whisk. For the next few minutes conversation was impossible. When the cream was standing in soft peaks, I said, 'It slipped my mind.'

He put four tomatoes in a bowl.

'There's a private clinic,' he picked up the kettle and poured boiling water over them. Tendrils of steam rose into the air. 'In Perthshire.'

We both knew it had to happen, although neither of us had raised the possibility until now. It was a solution – perhaps – but also irrevocable acknowledgement of The Problem.

'They get results,' he said.

'By cherry-picking their customers.'

'So if they take us we'll know we're in with a chance.'

Silently the tomatoes split their skins. I lifted the pan lid and checked the pearly mush of garlic and onions.

'This is about both of us, Freya.'

I knew what he meant, and knew he was claiming the moral high ground by not saying it.

We had reached that stage of material comfort where the only thing that mattered was the thing we could not have. And since we could not have it, we could not allude to it. And since we could not allude to it, it was all we talked about, but in ways we couldn't anticipate until the words jumped out of our mouths. Everything meant something else. We weren't just having friends to Saturday lunch, we were having them to lunch so they could bring their children, so Frankie could play at being a dad for the afternoon. A bittersweet pleasure. He hadn't forgotten to buy the pecorino: the Frankie who feared he'd never be more than a make-believe dad was registering his protest at the dietary hoops I was putting myself through, the pointless disruption of our old easy routine. And there was an extra layer of meaning, apparent only to me. Should I ever fulfil his heart's desire and bear him a couple of children, he would do his best, but he couldn't promise to notice when their nappies needed changing. He might forget to pick them up from nursery the odd day, or take them somewhere without a bottle, or leave them strapped in their car seats in a heat wave with all the windows closed. His fathering would have much in common with his style of partnering. He would love his offspring dearly, and play with them – when he wasn't distracted by work – and his sense of who he was would change forever, but the responsibility would all be mine. Just thinking about it made my blood pressure soar as if I were already half-dead with sleepless nights. So it was no trivial oversight to suggest I patronise a deli that sold listeria in the guise of unpasteurised cheese. Why would he do it? The only answer I could come up with was that he was no less angry with me.

Every morning I reached down to check the consistency of my mucus, waiting for it to pull between my fingers in jellied strands. For the next five days, before and after work and last thing at night, Frankie and I made love – or, at least, had sex. Unfailingly, the following week I felt a tenderness in my breasts. The smell of cigarettes made my gorge rise. I had never realised there was so much meat in the world. Neighbourhood barbecues on sultry afternoons, Sunday mornings greasy with bacon and egg, commuters on the station platform wolfing down their roll and sausage. Once these smells would have revolted me, now I gulped them in with the greedy thought *perhaps I'm craving*. For the last week of the cycle I was unbearable, yawing between joy and savagery, shopping for sleepsuits one minute, the next cursing myself for having dared to hope. And finally came the monthly rage, a physical need to destroy, or fuck, which in its orgy of blood could look like the same thing. The best sex Frankie and I had these days was when there wasn't a chance in hell of conceiving. And then it all began again. The waiting; the grim, timetabled coupling; the heightened sensory awareness; turning in front of the mirror to see if I had bigger breasts...

Yet for most of my life I had managed fine without biology. Except at school, where it was one of my straight As. I was never one of those hormonal women, the type who referred *sotto voce* to 'the time of the month' and burst into tears for absolutely no reason, taking the next day off work or, worse, soldiering on bent double over their desks. I'd been deaf to the ticking clock. Which was where I heard Frankie's unspoken accusation: I had frittered away my fecund years only to decide at the age of forty that I'd like to have a baby. And if he too had been late in this realisation, he wasn't the one

13

whose reproductive equipment was nearing its use-by date.

He crossed to the stove and turned down the gas. 'It's three hundred quid for the first consultation. I'll pay it.'

'I thought this was about both of us.'

'You'll need to be there.' He took the skinned tomatoes out of the boiling water and added them to the pan. 'If that's OK.'

'You hate private medicine.'

'You're forty-three. The NHS won't touch us.'

His phone rang. It was on the shelf. We both grabbed but I was quicker. I handed it across.

'Frankie here... how're ye doin', doll?'

It was Lauren at the studios, I could tell by his sexy growl. He walked into the hall, closing the door behind him. I started clearing the debris off the worktop.

He came back into the kitchen, slipping the phone in his pocket.

'What?' I knew what, had made a little bet with myself that this would happen.

'There's no one to cover the Aberdeen game.'

I was careful not to react.

'Dougie's got a bug. He can't move more than six feet from the cludgie.'

'Sounds messy,' I said.

For a couple of seconds nothing happened, then I lost control and laughed. It wasn't just that he was unambiguously in the wrong. My refusal to point this out was such a deniable form of goading.

There was a suspenseful moment before he, too, saw the funny side.

'You'll never get to Aberdeen in time,' I said.

'They're playing in Paisley.'

'You can stay for the first hour with Kenny and Ruth, then.'

He confiscated the cloth I was using to wipe the counter and stowed it out of reach, but in a matter-of-fact way that broke the chain of provocation linking him forgetting the

14

pecorino, me driving to the supermarket, his cooking mess, and my martyred decision to clear it up.

'C'mere.' He put his hands on my shoulders.

We eyed each other, wanting reconciliation but still close enough to our fighting selves to be wary of premature embraces.

'You're a wee bitch,' he said tenderly, 'aren't you?'

I shrugged modestly.

He sighed. 'And I'm a lucky bastard to have you. You chose me over every other guy you could've had – I'm fucked if I know why, but you did. You think I take it for granted?' He pulled me close, his lips warm on my ear. 'I love you, Freya Cavalle, and if you give me a wean I'll be the happiest guy in Glasgow.'

We heard a knock on the window. Ruth, Kenny and the kids were grinning at us from the other side of the glass.

'Just don't turn into your mother,' he murmured, as we broke apart from the kiss.

Soap

'Darling!'

Princes Street was packed with tourists, shoppers, pipers, police and placard-carriers, but it took me all of three seconds to locate Lilias: she was the one everybody was staring at.

'Over here, darling!'

She was wearing a soft leather skirt and a white linen shirt secured at the neck with an antique silver brooch. Her white-gold hair, pinned in an Edwardian cloud, was a scene-stealing melodrama of elegance and escape. I caught the blueish translucence under her eyes, the cream, pink, white of skin, lips, teeth, and familiarity filled in the rest. Radiance, vivacity, a touch of Lady Muck. She would be seventy in November. She was my mother.

We grazed cheeks and she held me at arm's length. 'Is it safe for you to be here?' Her eyes flicked to a couple of farmhands eating ice creams. 'They're everywhere.'

'Looks like they left the pitchforks at home.'

'You won't be laughing when they recognise you.'

'They won't be recognising me.'

'It's very *petit-bourgeois*, darling, this shrinking violet thing. I can't think where you get it from.'

'Children pick up all sorts of bad habits when they don't have a mother for nine months of the year.'

I was sorry as soon as I'd said it.

She glanced over at the columns of the Royal Scottish Academy, a trick she'd learned from Gielgud when they met doing commercial voice-overs: focus on something beautiful, forget the fluffed take.

'New coat?' she asked.

'Not really.'

'I approve. Very slimming.'

Lilias always looked the same to me, but I took a punt on the brooch. 'Is that art deco?'

'Hardly, darling, with a pie-crust edge.' Her upper lip lifted just high enough to show her perfect teeth without disclosing the worrying things happening at the gum. 'You are funny, I've had this for ages. But I do have something to show you. I've had a few repeat fees, thanks to good old Gold, and Susie Lennox is always telling me about this marvellous man in Stockbridge who's so clever with his hands, so I thought I'd give him a try.'

She turned, presenting me with the back of her head, and I saw the silver clasp in her hair.

'You wouldn't believe the palaver I had to go through to get it. I nearly bought myself a Nicole Farhi coat instead. He wouldn't take a detailed brief – he wouldn't even show me a sketch. I had to trust him.'

'It's lovely.'

'You don't like it,' she said.

'No, I do. It's lovely.'

She shrugged and looked away.

Belatedly I found the line she had scripted for me: 'It's very you.'

The face she turned towards me was flirtatiously combative. 'I told him, "You don't even know me, you can't expect me to commission a piece on that basis." I was ready to walk out, and he was ready to see me go. He's a proud man. He'll work for you, but you have to give him his due as an artist. We're very alike in some ways. We talked about it.'

'So who won?'

I saw her jib at my choice of verb. In Lilias's world everybody was happy when she got her own way. 'We compromised. I said I didn't need a drawing, but I wanted at least three adjectives, and he said it was going to be romantic, traditional and absolutely contemporary.'

We laughed, not necessarily for the same reason.

A gang of farmers' wives swept along the pavement towards us in fashion-crime jeans with sleeveless body-warmers over their sweaters. I caught the reek of mince and onions as they passed. Lilias moved out of their way without seeing them.

'I thought we'd have lunch at that little place in Bruntsfield,' she said.

'I'd rather eat in town—'

Her expression acquired a bright fixity of purpose.

'It'll take us for ever to get out there.'

'I'll be going there anyway.'

'Yes, but *I'll* have to get back into town before spending an hour on the train.'

'No one likes a whiner, darling.'

That shut me up.

She glanced down at the half-dozen carrier bags she had accumulated in the course of a morning's shopping. 'Do you think you could give me a hand?'

We walked the route of the march in reverse, so I saw it all: the tractors and combines in their clouds of exhaust, the T-shirts proclaiming farmers an endangered species, the banners opposing the closure of village schools and post offices, the cow with '30p a pint' shaved into its coat.

'Don't stare, darling.'

Lilias looked bored, having the professional's intolerance of amateur theatrics, but I was agog. The mounted contingent was at least a hundred strong. Hunt masters bulging out of their red coats, pony-club sweethearts, a posse of giants on Clydesdales who looked like rugby players up for a laugh. Then came the infantry. Men with straw on their boots and faces weathered to a beetroot flush. Solid, square-jawed lairds squiring dowdy women with long necks and high, intelligent foreheads. And everywhere I looked, the unbelievably old: bodies aged beyond gender, whittled down to liver-spotted skin and bone, but still very erect in their bearing. Who were these people? They never showed up in the peat-heated country pubs where Frankie and I ate Sunday lunch. They weren't in the car commercials filmed in the Highlands, or the fashion spreads shot in the glens. They were barely a statistical footnote in the reports that crossed my desk, and yet here were twenty thousand of them parading the streets of Edinburgh.

'I hope Colin's had the good sense to stay away.'

Colin was the Minister for Rural Affairs, whom she'd never met but, trading on my notional connection, called by his first name.

'He's up in Easter Ross, opening a community learning centre.'

'Wise man. Perhaps you should have taken a leaf out of his book.'

'Why?'

She looked at me.

'It's not even my department, Ma.'

'You're in power.'

'No, no I'm not. *Politicians* are in power, I'm a middle-ranking *civil servant*.' I heard my voice and hated its sarcastic measure, but I had lost count of the number of times I'd tried to put her right about this. 'I don't take political decisions, and I don't have a well-known face. *Frankie* is famous. He appears on *television*. The *Herald* once printed a picture of my *shoulder* when I was sitting next to Frankie at a testimonial dinner for Norrie "Nutmeg" MacAllister, but it's not very likely anyone's going to recognise me from it.'

I took a breath. I'd said enough. No one recognised Lilias either, unless they had a photographic memory for corpses. Over the past decade her most reliable source of income had

19

been police dramas. If she was lucky, there was a suspenseful scene before she met the killer, or an explanatory flashback at the end, but often her performance consisted of lying sheeted and immobile on a mortuary slab. It was true she turned heads on the street, and that some of these people thought they knew her, but only because she put so much effort into making them look.

'I've been thinking,' she said, 'Colin should get himself a Barbour.'

And then I saw them: a woman in her thirties and a teenage girl, uncannily alike, so it took a moment to pinpoint the details that made the elder seem a flawed copy. A pouching in her face, heavier breasts under her baggier sweater. They were leaning in to each other, like best friends it seemed to me, although another observer might have described them as exactly like mother and daughter. The girl was having trouble getting her words out. Each time she tried to speak, her mouth quivered. She pinched her lips together, but it only made her giggle all the more, while the older woman waited, her calm enclosing the two of them in a bubble of impregnable space. I had been watching mothers and daughters for as long as I could remember, but that day I put myself in the mother's shoes, with the light of the girl's wide-open gaze on my face, and her body angled towards mine, and my heart overflowing with pride and love. Could I give a child that absolute attention – not just for an afternoon, but every minute – or would I discover I too carried the Medea gene? The girl straightened up and finished her sentence, and the bubble that enclosed them became a vacuum of suspense, until the mother's composure cracked in uproarious laughter and, turning her head, her shining eyes grazed mine.

'I think our waiter's taken a fancy to you.'

It was four o'clock. I had heard a great deal more about the silversmith who was so clever with his hands, and Roderick

20

who was writing a screenplay for her, and the butch lesbian who loitered in the changing room when she took her Tuesday ballet class. They were casting the older Fonteyn in a miniseries. The script didn't call for dancing but she wanted to colour every gesture with authentic grace. I had failed to mention any admirers, manually adept or otherwise, and had no social or professional triumphs I cared to report: obviously I needed the fillip a smitten waiter would provide. As far as I could tell, he had no interest in either of us.

He approached with the bill and she gave me an arch look. He took this to mean that I was paying.

'Thank you, darling, that was lovely.'

'Lovelier than all the other undressed chicken salads I've watched you eat?'

I said it teasingly, but she pulled the barely-perceptible frown she used to minimise facial lines. 'Didn't you like your crème brulée?'

'I wasn't mad on you correcting my pronunciation when I ordered it, but the crème brulée was fine.'

'You didn't finish your soufflé.'

'It was a bit on the rich side.'

'Oh dear,' she said, in the voice she used when I was being difficult.

Lilias always encouraged me towards the heart-attack dish on the menu. Frankie said it was vicarious self-indulgence, but I knew better. It wasn't enough to keep herself slim: others had to grow fatter.

Still, I got my own back every once in a while.

'It's bad for you, you know: always eating the same food. You need a varied diet.'

She shrugged. 'We all have to die of something. Even me, you'll be relieved to hear.'

I must have looked surprised.

'Just a joke, darling.'

I squinted at her. For a moment the air had buzzed with

21

the static of improvisation, but Lilias was an actress of the old school, she always worked to a script. Until now lunch had followed its usual course. For the first hour she had done most of the talking, growing even more animated with her second glass of wine. When she was hungry enough to want me to take over, she had asked for my news, and I had drawn a blank. (Once, long ago, I'd boasted of a complimentary memo from the Perm Sec, and she'd replied, 'Will they give you gold ink for your rubber stamp?') She had not yet recommended a skin consultant or personal shopper or trainer in the Alexander technique, but when she did I would refuse to write down the name, and she would give me a lecture on sagging pores or slouching or dressing like a Jehovah's Witness, or *this shrinking violet thing*. Lilias believed in recycling every word of praise that came her way. The youthfulness of her feet, remarked on by her pedicurist. A wardrobe mistress's surprise at her slender waist. The casting director who compared her singing voice to Streisand's (though he didn't offer her the part). There was always at least one man in her thrall, to the chagrin of a fatter and less charming woman. It's possible she reported these tributes in the hope that I would follow suit, but I was a bureaucrat, working with other bureaucrats. We didn't spend our days exclaiming over each other's feet.

Between mouthfuls of crème brulée (mine) and sips of unsweetened black coffee (hers), we had discussed her next audition. A spinster of the parish due to meet her maker at the hands of a cross-dressing curate in one of those English murder mysteries that sell so well on the Pacific Rim. She was wondering if RP would suit the character better than Mummerset? Would a stammer be gilding the lily and, if so, how about a lisp? Once, in my door-slamming, denunciatory adolescence, I had accused her of being more convincing as an actress than she was as a mother. If anything, she had seemed pleased.

Yet I always looked forward to these lunches, always hoped the next time would be different, and her eyes would light up with unfeigned delight while we took turns on centre stage, the air around us shimmering with all the things we had to say. And once in a while it was almost like that. I'd be less shrinking and she less *large*, and a snatch of dialogue overheard at the next table would trip us into laughter. 'What did I tell you?' Frankie would say when I got home. 'You just need to give her a break.' But at our next meeting she would be her usual all-singing, all-dancing, all-oxygen-stealing self, while I sat and watched from the other side of the table.

'Before I forget, darling—'

She reached down for a cream cartridge-paper bag with the name of an unfamiliar store woven into its ribbon handles. I made ready to admire another present to herself.

'I bought you a little something.'

She had faultless timing, have I mentioned that?

'Why?'

She gave me her amused-indulgent look – *does there have to be a reason?* – and I felt the helplessness that overcame me whenever Lilias displayed anything construable as affection.

'You didn't need to.'

'I know I didn't *need* to.' She leaned towards me, lowering her voice as if sharing a secret. '*I wanted to.*'

As I broke the monogrammed sticker sealing the bag I guessed what was inside. Every Christmas without fail she gave me five tissue-wrapped Bronnley lemon soaps. As a child I had loved their Anna Neagle-ish whiff of post-war London. She'd kept three in her green theatrical trunk along with all her old programmes bound in pink ribbon, a tin of Crowe's Cremine, and several fluff-furred sticks of Leichner No 9. Tempted by the mimetic shape and scent, not so very different from the smell of sherbet lemons, I had actually licked one of these soaps. Not a mistake I made twice. But that was thirty-odd years ago. So why did she persist? Laziness? A coded

23

attempt to civilise me? Or was it a reference to a moment in the past when I had actually approximated the child she wanted? This remote possibility was the reason I could never tell her I had accumulated close to a hundred Bronnley lemon soaps in a bin bag at the back of the hall cupboard. I'd used them as drawer-fresheners for years until I worked out the connection between my anomie in the mornings and the fact that all my underwear smelled of Lilias.

I lifted the bag to my nose and inhaled. 'Thank you, Ma.'

'To tide you over until Christmas,' she said.

The presents I chose for her were a little more ingenious, but not much. Each December I bought the ghost-written memoirs of some awful old ham. Whatever the cover price, there was a cheapness about these books: the jaunty title (as often as not, the catchphrase of a 1970s television sitcom); the flashlit black-and-white photographs of the subject standing next to a glassy-eyed theatrical knight, or shaking hands with Jim Callaghan, or peering down Diana Dors' cleavage; the blurred print on substandard paper; the way the pages fell out when the spine was cracked. With the books I gave Lilias this didn't tend to happen, so I knew she never read them, but she had fifteen minutes of pleasure looking herself up in the index.

For a few moments we stared at each other across the tablecloth. Lilias's silences were almost always a cue, but this one felt empty, and full, and frightening, a pause that neither of us controlled.

A rhythmic chanting from the march carried through the open window.

'I nearly married a farmer,' she said.

She collected proposals. Architect, doctor, concert pianist, racehorse trainer, hotel manager (a wee bit below her usual standard, but it was a five-star hotel). Now I had to add a farmer to the list.

'What went wrong?'

24

'He was a *farmer,* darling.'

'He must have thought he was in with a chance.'

'He was very good-looking.' She traced the pattern of the damask tablecloth with the tip of her ring finger, a familiar piece of stagecraft. I prepared myself for the usual story of extravagant devotion, the broken engagement to another woman. She made the breath catch in the back of her throat. 'Very cruel, country people.'

The waiter returned with my change. I thought how seldom Lilias had given me anything outside Christmas and birthdays. I wanted to reciprocate in some way.

'I've something to tell you.'

She was watching herself in the mirrored wall and took a moment to adjust her gaze.

'Frankie and I have been trying for a baby.'

She sparkled her eyes in congratulation. I ploughed on.

'But we don't seem to be getting anywhere, so we're going to look at this place that does assisted conception.'

The sparkle faded. Oddly for a woman who had made a career out of artifice, she disapproved of tampering with nature. Botox, eye-lifts, tummy tucks, test-tube babies. There was a moral difference between making the best of oneself and loading the dice.

Opening her handbag, she took out her powder compact and used the mirror to retouch her lipstick, bringing her lips together with a faint practised smack. After inspecting the result, she closed the bag and, demonstrating once again her genius for the *coup de théâtre*, said,

'Darling, I've got cancer.'

I made the five o'clock train back to Glasgow with seconds to spare. It was drawing away from the platform before I'd sat down. The carriage was packed with commuters and shoppers, an obstacle course of laptops and Harvey Nichols bags along the aisle. One seat left, at a table. I took out some paperwork. In the seat next to mine a small girl was fiddling with a device which emitted continuous electronic arpeggios. I put the file back in my case.

On the other side of the table, the mother gave me a rueful grin. Twenty-five going on forty. Tired, too thin, doing her best, smelling of the detergent the clapped-out machine no longer rinsed from her clothes. I was surprised she could afford the peak-rate fares. In the window seat beside her was a child of uncertain age, toddler-size but lacking a toddler's doughy features: a perfectly-proportioned wee man. He was sleeping, not the way adults sleep on trains – head lolling, body still defended – but wholly abandoned, deep in his dreams. His mother watched over him, and I watched with her, noticing the long lashes at rest on his pale cheek, a faint rosy tinge around the delicate nostrils, the translucent curl of his one exposed ear. His mouth was more taupe than pink, with a shallow scoop in the upper lip. I too had the urge to run a fingertip down his nose, tracing the line of that heart-breaking profile. He stirred, twitching away his mother's touch, burrowing deeper into the dusty plush. She caught my eye, biting her lip in mock-remorse, her pinched face flooding with tenderness, and I thought: *there is nothing I wouldn't give to change places with you.*

1972

That first morning Lili rises early, tiptoeing past the kitchen where Mrs S is clanging pans on the Rayburn, cooking pigs' blood or salty porridge or whatever they have for breakfast on a farm. Life could be worse. She could be in Edinburgh, tucking a cryptic note under Brod's windscreen wipers, some grubby little private dick breathing down her neck. This way, he'll get his divorce without being taken to the cleaners, and the next time she sets foot in George Street she'll be as svelte as the day she left. And absence makes the cock grow fonder. Meanwhile, it's cheap here, and anonymous, and Mrs S shows no inclination to chat, thank God. (Lili could never befriend a woman who sits down to dinner in a pinnie and wellingtons.) Eggs from the henhouse. Butter from the churn. Three meals a day cooked by someone else.

But what the hell is she supposed to do with herself?

The turf-scented breeze is a godsend after the farmhouse smell of coal fires and last night's stewed meat. She can't risk the yard in case she's seen from the kitchen, so she goes the other way, round the corner, between the dairy and the grassy triangle of paddock ruled by Ronnie the chestnut gelding. A shaven coat with the gloss of polished rosewood, his mane and tail blueish-black, a white star on his forehead like a promise of sweetness, the effect rather ruined by his tobacco-brown teeth.

Showing Lili around the farm yesterday, Mrs S addressed him as a *naughty boy* she really shouldn't indulge, passing by the paddock with a couple of Victory Vs in her pocket, but who could resist? It was hard to reconcile her *coochy-coochy* tone with the malign presence in the three-sided field. (Not to mention the presence of his enormous purple erection.) He kept shaking his head. To get rid of the flies, Mrs S said, but there weren't any flies, just a sliver of white in his rolling eyes, and his lips curling back from those revolting teeth. When they moved on to the byre, Lili glanced over her shoulder. He was still watching. His front hooves drummed a tattoo on the grass before rearing up to churn the air.

After dinner she went back. The light was fading. The sky was full of rooks flying home to roost in the three-hundred-year-old oak. She walked up to the fence. He came to meet her but would not let her pat him even when she yanked up a clump of long grass and fed it to him, soil-clogged roots and all. But it's morning now, one of those mornings when everything is made new. The sun is warm on her bare arms, the sky is duck-egg blue, the cropped grass has a mossy sheen. Walking towards her from the far end of the enclosure, Ronnie could be a painting by Stubbs.

'Hello, Ronnie,' she says, 'or are you Reggie today?'

Ronnie regards her with his intelligent gaze for several seconds before his powerful neck reaches over the fence and his long head lunges at her groin. She leaps back, startling the horse, which wheels away from her, shaking his head, turning one way, then the other, in a tight circle of agitation. His rolling eyes show their unnerving crescent of white.

'He thinks you've something in your pocket for him.'

She turns. It's the son – what's his name, Jake? – in the sweater he had on last night, the same sweater he was wearing a fortnight ago. That same dirty face, too. What are the chances? Even now she can hardly believe it. She should have left the moment she spotted him, but the room was so astoundingly cheap, and she had been looking all day. Even after seven hours' sleep, the thought of having to find somewhere else exhausts her. It's awkward, of course, but she'll bring him round. Actors talk a lot of rot about their craft. It's mostly a matter of getting people to like you.

'You don't want to be frightened,' the boy says. 'He's big, right enough, but he reckons you're the threat.'

'I'm not frightened. He just made me jump.'

'Is that right?'

The sun brings out the suppleness of his skin under his high shaving line.

Lili gives a charming half-shrug. 'Well, perhaps a little bit frightened.'

'You'll need to get over that.'

He takes hold of her wrist. The horse's alarm has subsided, but his ears still twitch. The velvety nose sniffs her palm with a tickle of warm breath. She shivers, pulling free of the boy's grip, but her nerves remember the light, sure circle of his fingers around her wrist.

'What do I do now?'

'It's not what you do, it's what you are. If that's right, he'll smell it on you—'

She raises an eyebrow.

'It's like any relationship, when you get down to it.'

Gingerly she places the flat of her hand on Ronnie's muscular neck. The chestnut coat is coarse and warm, faintly gritty. She takes in the veins standing proud on his gleaming haunches, the carved muscle of his breast, and smiles. It's the first time she has felt at peace for weeks. Stroking a horse. Such a banal act, yet it holds her completely absorbed. Or almost. A part of her remains aware of the boy's eyes, so dark they seem all pupil. The ragged knit of his black brows.

'How're you doing?' he asks.

'All right,' she says, echoing his level tone.

'That's how he's all right. He likes you.'

The horse's head lifts, the black lips pulling back in a gum-baring sneer.

Seeing her unease, Jake takes hold of her wrist again. 'He's flehmening. It's how he knows if a mare's in heat.'

Is this what passes for a chat-up line hereabouts?

'Your mother said he'd been gelded.'

'He doesn't know that.'

'Presumably he was there at the time.'

His laugh gusts against her cheek. 'It's years ago now. He's forgotten. He's not too keen on the vet, mind, but the instinct's still there.'

'I thought the whole point was to get rid of the instinct.'

He laughs again. There are men who find her hilarious whatever she says, though it's not their sense of humour she tickles.

By now she is gaining confidence with the horse. She runs her hand down his neck, pressing into his warm flank. Without moving, Ronnie seems to return the pressure. It's so easeful here, the sun on her skin, her thoughts lost in the rhythm of her stroking. The long head moves towards her, the nose furrowing, brushing her bare flesh. Soft lips nuzzle her elbow with the slight suction of a kiss, a rasping-tender tongue licks the salt from her skin. The brown teeth part around her arm. With a cry she jerks away, and the horse, startled – or thwarted – backs off, tossing his head.

'I thought he was going to bite.'

'He was.'

Even with the sun in her eyes she can see the boy's grin.

'You told me...'

'I never told you to let him get a taste of you.'

'*It's a relationship*, you said.'

'You need to show him who's boss.'

'And that's your idea of relating?'

'It's good advice if you don't want bitten by a horse.'

Reluctantly she laughs.

'You'll know next time,' he says.

'Oh no, he's had his chance. There won't be a next time.'

As if to demonstrate his indifference, Ronnie drops his head and begins cropping at the grass.

Jake hoists himself up to sit on the paddock fence. His hands, with their intricate pattern of cuts and calluses, hang between his open thighs.

'I could teach you to ride him,' he says, his voice so soft it's almost a croon.

This is when it hits her: how utterly grotesque! To have met in that place, under those circumstances, and still they're scratching the old itch.

'How long are you staying?'

She doesn't even try to keep the bitterness out of her voice. 'Until nature takes its course.'

He quizzes his brows, puzzled by the change in her. It's almost as if he hasn't recognised her. She dismisses the thought as too preposterous. She could list the music that was playing on the radio, reproduce the swirl of the carpet, describe the clothes he was wearing. Every detail of that day is burned into her memory. She folds her hands across the flat of her stomach. His glance drops from her face, and a bolt of understanding passes through him, leaving – she sees it clearly – its scorch-trail of shame. The next moment his supple skin seems to petrify, the sootiness she took for dirt revealed as a freakish darkness in the pigment itself. His eyes, so alive till now, are suddenly opaque. He blames her, that much is clear. For turning up to remind him, for putting him to shame, maybe even for the unspeakable thing itself.

'I usually make more of an impression,' she says, her tone overfamiliar now, though a moment ago it sounded quite natural.

He jumps down from the fence and walks away.

31

Wink

The Everyday Miracle Clinic was tucked away in one of those country towns that smell of warm rolls and sweet tea first thing in the morning. We crawled the length of the main street behind a flatbed lorry stacked roof-high with haybales, Frankie cursing at the wheel while I gazed into shop windows stocked with fishing tackle and embroidery silks and patent leather court shoes. How could anything provided here be better than the equivalent service in Glasgow or Edinburgh? It was an objection the clinic seemed to have anticipated. A pair of Victorian villas connected by a brick extension, the place was a warren of ramped floors and winding corridors cluttered with so many Sanderson curtains, and skirted armchairs in toning chintzes, and Oriental vases under lampshades of slubbed silk, that I yearned for the squeak of lino and the tang of disinfectant. It was all so knowing, every detail calculated to reassure the sort of cash-rich, time-poor metropolitans who liked the idea of country air but panicked when they couldn't get a skinny decaf latte. In short, people like us.

'Through here are the relaxation rooms.'

The doctor reached for the door but Frankie got there first. She dipped her knees in a sort of curtsey and I noticed again how coltishly long-limbed she was, how those sky-blue scrubs brought to mind a larky child in her pyjamas. *To your mind*, said Frankie's voice in my head. At some point on the drive home he was going to give me a lecture about negative thinking, and he'd be right. If we were going to spend all that money, I had to give them a chance.

'And this is where it all happens.'

I don't know what I'd been expecting. Maybe a sci-fi laboratory, masked professionals working silent as ghosts in the brilliance of steel and glass. Certainly not this.

The cream-papered walls and vinyl floor did nothing to disguise the fact that we were standing in what had once been a master bedroom. One wall was lined with what looked to me like kitchen units: cupboards and drawers. There was a vibration-proof table with a high-powered microscope, a freezer, an incubator, a clutter of metal boxes and moulded-plastic paraphernalia. While I couldn't identify all the equipment, the feel of the place was deeply familiar. The technicians chatting in a corner (clearly not about work), the white surfaces scuffed from years of use, the tendency of the British workplace to drift into a state of controlled chaos. Any minute now, someone was going to tell us, 'It looks a mess but I know where everything is.'

Frankie put a brave face on it, but I could tell he too was disheartened. 'So this is what we get for our ten grand?'

The doctor shed her girlish air. 'And the best record in the country for working with peri-menopausal mothers.'

I caught his eye, making a *that's told you* face, although we both knew I was the one who'd been put in my peri-menopausal place.

Frankie MacKewon was the first boy I ever kissed, a two-minute slather under the mirrorball at our high school Christmas party. He was drunk on vodka he'd smuggled past the teachers in a Coke bottle. I can still feel the sting of it on my mouth ulcer. Next morning I asked Lilias, who happened to be around, if people always kissed with their tongues, and she answered with enough autobiographical detail to make me sorry I'd asked. Frankie was a wet-lower-lip kisser. Not perfect but, as I was to discover at my next Christmas party, preferable to an out-and-out drooler. We had never spoken that I remember, but we'd sat through spelling and sums and story-writing together, stroked catkins, decorated Easter bonnets, glued collages of autumn leaves. He was there the day I started at St Ursula's Primary: a stocky child with ginger hair. At high school he turned semi-tough, as teenage boys had to if they wanted to survive, growling at the back of the class with a couple of pals who supported Celtic. By the time we'd turned sixteen, the genuine toughs were gone and he could safely boast of reading *Lord of the Rings* twice and knowing the words to every Billy Bragg song. The possibility of talking to boys was one of the revelations of the fifth year – almost more of a revelation than that it was possible to kiss them. On Tuesday afternoons our free periods coincided and we'd sit in the common room, pulling chunks off the foam-rubber seat cushions where their covers had split, discussing abortion and capital punishment and whether Joey Donnelly had really had sex with Mrs Wintour.

We went to different universities but bumped into each other between terms. In the Ashoka one Sunday, at a Waterboys gig everyone had tickets to, outside Boots on Byres Road. He seemed taller to me. He admitted years later I'd had noticeably bigger breasts. We'd have ended up the sort of acquaintances who smile and wave and pretend they're in a hurry when they pass on the street if we hadn't both found jobs in Edinburgh. I was a trainee civil servant, he was a cub reporter on the *Evening News*, both of us homesick for Glasgow. One day I stood behind him in a supermarket queue and we went for a drink. It wasn't like a date, more an extension of those chats amid the shredded foam rubber. We fell into the habit of meeting mid-week and sometimes catching a movie on Sundays. Then my landlord started knocking on my bedroom door at one in the morning and Frankie offered me his spare room.

Every Saturday he'd stand in a sparse crowd of fathers and wives watching a different team of butchers and fitters and photocopier salesmen with dreams of promotion to the second division. If I had nothing better to do, I'd keep him company. We operated a points system. Two for a striker with lovebites, three for lovebites *and* a black eye, four for a manager in a sheepskin coat, five with a gold signet ring, six if he smoked a cigar. It was part of the joke that we were no less faithful to the clichés of our respective trades. Why else did I wear all those prissy little suits? As for Frankie, he passed his days in a pink-eyed jitter of nicotine and adrenaline, chasing sirens, having doors slammed in his face, poking his nose into everybody's business in case it turned out to be news. Night after night of council committees and residents' action groups. Even the hanging around had a sour-tasting glamour for him. If we'd been boyfriend and girlfriend I'd never have tagged along, but I was home from work by ten past five with seven empty hours to fill, and who remembered that Christmas kiss? Not me.

I learned to drink pints of heavy, and flirt with men in uniform, and make the tyres squeal as I accelerated away from the kerb. One Saturday morning I hung out of the passenger window of Frankie's Ford Escort spraying antifreeze on the iced-up windscreen while he sped blind along Lothian Road. When his cousin from Galway came to stay, I slept on the floor in his room. I can't remember how we undressed, but I know it caused us no more awkwardness than getting changed into our shorts and plimsolls at St Ursula's. I'd met a man by then, an academic with a pile of post-structuralist journals by the lavatory and a way of cocking his head to dissect the subtext of my least-considered remarks. That summer I moved to London without a backward glance.

Ten years passed before we met again. Simon and I had discovered there are only so many times a couple can get back together, and devolution had created opportunities for clever women at St Andrew's House. I got myself posted up from Whitehall, only to be shocked by how little Scotland felt like home. One night I turned on the television and caught the end of the local news. A gum-chewing boy in a Rangers strip was expressing smirking repentance for a spectacular foul. There was a cutaway shot to the interviewer. His face gave me the first thrill of recognition I had had since coming north. At the end of his report he delivered a tricksy little summary while walking towards the camera. I say I recognised his face, but it was the way he moved my body remembered. A whole physical life was encrypted in that walk: the heel of his hand on the steering wheel as he reversed the Escort; the receiver clamped between chin and shoulder, dictating copy down the phone; that chimpanzee grin he used for satire. The next morning I tracked down his number and we talked until his boss grabbed the phone out of his hand and told *whoever you are*, 'He's supposed to be working.' We arranged to meet that night in a bar that hadn't existed a decade before. He was waiting for me in a suit that looked too expensive for work, even work in television. I glanced around at the Corinthian columns made of glass, the flame velvet sofa.

'Where's the spittoon?'

'No spittoon.'

'Beer mats? Overflowing ashtrays?'

'I packed in the cancer sticks four years ago. I don't smoke, I don't drink in shebeens, and I don't run after flashing blue lights.'

'Are you sure you still want to be seen with me?'

At least his smile hadn't changed. 'You don't have a scoobie, do you?'

'About what?'

His eyes caught mine with a different sort of smile, until I dropped my gaze.

The restaurant had been fully booked; he'd got a table because he knew the owner. He was on first-name terms with the First Minister, coached a team of East End neds as a favour to someone I should have heard of who'd just had a Hollywood smash. I mentioned my secondment to the Cabinet Office and the lecture I'd given to MBA students at Fontainebleau. It was at least thirty minutes before this territory-marking was abandoned for common ground, and another half hour before I could relax in the certainty that, underneath, we were still the same. Though he had never offered me his jacket before when I said I was cold, or touched my waist to steer me across the road. At the end of the evening I found myself standing at the taxi rank with my arms around his neck and his lower lip (drier than I remembered) on mine.

Cue the happy ever after. He was a full-time sports reporter by then, covering the sort of fixtures to which I couldn't tag along. In due course he became a presenter, one of those gruff, poetic men's men whose aftershave seems to leach through the television screen. Of all the fans with typewriters, he was the most intellectually nimble, a turnstile philosopher famed for the extended conceits in his match reports. No European Cup was complete without Big Frankie waxing lyrical on national pride, his perma-flush set off by an ice-blue open-necked shirt. Alone together we were the same old Frankie and Freya, but the world around us had changed. Every man in Scotland watched *Extra Time*. When Frankie cracked a joke in the studio half a nation laughed with him. Strangers clapped his back in the street or jabbed a finger in his face, insisting the ref had been wrong. One day he phoned me at work to say, 'Guess what?' He'd signed an £80,000 contract, with half as much again to be earned on the after-dinner circuit. I thought he was joking. I couldn't see Frankie as a totem of Scottish manhood. To me he was still Kewie, the ginger kid with chubby knees.

There were five other couples in the waiting room. Two corporate-looking women ignoring their pinstriped husbands, an orange-skinned blonde squired by a Glaswegian with a silver ponytail, a mousy woman kneading the hand of her edgy other half (like us, I guessed, waiting to be given the hard sell), and a fat girl barely out of her teens whispering with her beanpole boyfriend. The clinic boasted an eleven per cent success rate per cycle for women of my age: if we oldies had two shots each, one of us was in with a chance. Discreetly I eyed the competition, grading the elasticity in their skin, the gloss of their hair, and anything else that might indicate fertility. For all the girly inclusivity of those fashion magazines, the framed notice offering spa treatments, the upmarket snacks in the vending machine and the endlessly-smiling staff, we all knew there were two classes of women: those who could make babies, and the rest.

'Is it midgie repellent?'

'Ssshhh.'

The fat girl and her boyfriend were giggling in the corner.

'Fly spray?'

'No,' she hissed.

'Toilet Duck?'

She sniggered. '*No.*'

'It can't smell like that and not kill something.'

They were talking about somebody's perfume. Mine, perhaps.

'I think it's nice,' the girl said.

'If you like Vapona.' His accent was posher than hers, even with a mouthful of chewing gum, but their bodies did that unselfconscious mirroring you only get with a good match. 'What's wrong with the smell of—'

She clapped her hand over his mouth so we all knew what he'd been about to say.

'You know what they make it out of?' he asked, when she lifted her hand.

She gave him a sidelong look.

'I'll give you a clue. It comes out of a cat's arse.'

'Shut *up*.' She flounced across the room to choose a magazine. He sprawled in his armchair, watching her.

'You reading that?' She pointed at my lap. 'That *Vogue*.'

'No.'

She took it with her left hand. The diamond was small, the rose gold keeper looked antique. They seemed too young to be married, and much too young to renounce nightclubs and hangovers and recreational drugs for the sake of the next generation. Though biology would disagree. According to biology, they were the perfect age.

She planted herself in the armchair beside me. 'This your first time?'

'Yes.'

I felt Frankie tensing on my other side.

She brought her thumb to her mouth and gnawed at a hangnail. 'Boring, eh?'

'They could manage their appointments system better.'

She stared at me as if I'd arrived from outer space.

'There's no need for us all to be here at the same time.'

She thought about this for a moment. '*Aye*. Most days you're in and out, half an hour. I've left the dinner in the oven.' A bright spot of blood had appeared on her thumb. She sucked it. 'I'm Nikki by the way.'

'Freya,' I said.

'Is that foreign?'

There was a muffled snort on the other side of the room. I gave her husband a cool stare. He looked up, still chewing, and winked at me.

It may be Nikki mistook my silence for nerves. 'She's all right, Doctor Ross, when you get used to her. Better than that woman they had before. I could see her far enough. It'll be worth it in the end, eh?' She gave a heartfelt sigh. 'It better be.' Across the room, the gum-chewer had taken out his phone. She leaned towards me, dropping her voice. 'If it was

39

my choice, we'd leave it for a couple of years, but somebody doesn't want to wait.'

She wasn't truly fat, I saw then, just scaled-up. There was a waist between her Amazonian hips and that eye-catching bust. Her brown hair was pulled back and twisted into a plume secured with a plastic clip, and the smooth acreage of brow and cheek so candidly exposed was beautiful. I felt a sneaking admiration for her spray-on jeans in that *Homes and Gardens* setting.

She glanced at her husband. 'It's worse for them, this place.'

'Is it?'

She moved her hand in close to her belly and waggled her pinkie.

Sneaking admiration gave way to the hope that no one else had seen, but she had a point: these men could have been awaiting summons to some evolutionary court. They were almost comically anxious to avoid each other's eyes: the silver ponytail thumbing out a text message, the nervy type staring at his wife's hands, one of the suits studying the *Telegraph* crossword with ferocious concentration, the other checking his watch. Even her husband's cockiness could be read as a smokescreen for embarrassment. Blond hair curled into tendrils below his black beanie. An ironic tuft of beard under that mouth-breather's pout. A naughty-boy glint in his eye that brought back double maths and Mr Wilson in a lather with Craig McBurnie. Craig McBurnie, Stephen Lynch, Matthew Doherty. Funny that I still remembered their names. For a good twenty years I hadn't given a thought to naughty boys, and now I saw them everywhere. My godson. Ruth's eldest. Miranda's four-year-old twins. Who knew, I might yet give birth to one myself. The child in me could still recall that anxious twist in my guts, but the mother-in-waiting was a pushover for their bold-eyed mischief.

As if sensing my interest, Nikki's husband looked up.

Our glances connected, he looked away, and I felt a pang of slighted vanity that was almost like loss.

Nikki dropped the copy of *Vogue* back on the magazine table. 'Do you stay round here?'

Her husband shot her a look. I wondered if she was deliberately winding him up.

'Glasgow,' I said.

'There's nowhere nearer?'

'Not with a reputation like this place.'

'Cool.'

I felt something new in the air between us.

'We're NHS.'

'Lucky you,' I said.

Her glance strayed towards Frankie, then veered away, her mouth crimping in a smirk. 'What does your husband do?'

Ah.

I looked her in the eye, not bothering to answer, since she knew.

It didn't happen so very often when I was with him. I suppose my presence put them off. Mostly it was men who made the approach. A look on their faces as if they were the ones about to be recognised. As, in a sense, they were. He'd give them their two minutes of manly banter before explaining he was out with the wife, *you know how it is.*

'Frankie MacKewon?' Nikki's husband crossed the carpet towards us.

A fraction of a second later than he might have, Frankie looked up.

The boy extended his hand. 'Kit Oliphant.'

If he was going to shake hands, Frankie had to put down his phone. I watched the possibility of a snub register in the boy's eyes. He seemed to remember where he was, the implications of meeting in that place, what it might say about him, or about Frankie, how this could mar the innocent pleasure of two Scotsmen talking football. Each knew more about

41

the other than the other wished to be known. Even if they exchanged the benefit of the doubt, taking it for granted neither was any less of a man, each knew the secrets of the other's bedroom, the joyless fucking dictated by the ovulation kit, and neither wanted to shake hands with the sort of man who'd put up with that. But it was too late now. There was an audience to consider, the women mildly diverted, the men transfixed and waiting for a sign.

Frankie slipped the phone into his pocket. 'How're you doing, Kit?'

Sperm

The consultant was a short, fleshy woman dressed in expensive shades of sackcloth and ashes, with blonde highlights in her hair and a faint mousy down where the light from the window caught her cheek. It was hard to put an age to her. She looked as I imagined a Roman fertility goddess would look, if fertility goddesses banked a hundred and fifty thousand a year.

'Mr and Mrs MacKewon, I'm Doctor Ross.'

She sat straight-backed behind her antique desk, while Frankie and I fought to remain upright in the maw of a loose-covered sofa.

'Actually,' I said, 'I use my own name, Cavalle.'

Frankie leaned forward. 'Call us Frankie and Freya.'

She opened a folder. 'The first thing I have to tell you is your count was extremely healthy. Usually in a first consultation I'm saying cut down on alcohol, start wearing boxers and take a course of selenium, but the best advice I can give you is just carry on as you are.'

She broke off. I was staring at Frankie.

'I had the test last week. What's the point of sitting here not knowing...'

'...whose fault it is,' I finished for him.

'It's not about blame,' he said.

But it was. It had to be someone's fault, and I so badly wanted it not to be mine. I knew he felt the same. Despite the solicitous body language on show in the waiting room, in their

43

uncoupled hearts every one of them was praying *please let it not be me*. The past year, the rockiest in our marriage so far, now seemed like paradise. While I wasn't in the first flush of youth, male infertility was on the rise: it could have been either of us. But now we knew, and everything had changed. The best part of me was pleased for him. I just wished there was some way he could have been normal without confirming my lifelong suspicion that there was something wrong with me.

Dr Ross placed her hands on top of the desk. 'At this point we can't say why it hasn't happened.' She glanced down at her notes. 'Your GP says you're ovulating, but we don't know if the egg is getting to where it needs to be to meet the sperm, so I'd like to book you in for a laparoscopy. We have an arrangement with a private hospital down the road. The surgeon's very neat. He goes in through the tummy button and has a look round for—'

'Damage to the fallopian tubes,' I said. 'Endometriosis, fibroids, adhesions or malformations.'

Frankie grinned. 'I should have warned you, my wife's a technocrat.'

Dr Ross returned a sporting smile. 'There's no guarantee he'll find anything. Conception is a delicate business. There are plenty of couples with everything in full working order, but something between them just doesn't click. And that's where we come in.'

Hidden from her by the depths of the sofa, Frankie squeezed my fingers.

'On the other hand, there may be a very simple reason why you're not conceiving.'

'Is this you checking I'm putting it in the right hole?'

It was the sort of joke a television sports personality could get away with. She flashed him a roguish glance. 'Misunderstandings are more common than you'd think, though generally it's a question of timing. I remember one highly-motivated couple...'

44

I caught her eye.

She cleared her throat. 'The approach we take is rather different from anything you'll find elsewhere. Our fee scale is a little higher than some clinics per cycle of IVF, but we offer a much better chance of conceiving in the first or second cycle, as opposed to the third or fourth. It may not come to that, there may be a way we can help you conceive naturally.' Her left hand spanned my notes and I had a vision of those slightly rubbery fingers probing my body's secret crevices. 'But if IVF is the appropriate option, we strongly recommend you live locally for the duration of the treatment.'

I didn't need to look at Frankie to know this had thrown him.

'Both of us?' he queried.

'We need you to do your bit, but the deep freeze is a wonderful invention. It's up to you: whatever Freya would find most restful.'

'Now you're asking,' he said.

'Can't I just commute?'

I guessed she used this rueful pucker with all her awkward customers. 'As I said, conception is a tricky business, none of us fully understands why it works in some cases and not in others, but one of the reasons we tend to do better than most clinics is because we encourage our mothers to give themselves over to the process. We need to see you *every day*. Most days, you'll be here for under an hour. That might seem like something you can squeeze into your normal routine, but trust me: I've seen what happens when clients go down that road. It's enormously stressful for them, and rarely ends in a happy outcome. This is not a trivial procedure.'

I knew what was involved, but she went through it anyway. A week of injections to shut down my cycle, three weeks of hormone jags, blood tests to make sure I didn't get ovarian hyperstimulation syndrome, vaginal scans, more jags, sedation while they collected the eggs, implantation of the embryo

45

three days later, and another fortnight of progesterone injections before the pregnancy test.

'It's perfectly safe, we monitor you very closely, but these are powerful hormones we'll be putting into your body.' She paused, the saleswoman in her taking over from the doctor. 'And after all, we're talking about a very short space of time. A matter of weeks if everything goes to plan. Book yourself into somewhere comfortable where the food's good, pack a few beach books, some music you find relaxing and, ah, leave us to worry about the technical details.'

'Sounds good to me,' Frankie said.

She glanced at a photograph on her desk, twin girls a couple of years older than the heartbreakingly-cute babies decorating the corridor walls. They had that rosy-cheeked, tousle-haired, just-bathed look: the excitement of small children in their pyjamas before the great adventure of bed. 'It'll be your last chance to lie around doing nothing for a long time, take it from me.'

I thought about *a matter of weeks* kicking my heels in the middle of nowhere. My career on tick-over while Frankie worked his usual fifty hours. Country hotels. The traditional Scottish breakfast cooked at six and microwaved back to searing heat at nine. The shoebox en suite with its extractor fan droning half the night. The framed prints of local beauty spots and the window overlooking the bins. How could any of that facilitate *the process*? And I had never read a beach book in my life.

'There's one other thing I'd like you both to think about.' Her right hand came to rest on top of her left, an obscurely ominous gesture. 'Our clients tend to find it useful to have a fallback plan.'

'We're not interested in adoption,' Frankie said.

'I'm talking about other reproductive technologies. For example, would you consider using a donor egg?'

This was something I hadn't researched.

'It's only fair to warn you there are currently more women wanting eggs than there are donors but, assuming it's a possibility, how would you feel?'

'I'd have to know a lot more about it,' I said.

'We can steer you towards the relevant information. What I'd like to know now is whether you're open to the idea in principle?'

'It's not just my decision.'

'Of course.'

I turned to Frankie.

He shrugged. 'If you don't mind, I don't mind.'

'And that's your considered opinion, is it—?'

The consultant moved her right hand in a tactful gesture of curtailment.

'How do you know my body would accept another woman's egg?'

Frankie dropped into the droll growl he used sometimes on camera. 'It's your head she's asking about.'

Dr Ross pressed her lips together but it was too late, I'd seen the smirk.

'Well,' she said lightly, drawing the consultation to a close, 'it's one option. There are various paths you might take.'

Brogues

My title was Head of Transparency, in charge of a tiny autonomous unit squeezed on all sides by departmental big spenders. Anyone with an interest in, well, anything at all, could log on to our website and track the history of their chosen issue, the part played by Brussels, Westminster, Holyrood and their local council, decision by decision. If you wanted to know why your granny died after her hernia operation, why prisoner number 666 couldn't follow the 5:2 diet, why hedgehogs were being culled on Uist, it was possible to find out from the comfort of your own home. As an idea this was hardly radical, merely the logical next step from Freedom of Information, but the IT boys had always blenched at the sheer volume of data, the mind-boggling complexity of the pathways involved. For years it was regarded as an insane piety. Then I volunteered to take it on.

I never doubted it was possible. All it required was clarity of thought, a clarity that would spread through the government, reforming administrative practice. After all, taking the right decision for the right reasons, and logging them as you went along, was a hundred times quicker than trying to post-rationalise a moment's sloppy thinking. Inevitably we weren't popular with everyone. Those who refused the carrot of transparency had to be shown the stick. In some offices we were known as the 'rubber heels squad'. The job had its pressures. My staff turnover was higher than average, which is how I happened to be interviewing for two vacant posts that Wednesday morning.

I was just in the door when Kelly called me over and nodded towards a figure sitting under the atrium. 'Mr Smith.'

I squinted in disbelief.

Kelly laughed. 'I did wonder.'

'And he's not due for another forty minutes.'

'The keen type.' She was enjoying herself. 'That's good, no?'

'The keen types get here bang on time. It's the game-players who arrive early.'

He half-turned in his seat, looking towards us, and I had the strangest feeling.

'You know him?'

Kelly was wasted on reception, but she wouldn't consider another job.

'He reminds me of someone.'

'Who?'

'I've no idea.'

He was wearing a cheap, black, narrow-lapel suit with a black shirt and black tie. A thirtysomething might just have got away with it. On a man twice that age, however tall and spare, it was embarrassing. Like an ageing theatrical knight convinced he had one last *Hamlet* in him.

I walked across, expecting him to stand, if not out of ordinary politeness, then from interview nerves.

'Mr Smith?'

He remained seated. 'Are you Miss Cavalle?'

There was something about the way he said it. Now I was close enough to study him, his long face troubled me. The directness of his gaze behind those wire-rimmed glasses, the starburst of white at the outer corner of each eye. Elsewhere his skin was a toughened liverwurst brown. A weekend Munro-bagger, I guessed. Almost an old man, with fleshless shanks and clumps of wiry hair in ear and nostril, but I could

49

tell from the way he was sitting that his body was not yet a burden.

His stare let me know that I too was being judged.

Generally I didn't talk to applicants outside the interview room, but Mr Smith had already ruled himself out as a candidate, and I was curious.

I took the chair diagonally across from him. 'Have you come far?'

'Perthshire.'

'You must have had an early start.'

'It's a fair walk.'

I saw this was intended to elicit just the swift look I gave him.

'And you?'

'I'm sorry?' I said.

'Where do you bide?'

'Glasgow.'

'You won't see much of your bairns.'

I composed my features into a pleasant expression. 'Do you have family yourself, Mr Smith?'

'None I know of.'

I had to look him in the eye to check if this was another joke.

'Never say never, eh?' His upper lip had that overdefinition I had noticed before in older men, almost as if he were wearing lipstick. It brought out the yellowness of his teeth. 'We've one over you there.'

'We?'

'Men.'

We sat for a few moments holding each other's gaze. When I told Frankie, over dinner that night, he said, 'The guy was flirting with you,' but it didn't feel like that.

When we had watched each other for long enough to establish that neither of us was going to look away, I said, 'What age was it you put down on the form?'

'I cannae mind.'

'Thirty-two.'

He looked very pleased with himself.

'Do you have a degree, or was that a fiction too?'

'University of life,' he said.

'And the rest of your CV?'

He didn't bother to reply. I checked his body language. Legs modestly apart, hands spanning his thighs, no armpit-flaunting or groin-airing, but a definite challenge.

'Your application form was very well done.'

'Ticked all the right boxes?'

His stare made me itch for a mirror. Lipstick on my teeth? Pigeon shit in my hair? I waited.

'It's amazing what you can find on the worldwide web,' he said.

I nodded. 'Why?'

For the first time he smiled. 'Is it not your job to work that out?'

'Actually no. As long as I weed out the time-wasters, the government doesn't care. But since you're here, why would you go to all that trouble when you knew you'd never get the job?'

His smile acquired a cunning edge. 'Because I'm too old?'

'Because you're a liar.'

'I've owned up.' As if that made it all right.

'You violated the ethos of the unit you say you want to work for.'

His eyes were suddenly huge. I saw their Spam-pink rims, each blue iris swimming in its greying sclera, and I wondered if he was having some sort of attack. Then I realised he was wearing bifocals.

'You don't like folk showing initiative?' he said.

'You lied. When applying to work for the Transparency Unit. That could be construed as a failure of intelligence.'

I sat back in my chair to break the charged space between

51

us. Professional detachment came naturally to me, I wasn't sure how he'd got in under the wire.

After a moment, I asked, 'How did you think I'd react?'

'Is this part of the interview?'

'You're not going to be interviewed.'

'Ach well,' he pushed the glasses higher up his nose, 'maybe that's a failure of intelligence in you.'

I had never been mocked by an interview candidate before. At least, not to my face.

'You'll lose some good folk, being so pernickerty.'

I could have explained that *being pernickerty* was what the Transparency Unit was all about, but why waste my breath?

'Like now. You're thinking, he's interesting, but I don't like him making a monkey of me.'

'I'm not employed to hire people I find interesting, Mr Smith.'

'Be better if you were, Miss...'

'Cavalle.' We said it together.

His eyes loomed large behind those distorting lenses. 'You're not related to Lili Cavalle, the actress?'

'She's my mother.'

'I saw her the other night.'

My pulse picked up speed.

'On television.' He smiled again, showing his yellow teeth. 'A repeat of *The Protectors*. She was a perfume-maker. Blew herself up with a bottle of scent.'

'I've not seen that one.'

'You should look out for it, she was very good.'

'I'll tell her you said so.'

'Aye, you do that.'

Who the hell remembered Lili Cavalle these days? She didn't even call herself that any more. I had a sixth sense for actors, the high hum of their presence, the salivary repartee: Mr Smith wasn't a pro.

Out of the corner of my eye, I noticed Paul standing beside Kelly at reception.

'I have to get back to work.'

He, too, stood up. 'Do I get my expenses?'

'What do you think?'

He gave a wry cough. 'It was worth a shot.' The eyes swimming behind his glasses softened. 'I've met you, anyroad.'

Before, he had shaken my hand, now he held it. His liver-wurst-coloured fingers were rough but warm around mine. His nails, I noticed for the first time, were rimmed with black.

And then it dawned on me who he reminded me of. Myself. For years I'd stared at strangers just as Mr Smith was staring at me. I travelled all over the south of England, Guildford, Exeter, Bristol, the London West End, monitoring my body for the tell-tale frisson, running through the checklist in my head. I spent a fortune on theatre tickets, waited hour upon hour across the road from the stage door before trailing them to the pub. A new suspect every week, each as plausible as the last, but never quite conclusive. As with any addictive behaviour, it was the impossibility of satisfaction that had me hooked. I had to move back to Glasgow to break the habit. One of the few facts she'd let slip was that he wasn't a Scot.

'I'll be off then,' he said.

Since my mother had entered the conversation he seemed a different person, his unfortunate manner replaced by something almost like tenderness.

'I'd never have guessed, if it wasn't for the name.'

'No, we're very different. I, ah...' My glance dropped to the floor, to the brown brogues under his black trousers. I was distractingly aware of Paul watching us from the other side of the atrium. I gave Mr Smith an awkward smile as I tugged my hand from his grasp. 'I suppose I must take after my father.'

Cat

My mother told me she went into labour in act four of *Macbeth* during a Saturday matinee at the King's Theatre in Edinburgh. I was lucky in my Scottish birth. A week later and I'd have been a Geordie. A fortnight after that, Liverpudlian. Lilias, always a slender woman, was living on black coffee and untipped cigarettes. The director had no idea she was starving for two. I like to picture her with clunky wrists and hollowed throat, her discreet bump upstaged by a spectacularly pneumatic bosom. In a linen smock and blood-red surcoat cut to flare from those milky breasts, she was the perfect Lady Macbeth, even in her seventh month. If only I'd hung on for another half-hour I'd have saved the house from her understudy, a dumpy girl with ginger hair who had to wear Lady Macduff's dress (Lilias's waters having broken over the surcoat). There was talk of naming me Hecate, to be shortened to Cate, but Banquo persuaded her it might not be the luckiest start and instead I got Freya, the Norse goddess of love. I heard this story told dozens of times as a child, drinking orangeade in pubs where the barman turned a blind eye because we were his only afternoon custom. There was always a moment when Lilias looked to me for confirmation and, because I loved to be included and had heard the details so often I almost believed I did remember, I would nod at her, mugging a little, renewing the gales of laughter.

In term time I was packed off to Uncle Nellaney in the house of ticking clocks, but the rest of my childhood was spent 'helping' boarding-house landladies with the house-work and walking the arthritic hind legs off their bug-eyed King Charles spaniels. Where the accommodation did not include free child-minding, there were railway waiting rooms, bus station cafes, public libraries and municipal art galleries where the staff, recognising a fellow time-passer, let me alone. Only if we found ourselves in a burgh too mean for roofed and heated public space would I end up backstage. Every school holiday brought a different town, sometimes two or three: throwing the Gordon rug over the latest greasy sofa, buying a bunch of fresias for the ring-marked table, propping the photograph of my father as Othello on the mantelpiece, and telling myself this was home.

It wasn't a slapdash upbringing. I never sang at the table or ate in the street. To this day I am innocent of the taste of bubble gum. We said 'lavatory', not 'toilet' – and certainly not 'cludgie'; 'street sweeper' not 'scaffie'; 'going to' not 'gonnae'. Farting was euphemised as 'having an affliction' and well into my teens I believed this to be the correct, if recherché, phrase. 'Common' was another proscribed word, with its whiff of shopkeeper-class petty-mindedness. In hindsight, I can see that Lilias was just another parvenu: an ambitious, pretty woman with a Frenchy made-up name. But as a child I was convinced there was no one else like her. And I never met anyone else's mother who dished up Shredded Wheat for dinner or pegged used towels on the line for a 'fresh-air wash'. My mother was that trickiest of combinations, a bohemian snob. I once asked her why she didn't wear a boob tube like our landlady that month, a divorcée whose gold slingbacks and cerise toenails struck me as the ultimate in glamour. I don't remember committing this crime, but I do remember hearing it recounted in a series of green rooms, and being scorched at each telling by my mother's tinkling laugh.

There was a fixed way to dress, to smile, to enunciate, to deal with bus drivers and box office managers, to converse with our fellow boarders and, if need be, to ignore them. And although the memory of all this was a source of corrosive resentment throughout my twenties, it was a kind of structure when everything else was in flux. I never knew when I went to sleep if I would wake up in a bed, or on somebody's sofa, or in the back of a van speeding down the M1. Whether there would be scrambled eggs for breakfast, or (since Lilias remained an erratic dieter) nothing but frozen peas. Whether I would be spending the day with Cordelia or Goneril, Mrs Warren or Eliza Doolittle, Dorothy or the Wicked Witch of the West.

'Come on up, darling.'

The buzzing door yielded to my touch and I smelled the burned-plastic stink of Casablanca lilies. There they were on the hall table, caught by the ruby light from the stained-glass window. Every time I came here I'd glance down at the polished-brass stair rods and up at the wedding-cake cornice, caress the seductive curves of the newel post, and have the same thought: after all the rootless years of my childhood, *now* she gets herself a home.

It was a Victorian villa converted into flats. Lilias had the billiard room, with three adjoining closets for cooking, washing and sleeping. It felt cavernously empty, partly due to the antique, gilt-framed mirror that doubled the size of the room, and partly through lack of furniture. She owned a white linen sofa, a glass dining table and six metal chairs, a portrait of her by Robin Philipson, and little else. There were no carpets, or blinds at the windows, no photographs, no keepsakes, not even books. (The showbiz biographies were hidden in a cupboard.) No one could call it homely, or even particularly comfortable, but she loved it: her very own stage.

The lights were off, though the day was overcast. Blurred shadows converged on the walls as I handed over the brown paper bag.

'I haven't had figs since I was Cleopatra.'

I tried to tell myself this was said by way of thanks. Food was always a gamble, but what else was I to bring? Flowers she dumped in the sink because she didn't own a vase, and all the scarves I'd ever given her were still folded in their original wrapping at the bottom of one of her drawers.

I noticed a script on the glass table. 'Am I stopping you working?'

'Yes, but half an hour won't hurt.'

We sat on the capacious settee, leaving a cushion's width between us.

'How are you?' I asked.

Her mouth performed that impatient lateral twitch a stranger might have taken for a smile. 'As you see.'

The day she moved in I'd spent hours shifting the sofa until we found the perfect spot, but that afternoon she was beyond any trick of the light.

'You look tired,' I said.

She wiped a speck of matter from the corner of one eye. 'I shouldn't wear grey, it doesn't do anyone any favours.'

'How do you feel?'

'Oh darling, I feel fine. What about *you*, how are *you* feeling?'

'OK.' I looked at her left breast, girlishly small under the grey linen shirt, neatly symmetrical with its partner. 'But I'm not the one with cancer.'

A gust of air through the open window rustled the pages of the script.

'Frankie popped in yesterday,' she said, as if I hadn't spoken.

This was news to me.

'He told me that place is charging you ten thousand pounds—'

And that was just for starters.

'Are you sure you want to do it, darling?'

My eyes narrowed in disbelief that she could ask me this but, in fairness, how was she to know what I felt? I had never told her about the conversations I had with my future daughter, how she was beside me every step I took, how we shared little jokes, how I'd bought her replacement copies of my old favourite books (*Anne of Green Gables*, *Elidor*, *The Secret Garden*), how I was going to tuck her in and read to her and always kiss her goodnight. I could have said some of this now, but Lilias would only have heard the reproach in it, so instead I replied, 'I suppose we could spend the money on a conservatory, or a cruise, but on balance we'd rather have a baby.'

'But do you really...' She saw the look on my face and took a tactful breath, the sort of *ah* that carried to the back of the stalls. 'What I don't understand is why you have to do it now?'

'If we leave it any longer it won't be an option.'

'Yes, but you *have* left it. You've been married nine years. It's a bit,' another tactful breath, 'late.'

'Maybe I feel the need to make the numbers up.'

If I'd had to supply one adjective to describe my childhood I would have said 'lonely', but I had never felt loneliness like the prospect of being the last Cavalle left alive.

'I don't want you to make a mistake you'll—' She broke off. I watched understanding dawn in her eyes. 'I'm not planning on kicking the bucket just yet.'

A house fly settled on the wall behind her. Without looking she raised a hand to bat it away. I remembered all the other times I'd sat there. In winter the light from the cupola draped the room like a dust sheet, in high summer it poured like Chablis through the glass. The week I helped her redecorate I had watched it change hour by hour, vibrant in the morning, pearly in the afternoon, poignant at dusk, each shift a cue for Lilias to become someone else.

She reached across and touched my hand. '*Darling.*'

I was temporarily incapable of speech.

We sat like that awhile, me with my reddened eyes, Lilias's hand resting on mine, until I noticed her right foot rotating from the ankle. She liked to work on her flexibility in pockets of dead time.

'I've got some formosa oolong in the kitchen,' she said.

I made the tea in a couple of mugs, then spotted the eggshell china on the top shelf of the cupboard. Cups, saucers, teapot, milk jug and sugar bowl. I'd bought them for her sixtieth birthday.

'Oh,' she said, when she saw them.

'I rinsed the cups.' I set the tray on the floor, remembered not to put the milk in first. 'Do you know a man called Smith?'

'Hundreds, I imagine.'

'Tall, lean, charcoal-coloured hair. He applied for a job in the unit—'

She looked bored.

'Asked me if I was your daughter.'

Now she was interested. 'Was he good-looking?'

A detail I hadn't consciously noticed came back to me. He'd smelled of livestock. 'Too countrified for you, I'd say.'

Something happened in her face. I wasn't sure what, only that it was an event beyond her control. 'Smith?' she queried.

'Well, that's probably not his name. The rest of his application was a pack of lies.'

She fingered the puckered skin of her throat. 'How old?'

'Hard to know. I thought early sixties, but he could be older.'

I knew her face as well as I knew my own. The classic bone structure to which the skin still more or less cleaved. Her creamy complexion, with just a hint of old ivory tainting its translucence in certain lights. The handsome grooves around her eyes, like claw marks from a tiger's playful swipe. None of this was new, but there was a change in the way her features fitted together, as if the effort of harmony had become too much.

'What's the matter?' I said.

She lifted her cup from its saucer. 'Why would anything be the matter?'

Outside it began to rain. We chatted about her last audition and how the ballet was going (she was continuing with the classes though she hadn't got the part). She had been to a garden party at an Adam house near Selkirk where she'd managed to meet a lovely man, despite being there on the arm of the clever silversmith.

A tortoiseshell cat came through the window and sprang onto the cushion between us.

'Hello, Malvolio,' she sang. At the sound of her voice the creature began to purr.

I nodded at the floorboards to indicate the woman downstairs. 'Doesn't she mind you rechristening him?'

'I presume he still answers to Kitty or Tiddles, whatever he's called.'

'Toby,' I said, turning to check the tag on his collar as he prowled along the back of the settee. 'It must be very confusing, being named for two characters in the same play.'

'Oh he knows who he is, don't you, Malvolio?'

The cat came to a halt behind her and began to lick her hair. I waited for her to shoo him away, but she did nothing, even when he pulled back his lips and daintily bit her scalp.

'Has the hospital given you a date yet?'

'It's just a biopsy,' she said.

'I'll come over and drive you up there.'

'It's not for four weeks yet.'

'*Four weeks?*' The cat leapt to the floor. 'In that case you're going private.'

'Frankie's already offered.'

This, too, was news. 'That's settled then.'

'I said no. You've enough to spend your money on just now.'

I had no idea why she'd declined Frankie's offer, but I knew it had nothing to do with the state of our finances.

'It's not going to go away,' I said, as gently as I could.

'It doesn't have to be the nasty kind.'

'That's what we need to find out.'

As so often when Lilias and I seemed to reach a concensus, she veered off in the opposite direction. 'Once they get the knife into you you're done for. I've seen it happen. Robert Ap Robert had his gall stones done, four months later he had a stroke. Sarah Duff-G only went in for a hip replacement. The next thing we heard—'

'She'd had a heart attack because she was six stones overweight,' I said. 'Not a problem in your case.'

'I heard a programme about these full-body scans they're doing now. Apparently they actually lower life expectancy. They always find something, and then they want to intervene.'

I was familiar with Lilias's views on modern medicine. Before she got around to mice with human ears growing out of their backs, I said, 'The longer you leave it the worse it'll be.'

She inclined her head in graceful admission. 'I'm not the only one who puts things off.'

'It's not the same.'

'Life, death,' she shrugged, 'it seems fairly similar. Don't look like that, darling, you'll get lines. You have to admit, this baby thing is rather out of the blue.'

She was avoiding the issue by changing the subject, but what could I do?

'We've been trying for a while,' I said.

There was a muffled thump from the kitchen. She cocked her head and smiled. I recalled seeing a saucer of milk on the floor. She'd never managed to give her child a home, and now she was feeding the neighbourhood cats.

'It looks like I'm the one with the fertility problem,' I said.

'Well, you didn't get that from me.'

'Presumably I didn't get it from either of you.'

I watched her face. Nothing changed. But then, we had been playing this game for forty years.

'Did you never want more children?'

'I didn't want you, darling.'

I laughed.

'Of course I loved when you came.'

'Of course.'

'It was a difficult birth.'

'Yes I know. You missed the last act.'

'I was in second-stage labour for thirty-six hours. My blood pressure was through the roof.'

'Pre-eclampsia?' If there was a hereditary predisposition I needed to know.

She made a face that said pre-eclampsia wasn't the half of it. 'You don't know what pain is until you've delivered a baby. They wanted to give me morphine but I couldn't take the risk of being out of my mind and letting them cut me.'

I was surprised to hear Lilias talking like this. She was the sort of performer who draped herself in a variety of becoming poses on stage but acted from the neck upwards. For all her lip-smacking sensualism, she was reticent about matters *down there*.

'It was all so much more primitive in those days. I knew a man who'd lost his wife in childbirth. The midwife was completely out of her depth. "Won't be long now," she kept saying. She finished her shift and when she came back the next day I was still there. I saw the look on her face and thought, *I'm going to die. And this thing inside me.*'

'Me, you mean,' I said.

'You weren't you then.'

I wondered if this were true.

'What about the obstetrician, wasn't he keeping an eye on you?'

'It was the *seventies*, darling. No one kept an eye on anyone. The ward was like the *Marie Celeste*.'

'In Edinburgh, in the baby boom?'

For a moment she looked shifty. 'It must have been a quiet week. Anyway, in the end another midwife turned up, an islander. She gave me castor oil. Repulsive stuff, but it did the trick.'

'So you shat me out.'

'If you have to be vulgar about it.'

'And then what happened?'

'I rejoined the tour in Liverpool.'

'What happened *in the hospital*?'

'Oh, they took you away to the nursery. I needed to sleep.' She thought about how this sounded. 'And you were a bit sickly, so they had to keep you warm.'

I was disappointed, yet she had only confirmed what, in my heart of hearts, I had always known. There had been no joyful moment of connection. She had not guided my mouth to the nipple. We had not bonded skin-to-skin.

'Can I see it?' I blurted.

'See what, darling?' And then she realised. Her face folded with displeasure. 'I don't think there's any need for that.'

I should never have asked.

'There's nothing to see.'

'I know. I just…'

'Before they lop it off, is that it?'

I saw how far I had overstepped the mark.

'It's not even as if you were breastfed.' She crossed the room to close the window, her heels clacking on the floor. 'Anyway, that's the beauty of genetics: mine look just like yours. With another twenty-five years' wear and tear.'

1972

Eight o'clock and the sky is still bright, while the land below gathers shadow. Mrs S has gone out. Each time the farmhands cross the yard their eyes are drawn to the square of yellow light framing Lili at the kitchen table. Not to ogle her, as she thought at first, but to stoke their indignation. How hard they work. A good half of what they do is a mystery to her, but it's clear that the farm is a highly ordered space, a place for everything and everything in its place. Nothing is wasted, least of all time. Except by her.

Three weeks and still she's heard nothing from Brod. She imagines his wife finding her letters in the inside pocket of his suit, scanning the pages, taking everything in: the effort she has put into making him laugh, the part about touching herself in bed, the references to a shared future. However traumatic for all concerned, discovery would at least move things along. Do they call co-respondents to give evidence? Lili quite fancies standing in the witness box in her close-fitting grey suit. Scarlet lips, a spotted veil, the whisper of nylons as she crossed her legs. Every man in court would understand. Even the judge would blush. And then there'd be no reason to wait.

She hated it when people asked, 'Who are you playing next?' Apart from anything else, it was unlucky. But not that day. 'She's going to be Mrs Broderick.' The elation – or was it the shock? – hit her like a glass of champagne on an empty stomach, before the inevitable doubt: did he really mean it?

But he has said it so often since, in front of so many people. She likes to look back on the years before they met, not bad years, even if they seem lacklustre to her now. A day's shooting on *The Avengers*, two days on *The Saint*, beating Rowena to the role of Juliet. The weeks in between living on fresh air, until she surrendered to the treadmill of provincial rep. She nearly didn't go to that party in India Street. It would only be the same old crowd, and she was feeling fat. There was a man who arrived in a wine merchant's van. Too short for such a powerful head, she thought, as he joined her on the doorstep. She teased him about the tradesman's entrance and he looked at her with those tea-coloured eyes: 'We were not born to sue but to command.' Nine words, and she shed her old life like a worn-out coat. After that it was a five o'clock gin in the George every night before nipping back to the flat, supper in the Doric sometimes, the odd weekend down south while Rosie visited the sister he couldn't stand. Henley, Royal Ascot, someone's country pile. *D'you know Minty and Hugo and Roddy?* She does now. They've never asked who her people are or what school she went to. They know she's not pukka but nor is she really a pseud – it's her job to inhabit a part. And anyway, Brod belongs enough for both of them. He was at Glenalmond with Jamie Kelso and Johnnie ffoulks. He shared a set with Rollo Drummond at Cambridge. He passes the port to the left, and goes shooting on the Twelfth, and sells an awful lot of claret to the chaps' maters and paters. They know he charges over the odds, but he makes them laugh. And he chose Lili over all the triple-barrelled Susies and honourable Georgianas. Of course it was tricky, him being married to Johnnie's favourite sister. Lili could see that extricating himself would take time and tact, that Rosie already had half an idea there was something going on and could be an *absolute bitch* when her pride was hurt, that it would be better all round if Lili made herself scarce for a while.

If only she'd known how lonely it would be.

Behind her, Mrs S's ancient refrigerator gurgles into life. Under the table, the red-eyed spaniel whimpers in his sleep. Lili walks over to the Rayburn. The cross-eyed farmhand glances through the window to catch her filling the kettle. *Another cup of tea, and half a packet of digestives!* It's the hormones. She feels sick whenever her stomach is empty. Changing her mind about the tea, she opens the back door. It's good to be out, under a sky now pierced by the first star. The border collie approaches, wagging its tail, trailing its long tether of washing line, and she strokes it until her fingers discover a small, hard, unidentifiable something snagged in its coat. The dog gives her a reproachful look as she stands up. Her nipples are like steel bolts (the hormones, or the evening chill, or both) but she can't face returning to the house, so she crosses the yard to the byre.

What first comes to mind are the Christmas carols of her childhood. A humid, intimate warmth. The smell is surprisingly wholesome, the beasts' steaming breath and the sweetness of straw dulling the pungency of their droppings. The cattle are penned behind horizontal bars, leaving a narrow walkway beside the cold stone wall. As one, they turn, their globular eyes following her progress towards them. The light has a thickened quality. It takes a moment for her vision to adjust, allowing her to distinguish between them: black and brown, plain and patterned hides, the gradations of wariness and curiosity that make this animal retreat from her while that one edges forward to take its place.

What if Brod just wants her out of the way?

She has never stood so close to cows. Bullocks, she means. Or, what is it the farmhands call them – stirks? Such enormous heads. Cavernous nostrils. Muscular slabs of pink tongue. She remembers dissecting a bullock's eyeball at school. It was as big as an orange. She had a hell of a job hacking her way through the cornea. The thought brings another lapping of

66

nausea. Even the timid beasts have closed in now. They press together, flank to flank, just the other side of the steel bars, the nearest she has come to an audience in weeks.

Locking her jaw, she drops into a demure, Home Counties staccato.

'This can't last. This misery can't last. I must remember thet and try to control myself. Nothing lasts really. Neither heppiness nor despair. Not even life lasts very long. There'll come a time in the future when I shan't mind about this anymore, when I can look beck and say quite peacefully and cheerfully how silly I was.'

The bullocks chew the cud, unmoved. She puts out a hand. Some shy backwards, but the nearest sniffs at her, consenting to be touched. She claps the solid neck, then, growing in confidence, spreads her fingers in the rough mat of hair.

'You don't want to do that.'

Jake is standing behind her, his face in shadow and darkened further by a day's growth of beard. He must have been here when she walked in.

'Why?' she says. 'Is this one a biter too?'

He doesn't smile.

If that's the way you want it, she thinks.

Since that morning by the paddock they have not spoken, though he has watched her from a distance, as she watches him when he's looking the other way. No one minds a bit of spying, but damn him for eavesdropping on her Celia Johnson. If he'd spoken up earlier, or crept out without her noticing, she wouldn't feel such a twit.

'I was giving them a bit of *Brief Encounter*,' she says. 'You know, the old film?'

If he does, he shows no sign of it.

'I played Laura at Chichester opposite Alan Bates.'

Bingo. It's just a flicker, but she can see he's impressed. No need to tell him it was only a matinee. Susannah had a terrible hangover.

'You'll be missing all that,' he says.

'A bit. Not much. It's very different here.' In the pen a bullock lifts its tail, voiding a stream of greenish shit. 'Which is interesting.'

'But not as interesting as your job.'

She wrinkles her nose. 'Any job gets samey after a while. Yours too, I'm sure.'

'What would you know about it?'

She gives him a long look, head to foot. His hair needs cutting. He'd get away with it in Edinburgh, with a lick of mascara and an Afghan coat, but that's hardly his style. It's on the tip of her tongue to say, *I know all sorts of things about you*, but neither of them would benefit from a declaration of war. They are going to carry on pretending they had never met before she came to the farm. For all his growling, she's fairly sure he'll collude in the charade. Thinking this makes her smile. Deliberately, while the smile is still warm, she looks him in the eye.

He nods at the bullocks. 'What do you reckon they'll fetch?'

'I haven't the faintest idea.'

'We'll find out tomorrow.' There's a sly gleam in his eye.

She returns an enquiring glance.

'They're off to market. Next time you see him'll be on your plate.'

Oh for God's sake, he thinks she'll be shocked. As if you have to work on a farm to understand that the powerful do as they please with the weak. As if one moment of squeamishness has defined her for ever in his eyes.

'I don't eat beef,' she says.

He bares his teeth in derision. 'You think it's *cruel*?'

'I just don't like the taste.'

Why doesn't he clear off? They have said all they have to say to each other. He has made his position perfectly clear. There'll be no truce. The day they met they became enemies:

her virtue his crime, his lightness her burden. Under the circumstances, they can only wish each other ill.

She starts to move past him, towards the yard, but he does not step aside and now they're standing too close.

'Don't put your hand between the bars again. I saw somebody do that once, a farmer. He should have known better. The beast reared its head—'

He flicks his own in demonstration, the movement made faintly comic by the swaying of all that hair. His hand catches her forearm, jarring it against the metal, not so hard that it hurts, just enough to send a jolt of adrenaline through her.

'Snapped the bone like a matchstick.'

Card

It was six weeks before Frankie and I went to bed. After our midnight kiss in the taxi queue, he sent me home alone. The next night, too. And the next. After a week or so he came in for coffee and some clothing was removed, but it was all very unlike the runaway train that was sex with other men. In the end I asked. He had a girlfriend, a colleague who turned up for work in a silk blouse, tailored jacket, jeans and trainers. Garden-variety reporters were never filmed from the waist down. I tried to bear this in mind when I watched her on screen, but still she looked mimsy. He wouldn't sleep with both of us and he wouldn't dump her out of the blue: another fortnight of mood swings and she'd be ready for the bad news.

We finally did it on the night of my thirty-third birthday, in his riverside flat, with a bottle of bubbly and tulips in a vase and brand new sheets on the bed and, despite all this fuss, it was like we'd been lovers for years. No first night nerves. No watching myself from the ceiling or lying there walled inside my skin, wondering who on earth this other person was. He gave a soft gasp when I undressed. I was flattered, but also perplexed. Surely he'd seen it all before? Every inch of him was known to me. Those shoulders. The whiteness of his meaty buttocks. He laughed when I told him: he'd never guessed I was such a spy. I smiled and said nothing, because what was the point of explaining if it left him less pleased?

I wanted to please him. It was a long time since I had given knowing the gift would be so gratefully received.

Our friends said we were made for each other, but still I panicked when we named the day, thinking of that Aberdonian girl at uni who first saw her fiancé in a dream, and the woman I overheard on a bus saying, 'When we come I can't tell where he ends and I begin', and Lilias's Ophelia at Dundee Rep. I can't remember Hamlet's name but I believed she really loved him, for that matinee at least. A week before my wedding I sat up till dawn with a bottle of Bowmore and an A4 pad, drawing a line down each page to separate the doubts from the never-quite-symmetrical reassurances. Fifty years with the television on too loud. Back-rubs on demand. Stability. Predictability. Newsprint on my white sheets. The cheesy odour of his thermonuclear feet. The soft weight of his balls in my hand.

By morning I had scored out almost everything, reducing three and a half pages to a single line. *Waking up with my best friend.*

For our first anniversary I gave him a Celtic shirt with *Chomsky* on the back. He gave me a framed print of Elizabeth Barrett Browning's forty-third 'Sonnet from the Portuguese'. The artist had transcribed the poem in brown copperplate, embellishing the H of 'How do I love thee' medieval manuscript-style. In the border around the words were hand-tinted thrushes and finches, a tangle of briar rose and ivy, red admirals and fat furry bees. Barrett Browning would have had a great career in advertising. *The breadth and depth and height my soul can reach* – what a saleswoman! So, yes, I knew the gift was kitsch, but when I tore off the silver wrapping my eyes filled with tears.

From Lilias Cavalle's daughter to Frankie MacKewon's wife. 'Culture shock' doesn't come close to describing it. I realise everybody's childhood skews them in some way. Another personality might have survived – even thrived on

– the same upbringing, but I emerged at the hard-boiled end of the sweetie counter. And then I married Frankie. *How do I love thee?* God only knows, but he did.

He had what psychologists call emotional literacy. When he felt something, he told me: pride in my achievements, tenderness as he watched me sleeping, fury at the thought of anyone hurting me. He was a manly grappler with pals gay and straight, a cuddler of women, an unselfconscious kisser on the lips at meeting and parting. None of this was exactly sexless, but nor was it creepy: merely the overspill from a bottomless reservoir of affection. I had the knack of making him laugh. Silly things that had him collapsed on the sofa, emitting a high-pitched whooping I never heard him do on screen. There were times when I carried him with me, all through the working day, a secret warmth just under my skin. At lunch, hearing a colleague moaning about her unreasonable other half and feeling obliged to reciprocate ('I know, Frankie's the same'), I'd be struck by how soon my empathetic noises ran out. I *didn't* know, Frankie was *not* the same. When Lilias urged me to invest in a tube of concealer or a pair of magic pants, or told me the gym was giving me 'Russian shoulders', instead of feeling crushed or enraged, I would look at her and think, you've never had what I have.

I don't want to overstate things. Frankie and I remained different people who experienced what we had together in different ways. He was a born romantic. For all the joys of married life, he missed those decades of unrequited yearning. Two or three times a year he liked nothing better than an evening alone, some dingy hotel bar in Dortmund or Bratislava, his phone switched off, the camera crew not due until next day. A few delicious, lonely hours to stare into his glass and imagine me cooking a meal, opening a bottle of wine, back in Glasgow. *And, if God choose/I shall but love thee better after death.* I once asked him if he ever fantasised about weeping at my graveside, the minor chords playing softly in his head? He looked so horrified I let it drop, but I wouldn't have minded. Nothing really mattered if you were loved.

For seven years we carried on this way. Laughing, making love, seeing friends, doing up the house, fighting from time to time. It wasn't just his affections that lived near the surface, he had a temper that was quick to fire, but as quick to burn itself out. It's amazing how happy I was – and even more amazing, it occurs to me now, that I took such happiness as my right. I believed in the fairy tale ending, the lifting of the curse. Love, generosity of spirit, ease in my own skin: I'd cracked it! And for a long time it really felt like that. Then we decided to try for a baby, and it became clear to me that I was no longer the object of Frankie's romantic dreams. In fact, I was their impediment: the wicked queen to his lovelorn prince. Now, the one he yearned for was his unconceived child.

Meaghan blew a noxious-smelling bubble of strawberry gum and played the six of diamonds. I played the five. Torcuil stared at his useless cards, slapping a hand to his head in a nine-year-old's mime of despair. It was Frankie's turn. A glint in his eye promised mischief. The children waited, their faces primed for laughter.

'Now, shall I be nice, or shall I…'

He placed the two of diamonds on the table. Meaghan whimpered, reaching for the deck to pick up her extra cards, but he wasn't finished, he tucked in his chin to peer at his hand. Torcuil gave a snort of mirth. The two of spades was added to the pile. Meaghan squealed. Frankie squinted at his cards again, fingers hovering. Meaghan started to protest. He raised his eyebrows innocently and looked to me to play.

Five of spades. The queen. The nine. Frankie leaned over Meaghan trying to see her hand. She squirmed away from him, laughing, and got rid of the remaining three nines. The suit was now clubs. I played the Jack, Torcuil the ten. Frankie, casting a sly glance at Meaghan, put down a run of five, six and seven, which reversed the direction of play.

Torcuil warned us, 'He's nearly out!'

King of clubs. King of spades. Four of spades. Frankie played the ace, changing the suit. He had two cards left.

'Anything but clubs,' Torcuil instructed his sister.

Meaghan used the four of hearts. I'd followed her with the four of clubs before realising my mistake. Torcuil's face showed disbelief but he did not make a fuss as he would have done with Frankie. He had known me all his life, I had soothed his colicky screaming fits and wiped his bottom more times than I remembered, but I was a grown-up, while Frankie was an honorary child. It would probably end in tears and someone else would have to pick up the pieces, but till then I was Mrs Boring and my husband was Mr Fun.

Smirking at Torcuil, Frankie played the queen of clubs. 'Last card.'

Torcuil's small features distended in horror. 'We gotta stop him, guys.'

He played the eight. I played the three.

'*Pick up*,' they chorused.

I took my punitive card from the deck. With a cartoon villain's laugh, Meaghan played an ace to change the suit to hearts. Frankie mimed dejection, tutting and shaking his head, then turned his remaining card face-up. The five of hearts. The children yelled in gleeful outrage.

'Another game?' my husband said.

Ruth was pricking baking potatoes at the far end of her enormous kitchen-cum-living room.

'Can I do anything?'

'I think it's all under control.'

'Of course it is: you're a mother. I bet you multitask in your sleep.'

A shout came from the other end of the room. The game of Switch had been abandoned. Frankie and Torcuil were wrestling on the settee.

Ruth saw my face. 'It's different when they're your own.'

'*No? Really?*'

She jabbed me with the fork. 'You try original thinking when you've been up half the night rubbing somebody's sore tummy.'

Not all my friendships had survived the experiential gulf that opens between parents and the childless. Ruth and I coped by caricature. In our pantomime, my life was all nights at the opera and issues of national importance. She was the earth mother who couldn't remember the last book she'd read that didn't begin *Once upon a time*.

'Why isn't Kenny getting up to do the tummy-rubbing?'

She pulled the rueful-smug face I'd seen on every mother I'd ever known, apart from mine. 'They want their mum. Besides,' she glanced down at her thickened waistline, 'I'll need to get used to it again.'

While Frankie and I had been fruitlessly fucking by the book, Kenny and Ruth had got drunk on sweet sherry at her Auntie Mary's funeral tea, had a quickie before the school run and conceived what they called 'The Afterthought'. Fortunately, the bond between the four of us was strong enough to withstand the stresses of this irony. Ruth and I had shared a flat at university, in the days when she was going to save the world as a feminist psychoanalyst, if I didn't beat her to it as a Labour MP. She was, if not my oldest friend (Frankie was that), the only woman of my acquaintance whose husband Frankie could stand. Everybody loved Kenny. A whispering giant with a graveyard cough from forty a day, eczema from the patches, toothache from the nicotine gum, and the most therapeutic bedside manner in Glasgow. He was from Dublin, a first-generation immigrant to Frankie's second generation but, unlike Frankie, a Protestant. The social assets were perfectly balanced: Kenny the more echt, with that mellifluous charm that was the birthright of the native-born Irishman; Frankie the better physical specimen, descended from the peasants Kenny's ancestors had starved off the land. Every couple of weeks Frankie would wangle himself off work early, head for the bar around the corner from the surgery, and spend an hour humouring the star-struck drunks until Kenny shambled in mumbling about having lost track of time. It was just like Kenny to botch the contraception, forget to bring home a morning-after pill and heave his trademark sleepy shrug at the prospect of an extra seven years of child-rearing. Happy accidents were his forte.

'Actually there is something you can do.' Ruth rummaged through the bags on the counter. There was a moment of dead air and I knew she was searching for a new topic of conversation. Satirising the gulf between us didn't make it any less real. There were vast tracts of our lives that held little interest for the other.

'How's work?' she asked.

This was one of them.

'A pain just now. Some guy who didn't get promoted to prison governor thinks there's a secret agenda. I've been over and over it: it's rubbish. Now he's got a Labour MSP accusing us of political bias.'

Ruth clucked and emptied a bag of radishes onto the chopping board. Although angled towards me, she had one ear tuned to the other end of the room. One of the drawbacks of Frankie being 'good with kids' was that other adults were forced into a supervisory role.

She handed me a knife. 'I don't suppose…?'

She had been asking me this for two and a half years.

'No.'

Her face lost its optimistic cast.

'Alice thinks I should try African moon magic,' I said.

She looked like Meaghan when she laughed. 'African *what*?'

76

'You sleep with the light on to fool your ovaries into thinking it's a full moon. It's supposed to reboot your menstrual cycle, make you more fertile.'

'If it doesn't bring out your inner werewolf.'

Torcuil squealed. We both turned to look, but he was laughing. Frankie had a faux-quizzical expression on his face and a thumb and finger pincered on the tender spots either side of the boy's knee.

'Then again, do I really want to sign up for eighteen years with Frankie's inner child?'

'He'll make a great dad—'

I caught her eye.

'Once he realises it can't be fun *all* the time.'

'And if he never does?'

'You'll have to kill him.'

She bit her lip, looking over her shoulder to check we'd not been overheard. 'At least he's got some energy, he's not knackered seven days a week. And he talks to you. I haven't had a conversation with Kenny since 2008.'

'But you've got children. Anyway, I always know what he's going to say.'

Now I was the one casting a guilty backward glance. Yes, we still talked across the candlelit table when we ate out, or in the arts centre bar around the corner, and yes, we were each comprehensively familiar with the other's preoccupations. But every once in a while he'd introduce a thought I didn't know inside out, a concept I needed to concentrate to engage with, and my heart would pound as if he were trying to murder me.

Ruth took a salad bag out of the fridge, dumped its contents in a bowl, opened a bottle of Sainsbury's dressing and drenched the leaves. Before she had children it was always home-made balsamic vinaigrette.

'The clinic rang with a date for my laparoscopy,' I said.

'That's great!'

'It was next Tuesday. I'm giving evidence to the Standards committee.'

'So you rescheduled?'

I grimaced.

'You didn't reschedule?'

'I don't want to get started and then have to stall it again because I've got too much on. If I need IVF, I'll have to clear my diary for six weeks.'

'How is Scotland going to manage?'

'I'd like to see Frankie take six weeks off work with next to no notice.'

'Frankie doesn't have a womb.'

We both smiled at this thought. There was a pause.

'You don't want to do it,' she said.

I was used to Ruth's insights and the temptation to hear them as oracular.

'Of course I do.' I began to sculpt a radish. 'There's a risk of ovarian cancer.'

'You could always have a hysterectomy when you're done.'

'Great idea!'

'And the real worry?'

The years fell away and for an instant I glimpsed the psychology student with her bleached buzz-cut and cherry-red Doc Martens.

'Shall I lie on the couch?'

She folded her arms to show she was prepared to wait.

'I have these awful dreams, doctor.' I said it as a joke, although it happened to be true.

'What about?'

'I don't know. I can never remember when I wake up.'

'You don't believe in stuff like that.'

'No.'

'So?'

I regretted starting this conversation. 'How about, if it

doesn't work, we'll know it's never going to happen, it's the last card in the deck?'

'Use it or lose it.'

We burst out laughing.

'Maybe not the most tactful remark in the circumstances,' she admitted.

A high-pitched yelp announced that Meaghan had joined the tussle on the settee. This time neither of us bothered to look.

'Just think, you might be standing here in ten months' time showing off your new baby.'

'And then I find out I'm no good at it.'

'It doesn't matter.' Her glance fell on the radish I was carving. It was going to be a lotus flower. 'You still have to do it. And do it again. And again. And again. And after a while you can't remember a time when you did anything else. It's boring, God knows, but it has its own...'

'Zen-like satisfaction?'

'They need a routine. You supply one. You had a mother.'

I looked at her.

'OK, forget I said that.' She snatched the knife out of my hands and chopped the lotus flower in half, dropping the pieces in the salad bowl. 'We're going to eat it, not enter it for the Venice Biennale.'

I took the knife back and selected another radish.

'*Oh*,' she said, understanding.

I met her look.

In the dogmatic voice she used with the children sometimes, she said, 'Lilias is a one-off. When they made her they broke the mould.'

'Get his shoes, Meg!'

The game on the settee had switched to tickling. Torcuil's fingers strummed at my husband's armpit while he wriggled in a helplessness that was obviously feigned.

'*Torcuil, Meaghan, get off him!*'

The radish flew out of my hands, the knife clattering on the counter. Kenny was back from the off-licence. He wasn't a big man in the Scottish sense, his height was more of a lovable eccentricity, but just then his bulk filled the doorway. His eyes, generally slitted with amusement, were blazing. Torcuil and Meaghan disentangled themselves from Frankie and perched on the edge of the settee, knees together, beady-eyed with shock. For a moment Frankie's face showed the same stricken expression, then he recovered his poise.

'They're no bother, Kenny.'

'They're acting like little savages.'

Of all our friends, Kenny and Ruth were by far the most relaxed with their children, allowing them to relate to the outside world without the relentless policing of behaviour, the prompts of *please* and *thank you* and *pardon* contemporary parenting seemed to require. I decided something had happened while he was out, and he'd brought the frustration home with him. But if that was the case, why was Ruth watching my husband, not hers?

There was an amused, unruffled look Frankie wore sometimes when I was annoyed with him. I found it completely exasperating. He shared it with the children now. 'Your daddy's right, two against one's not fair.'

Torcuil's eyes slid towards him, sensing this was a joke but needing confirmation. Frankie winked. Torcuil smirked.

Kenny's arm shot out, yanking his son off the settee.

'Upstairs, both of you.'

Meaghan jumped as if slapped.

'Upto your rooms, *now*.'

The children fled, their trainers thundering on the stairs.

I remembered the last time we had been to Kenny and Ruth's, when Frankie bought a couple of ninety-nines from the van across the road and, before Kenny had a chance to say no, carried them up to the kids in bed. The time before that, he'd flicked a pea off his plate at Meaghan. They loved it when he crossed his eyes and stuck his tongue out, or made fart sounds and pointed at them accusingly. He could hardly get in the door before they were searching his pockets for their treat. All this currying of favour drove me crazy. I was so busy dealing with the way they preferred him to me, it never crossed my mind that I might not be the one he was competing with.

It was a storm in a teacup, uncomfortable in the moment but soon forgotten.

Ruth turned away to finish preparing the meal we would all sit down to quite happily in thirty minutes' time. 'Fancy a wee aperitif?'

'I thought you'd never ask.'

She resumed the conversation where we'd left off. 'Kids are tougher than you think. You had Lilias, and look at you now.'

'Is that meant to be a compliment?'

She raised her glass in a salute. 'Size twelve. All your own teeth. Good job. *Fantastic* friends.'

'So I should pull myself together?'

She grinned in the unrepentant way of people who spent their twenties mining the unconscious and by forty are back with common sense. 'If you really think you're going to fuck them up, bail out now. Otherwise, yeah, get on with it. For all our sakes.'

Doctor

How do you describe something you did a couple of thousand times? I say two thousand, it may have been more – but not so many more. All those nights we were too exhausted to touch, all those groggy mornings and listless afternoons I won't see again. We both preferred the daytime: a Sunday with the background hiss of childhood boredom, a chalky sky outside the window, the smell of lunch downstairs. Frankie was warm-blooded. I'd strip off fast and dive between the covers into his humid cave, a hot bath of flesh, his hands pulling me in to the furred breadth of his chest. 'Jeez, your feet are baltic,' he'd protest for the umpteenth time, and for the umpteenth time I'd turn in his arms, saying, 'Not as baltic as this.' So then he'd set about warming me and, when I was tingling and touch-drugged and drowsy, we'd kiss.

Ruth once told me she and Kenny could get from toothpaste to climax in fifteen minutes. We liked to take our time. It was the one advantage of not having children. In the beginning we were pretty evenly matched, I didn't think of him as especially good-looking. Then the years pass, and looking good is less about the extra you have than the basics you retain. Just as I was discovered by gravity, he found the Botox of fame. Like most women my age, I was intermittently gorgeous. The rest of the time I looked tired. Frankie was in a different league. No matter how tired, he still had those shoulders, a genetic fluke maintained with thirty laps of crawl a day. Those shoulders, the sandy brush-cut, that virile flush. It was a pre-feminist look. You'd never have guessed he owned a jar of moisturiser and cooked a mean risotto, which made him that most desirable of combinations, a sensitive type who looked like a brute. I saw the glances in the swimming pool: plenty of women would have given their eye-teeth to be warmed by Frankie's hands. I never worried. It wasn't just that he loved me. There was a streak of the altar boy in him in love with the idea of fidelity. Though he liked to ring the changes, in a monogamous context.

'*Take your clothes off, Mr MacKewon. All your clothes. Now, let's have a look. Stand still, please, eyes straight ahead. Broad shoulders, strong back, firm buttocks. Good. I'm just going to…* Sehr gut. *Stand still, I said. Muscular thighs. Turn around please. Strong definition on the pectorals, taut abdominals. Oh. What have we here? No need to answer, I can see what it is. Lie down on the couch.*'
    '*But, doctor…*'
    '*On the couch, please. I need to give you a thorough physical examination.*'
    '*But, doctor, you've nothing on under that white coat.*'
    '*Try to relax, I don't want to hurt you.*'
    '*What are you doing, doctor?*'
    '*I find it more convenient to work on top of the patient…*'

'That was nice,' he said.
    'Mmm.'
    'That was *very* nice.'
Afterwards we'd fallen asleep. I had dreamed of porpoises and whitecaps and jellyfish that flashed like neon. I was warm all the way through, still drifting on the incoming tide.
    His hand settled on my belly. 'Like the old days.'
    I bumped against the shore.
    '"Come round for breakfast," you said. I thought, coffee and a croissant. Bacon, if I'm lucky. *Fuck*. Then you went in

83

and did a day's work. I had to pull a sickie, go back to the flat and crash out.'

Above me the ceiling came into focus. There was a crack in the plaster I hadn't seen before.

'Eight in the morning. I couldn't believe it. A quickie maybe, but not the full *a la carte*. I thought, I'll be dead of a heart attack by the time I'm forty, but I'll die happy.' He gave a pleasurable shudder. 'What were you doing down there?'

'Just the usual.'

'No, it's different when the doctor does it.' His fingers combed the hair between my legs. 'Good job my ma's not alive to see me now. I was a good boy, till I was corrupted.'

'Not by me.'

'Must have been your twin sister, then.'

I said nothing.

He nudged my shoulder. 'It was your idea.'

'What was?'

'The doctor.'

'No it wasn't.'

'Aye it was.'

His fingers burrowed deeper, the other hand lifting to give me an unobstructed view of his reviving interest.

'Before I went in to the Western for my foot. I was joking about the nurses and you said, "It's the doctors you'll need to watch."' He nudged me again. 'Remember?'

'No.'

'Aye you do.' It was one of his standing jokes that I would never concede a point. 'Doctor Hess. "Herman," I said, but you said, "No: *Hildegard*. Works twenty-four seven, can't get a lumber, so she gets her rocks off with the patients."'

I did have a vague recollection of this conversation.

'You had your glasses on and that white pyjama jacket. I've not seen that for ages – you've not given it away to Oxfam? You started talking German. Aah, that rings a bell, eh? Go on, admit it.' He tugged provokingly at my pubic hair.

'*No.*'

He looked at me for a moment then took his hand away. 'What's wrong?'

'Nothing.'

'You're not still huffing about me working Friday night?'

''Course not.'

'What then?'

'It's not my style.'

'What's that supposed to mean?'

I waited until he worked it out.

'Fuck's sake, it's a ponytail and a German accent. It's not going to get you an Equity card.'

We were lying ramrod straight now, no part of our bodies touching. I could see him thinking it over.

'Why'd you do it, then?'

'I...' But the evasions that occurred to me seemed as damaging as the truth. 'You like it.'

'And you're just humouring me?'

I sighed.

'You hate it.'

'I didn't say that.'

'It reminds you of your *fucking mother*.'

I closed my eyes.

'Were you faking it?' he asked.

'You know I wasn't.'

'How? Tell me how I'm meant to know? For ten years I've been thinking you do it for pleasure.'

'Frankie...'

'You know: an equal party.'

I felt a flaring of resentment. If the charge was sexual bad faith, I wasn't the one who'd said '*like the old days*', as if I rationed it, or the missionary position had become our staple. As if we had both agreed the poverty of our intimacy.

'Yes, equal,' I said, 'not cloned. We are allowed different tastes. I never spent my weekends standing outside the changing rooms at Ralph Slater before I met you. I didn't listen to radio phone-ins about Luigi Moroni's groin injury. Now I do, and I quite enjoy it.'

'*Quite* enjoy...'

'I'm not talking about the sex.'

'*I am*.' He was shouting now.

'All right, I don't find the doctor–patient thing sexy *per se*. What I do find sexy is that *you* find it sexy.'

'Well *molte* fucking *grazie*.'

I was tempted to get up and walk out, but I knew from experience the sweetness of upping the ante was short-lived and the wait for retaliation unbearably suspenseful, so I lay there, nursing my sense of grievance. What was wrong with the reliable mechanics of marital sex? We still did it, for God's sake, and I knew plenty of couples our age who didn't. If it was a long time since either of us had felt an uncontrollable urge to rip the other's knickers off, surely that was inevitable, not an indictment of our relationship, a blight to be cured by pretending I was someone else.

In a calmer voice, he said, 'You think I don't know what this is really about?'

Here we go, I thought, *the joker card*. I played it too, now and again, but not half as often as Frankie. 'You know what I miss about the *good old days*? At least I used to feel you were arguing with *me*, not some sock puppet in your own head.'

He lifted his hands with a flick that said he'd tried to discuss this in an adult fashion, he wasn't going to try again.

Of course it bothered me, not knowing what he thought was bothering me. I reviewed the weekend. I'd griped about the empty honey jar replaced in the cupboard, the cardboard core of the loo roll left on its holder, but such things were so trivial to him they were wiped from his memory before I'd finished complaining. His working hours were a longstanding beef, but I'd lost that battle years ago.

I looked at him. He raised his eyebrows.

'Frankie, if you've something to say…'

I waited thirty seconds and got up from the bed. 'Right, OK.'

It worked.

'All that money we're paying, and you won't even give it a chance. But Freya Cavalle's never in the wrong. It's always got to be somebody else—'

So that was it. We had been discussing the clinic over lunch. I was prepared to book the time off work, if it came to that, but I refused to be exiled to some grotty country hotel. He thought I should be feeling guilty about this. Guilty enough to engineer a quarrel about sex to retake the moral high ground.

'Three years we've been trying. We know the clock's ticking. You won't even have the fucking laparoscopy.'

'I'm booked in next week.'

'What day?'

My face gave me away.

'What day, Freya?'

'I'll ring them tomorrow.'

He made a sound like a punctured tyre.

'They'll do it with no notice,' I said. 'We are paying *all that money*.'

'We can afford it.'

'And don't they know it.'

'They get results.'

'Apparently.'

'But you think they're ripping us off?'

'I think we don't know. If they're so fantastically successful, why isn't every other clinic in the country doing it the same way? You saw the IVF lab: they're not spending the money in there. If they see me every day, they can justify charging us over the odds.'

On the chest of drawers, his mobile started to ring.

'It's not just you,' I said, 'I want a baby too.'

'Do you?'

The ringing stopped. I knew it would be the studios.

'What?' I said.

'You say you do, and I used to believe you, but not now.'

I thought about looking into every buggy I passed, about the tugging in my chest when I saw a knitted mitten speared on a park railing. I thought about the first time I held Torcuil, and how tiny he was, and how the tension in my neck and shoulders relaxed as some comfort I hadn't known I could give flowed out of my body into his.

Frankie sat up. 'I know what you're doing,' he said, 'so you can cut it out.'

I didn't trust myself to speak.

'Cut it out, Freya.'

We were back on familiar ground. The way I turned his anger by acting hurt, my refusal to engage in any discussion that might end with me looking bad. And these were faults of mine, just as it was true that I had never given a moment's serious thought to uprooting myself to Perthshire.

He dressed quickly.

I knew when he strapped on his watch. 'You're going out?'

'There's a couple of things I need to do at work.'

'On Sunday afternoon?'

'And I've to catch the dry cleaners before they shut.'

His blue chalkstripe. I had forgotten to pick it up on my way back from the gym.

'I'll get it tomorrow.'

'I'm *wearing* it tomorrow.'

Blue chalkstripe or Prince of Wales check, it was hardly the end of the world. Come the morning, he'd admit as much, but at that moment it was game, set and match.

There were rules to rowing with Frankie. His rules. You gave it your all in the heat of the moment, and afterwards it was forgotten. No sulking or casting-up. I could see the sense in this. But to accuse me of not wanting a child, that was beyond forgetting.

'Frankie—'

He turned in the doorway. If he hadn't raised his eyebrows like that everything might have been different.

'Take a key. I'll be out when you get back.'

Trunk

The man I called Uncle Nellaney wasn't a blood relative. The connection was Gina, who'd dressed Lilias during her four-month stint in *Garnock Way*. Six years before her stroke, Gina met and married a naval officer, moving from her spruce tenement flat into a medieval towerhouse furnished with Chippendale and Hepplewhite. I'm not saying this was her only attraction, but Lilias never formed a lasting bond with any other wardrobe mistress. Gina had been dead seven months when I arrived. All her things were gone. The house was dark, and cramped by the thickness of the walls and all those antiques picked up for a song. You could leave a block of ice cream on the kitchen table in midsummer. In winter, I slept in my socks. After dropping me off at school every morning, Nellaney drove to HMS *Euterpe*, a bottomy vessel built to help Admiral Nelson defeat Boney, by then used for training in the Firth of Clyde. He didn't drink, or eat out, or drive a high-performance car, or care what he wore (cardigans, mostly, when out of uniform), but he owned a Bang & Olufsen turntable. If I wanted him to notice me, I had to replace Ashkenazy with Kajagoogoo or tamper with the chiming sequence of his fourteen clocks.

I foisted the familial nickname on him but neither of us was fooled. As long as I was tidy and polite and made him cups of tea and saved my tantrums for the school holidays, he was willing to have me there, but I knew his tolerance was thin. There would be no warnings, no sending to bed without supper, just a phone call, and my bags packed in the morning. Why did he take me in? Lilias paid him. Not regularly and not enough, but it covered the odd extravagance in the sale rooms. And maybe he was a little in love with the woman she performed for him. Until I was old enough to travel alone, she would turn up to collect me at the end of each term and stay the night so we could make an early start. I'd go up to bed leaving them playing cribbage in the drawing room. Next morning, when I went in to open the curtains, I'd smell her perfume and the peaty astringence of whisky over the usual fust of pipe tobacco, cracked leather and old wood.

It never occurred to me he might want company on the nights Lilias wasn't there, still less that he might be lonely for the daughter he'd never had. I would hear the click of his fingernails on the polished table, turning over the cards in game after game of Patience, as I slipped upstairs with my illicit packet of ginger nuts. Solitariness is the natural condition of a certain sort of child. I was happy enough, flopped on my bed amid the biscuit crumbs, and I wasn't completely alone. There was a man I used to talk to, a tall man with Othello's build and an intelligent, unblackened face. Yes, he was a figment of my imagination, but he was there when I needed him, as Lilias so rarely was.

I found her in bed, swathed in white. The room was small, the bed large and made larger by its avalanche of lace-trimmed pillows, the billowing duvet, all the veils, saris, fringed shawls and pashminas draped over the brass bedstead, the tray of cold coffee and biscotti balanced on the mattress and, rolling from side to side in an ecstatic stretch, Toby the tortoiseshell cat. She was wearing a white *djellaba* in some slubbed fabric that might have been raw silk, its open neck exposing the fragility of her throat above a long sliver of bloodless flesh. It was a while since I had seen her white-gold hair released from its pins, brushing her shoulders in a straggle her bewitched lovers would surely see as gamine. That's if she risked the seductive illusion by actually doing it these days. Could any woman, even Lilias, be promiscuously sexually active at sixty-nine? I chose to leave the question open, ignoring the silk scarves tied to the brass posts, their weave creased and stressed as if from knotting in bondage games. She was quite capable of dressing the set before I arrived.

'I know you're not asleep,' I said, 'you've only just pressed the button to let me in.'

Her eyelids fluttered. 'Hello, darling.'

I pushed the cat to the floor and took its place. 'Everything all right?'

She didn't reply. I felt the first stirrings of concern. 'What's happened?'

Again she made me wait, then keeked at me from under her eyelids. 'Nothing, darling. I'm just having a la-a-azy day. I've been out every night since Sunday.' She gave an extravagant yawn. 'And this morning I thought I'll just spend the day catching up. It's not as if there's anything else I have to do.'

I touched her brow and felt her recoil. Her skin was reassuringly cool, despite the guardless fire crackling in the dog grate. On the other hand, she was very pale.

'You've got to look after yourself.'

'I do.'

'Drinking every night? Staying up till all hours?'

'It's called pleasure, darling. You should try it.' She pulled the quilt higher, snuggling her chin into the fabric. 'It's good for you, boosts the immune system.'

I stood up. 'Well, you can go back to sleep now.'

We couldn't have lunch if she was in bed, she kept next to no food in the house, yet she didn't want me to go.

'I wonder how you'll remember me,' she said, musingly.

'I won't,' I said, 'I mean, I won't have to. You'll be here for a long time yet.'

'But not for ever.'

'None of us are going to be here for ever.' I saved her the trouble of correcting my grammar: '*Is* going to be here for ever.'

She did that little tilt of the head which meant *have it your way*, and I realised that, somehow, we'd switched roles. I was now the one making light of her illness.

I sat down again and sloughed off my jacket. It was too hot in there, hot and unwholesome: the clutter on her bed, the intimate smell of sleep and coffee and cat. Those flames suspended part way up the wall spooked me the way an actor lighting a cigarette on-stage or opening a beer with that unfakeable hiss can spook. With the obscene intrusion of the real.

'They're much better at treating it these days,' I said. 'The survival rates are—'

She cut me off: 'I wasn't a very good mother to you, was I, darling?'

I stared at her in astonishment.

'I wasn't like any of the other mothers. You didn't fit in. I know how important that is to children. You wanted a sock darner and cake baker, someone who had your tea ready on the table when you came in from school.'

I noted how little there was to choose between Lilias's neglected child and the classic domestic tyrant.

'I should have bottled my own jam and knitted you Fair Isle sweaters.'

'Kids with homemade clothes got picked on.'

She smiled briefly. 'But you wanted me at home.'

'I wanted a home,' I admitted. 'I could have compromised on how often you were in it.'

'*Ah*,' she said.

Yet she didn't give me away. She passed the parcel, but when the music stopped she always took me back. I could have been put up for adoption at birth, or later, once the novelty had worn off. She could have skipped the Easter holidays, whittled down her summers with me from six weeks to three. All it would have taken was a British Council tour of former colonies, and the precedent would have been set, but she stuck to the child-friendly British Isles. Which must mean something.

'My poor deprived darling—'

I heard the satire in these words but they touched me all the same.

'It just wasn't possible.'

We both knew what she was talking about, but I never thought she'd actually say it.

'Every child wants a father, of course. It's only natural. But I was surprised how single-minded you were. Most little girls would have wanted a sister or brother as much.'

I held my breath. I could feel him in the room, he had never been closer, but one misjudged word could banish him for ever.

'If I talked to the ASM for five minutes you'd be tugging at my skirt. "*Is that my daddy?*" It was terribly embarrassing.'

Through the open door I heard the cat snagging its claws on the linen sofa.

Carefully, I said, 'I needed a wee bit more than a photograph.'

'It was all I had, darling.'

'You had three years with him. You could have told me, I don't know, what made him laugh, his favourite food.' *Maybe even his name*, I thought, but we'd had that argument too many times for me to reopen it now. 'Something more definite than that he made his living pretending to be other people.'

'That is something definite, darling. You just don't like it.'

The cat reappeared in the doorway and leapt onto the mattress, where it sniffed at the plate of biscotti. I scooped it up and dumped it back on the floor.

'I've never really understood why. It's in your blood. You've got the voice and the height and there are always going to be character parts. You'd have made a good actress. Only you'd have to have learned how to feel.'

I thought of a couple of feelings I might express there and then.

'Did he know how to feel?' I said. 'My father?'

She gave a mirthless laugh. 'I suppose you could say that.'

I had been waiting all my life to hold this conversation, and now that the long-bolted door had cracked open I was paralysed by how much there was to ask. Why now? Was she clearing her conscience before it was too late? Or just playing out the scene because, well, she was an actress?

'Can I have it?' I nearly didn't ask, and it was the catalyst that changed everything.

'Have what, darling?'

'His picture.'

I felt the static crackle across her skin.

'I gave it to you,' she said.

'No: I wanted it, but you said he'd given it to you so you should keep it.'

'Did I?'

Of all Lilias's vocal tics I found *did I?* the most infuriating. A stalling tactic while she groped for her next line, it meant nothing, and at the same time it was the most revealing thing she said. Behind its urbanity lay a limitless indifference to the truth.

I knelt on the floor and peered under the bed. The theatrical trunk was still there, along with a crumpled tissue and a tube of KY jelly. I leaned in among the dust balls and grabbed one of the handles.

She raised her head from the pillow. 'You won't find it in there.'

I hauled the tin box across the floorboards, coughing in the lemon-scented dust that rose as I lifted the lid. When I was a child, this trunk had been my most illicit pleasure. Even now I felt it. The thrill of bypassing the smokescreen of her presence. All this archaeological evidence of my mother's actual self.

It was just as I remembered. The red Leichner tins, the gold-edged invitations smudged with lipstick, the bundle of programmes secured with pink ribbon, the crumbling newspaper reviews.

She pushed back the duvet and swung her legs to the floor. 'Freya.'

'Just making sure,' I said.

I riffled through the clutter. A platinum-blonde wig matted with spilled face powder. That tin of Coty L'Aimant talc I had coveted as a dolls' pillarbox. A Peter Blake sketch on a paper napkin (she'd approached him in a café, told him it was her birthday). Tickets for the Edinburgh Festival and the Oban Ball. The spare keys to all those long-forgotten boyfriends' flats. A body stocking still in its cellophane envelope. And her love letters, not separated according to sender, but tied together in a fervid, dog-eared millefeuille of desire.

'*What did I say?*'

I caught a glimpse of starveling breasts through the *djellaba*'s slashed neck as she slammed her hands down on the lid. If I hadn't braced my arms to stop it from shutting she could have severed my wrists.

'Ma!'

She sat on the bed. 'I don't have it.'

'I don't believe you.'

'I threw it away.'

She was hopeless at improvisation.

'Really,' she said, 'I didn't need it any more.'

'What about my needs?'

'You were the one I needed it for.'

The picture of my father as Othello had never had a frame. She wouldn't have tolerated the extra weight in her luggage. And I liked being able to touch the grain of the photographic paper. It was a monochrome print taken on stage but not, surely, during a performance. The lens was too close, the pose too visibly held, the other actor on stage (Iago, I surmised) artfully blurred. I first read the play when I was nine, and saw it performed in the late 1980s, by which time no one would have dreamed of casting a white man in the part. Watching that glamorous, Rada-educated Trinidadian striding about the stage, it seemed to me he was playing both the Moor and the man whose genes I carried. I only saw that production once, but I can still repeat the cadences of *It is the cause, it is the cause, my soul* note for note.

'What's this?' My eye caught something dark amid a sheaf of papers. There he was. Half of him, anyway. The whites of his eyes staring out of that boot-blacked face, his right arm intact, along with most of his torso in its doublet, his left arm severed just below the shoulder. The print had been torn in two, pinched between finger and thumb and ripped in a diagonal line straight enough to suggest considerable force.

I found the other half of the photograph face-down at the bottom of the trunk.

'I should have thrown it away,' she said.

I fitted the torn pieces together.

She took a deep breath. 'Darling, you're not going to like what I have to tell you.'

I met her eye.

'But I can see you don't like me much anyway right now.' She touched her tongue to her upper lip. 'It's not him.'

I kept looking at her.

'Your father. It's not his picture.'

I tried to calculate the advantage she would gain from this fiction.

'I found it in a second-hand book shop. I've no idea who it is. I never worked with him, and I couldn't find him in *Spotlight*. I think he must have been foreign.'

I could tell my silence was unnerving her, but I wasn't going to respond until she told me the truth.

'You were fine till you went to school. Then, too, for a while. It was when you learned to write. They showed me your compositions. I thought they were making a fuss about nothing: all children make things up. Especially if the teacher sets such unimaginative assignments. But there were so many, and they were so similar, scratching and scratching at the same itch. It was quite heartbreaking. You needed someone to love.'

Finally I believed her. 'So you found a picture of a professional pretender doing some pretending and pretended he was my father.'

'He could have been an amateur,' she said.

I wanted to hurl something and hear it smash, to snap my jaws and feel the teeth shatter in my head. I wanted to scream until my ears bled. But I suspected that, in her melodramatic heart, she too wanted me to do these things. And so I did not.

Little girls and their daddies. You see them everywhere these days. Shampooing hair at the swimming baths, rubbing sore knees in the park, leaning sideways to keep hold of a tiny hand. As a teenager I was obsessively interested in the sensory development of the foetus. One day I would be weaving through the crowd and a man's voice would stir the marrow in my bones. God knows why I told Lilias. She looked thoughtful for a few moments, then told me she went on tour the day after she conceived and, apart from the acrimonious phone call when she broke the news, they never spoke again.

She was watching me from the bed. I realised I was still holding the photograph together.

'There's a roll of Sellotape in the kitchen drawer,' she said.

I uncoupled the pieces and dropped them on the fire.

1972

Every afternoon Lili does a circuit of the farm. There's always something new to see, a buzzard on a fence post, a roe deer among the beets, and it passes the time, gets her out of the house. God knows how she filled the hours off stage before she came here. There was screwing, of course, but that never took long with Brod. Mostly they talked, and drank, and smoked. None of which she does now, what with her queasiness and the lack of company. She'll never have a better chance of finishing the last hundred pages of *An Actor Prepares*, if only she could concentrate.

All day every day the same thought circles in her head. When did Brod stop loving her? For all his talk of *being careful*, he took her everywhere last summer. All those parties. Didn't they have fun, walking into that walled garden in the Borders, the bricks still warm with the afternoon's sun, a glass of fizz, the smell of lavender and trodden turf, shaking hands with some chap whose great-granny's great-granny had *accommodated* Bonnie Prince Charlie? They all knew Brod was screwing her, but he liked to introduce her as a 'valued client'. It wasn't just insurance against Rosie finding out, the pretence turned him on. Having to watch while she flirted with his old schoolfriends. That time she danced with Roddy, he couldn't wait till they got back: he had her in the van. So she didn't think twice about telling him she'd been out all night helping Ludo with his lines. How was she to know he'd go round there fists flying? Those were the golden months, everything so deliciously new. Even their rows. 'Christ strike a light!' he'd roar, so marvellously quaint, as if he were bringing out the family silver to hurl in her face. Of course, she has other memories, less delicious, less marvellous. When had she lost her lustre in his eyes? Wasn't it around the time he started saying 'She's going to be Mrs Broderick'? In which case the spur was not love, but guilt, or even a devious impulse to extricate himself. He never said much about Rosie, just enough to paint her as a Martha type, all duty, no dereliction. Lili was a Mary through and through, yet as soon as he started referring to her as the future Mrs Broderick, she became a Martha too. So many things she wouldn't do if she got another run at it. Understanding him and showing it, anticipating what he would feel or say. It infuriated him, which made her nervous. 'Do you love me, Broddie?' She remembers the way he looked at her, measuring her weakness. She should have told him to go to hell. Only by then she was so confident the prize was within her grasp.

It never occurred to her he didn't want children. It seemed so obvious: giving him a son to carry on the Broderick name was just one more thing Rosie couldn't do for him. Not that Lili wanted to be tied to a baby, but the business was minting money, he could afford a nanny. (Some whiskery old boot, not a Scandi au pair.) She would never have plotted to ensnare him, but since nature had taken the matter out of her hands, it would have been wasteful not to turn the situation to advantage. And so she broke her news.

How could he be so proud of her one minute, and look so cold the next? Was she sure? 'Absolutely certain.' He made an excuse to go outside, said he'd left something in the van. When he came back, his eyes were a thousand miles away. She told him he could stop looking at her as if she were trying to blackmail him up the aisle: he was the one who'd knocked her up. Did he know how many parts there were for pregnant women? Precisely none, so thanks very much. She used to find it sexy when he lost his temper, the way his shouting stirred her bones. He had never laid hands on her in anger, unlike some. Lili has had her share of slaps over the years, but she'd never been really frightened. Until that night.

Afterwards he sent roses, and left her alone. She must have walked into a dozen phone boxes, but she knew better than to dial his number. He had to think he'd lost her. At last he got in touch. They met in the Café Royal. He handed over an envelope and ordered champagne. If she'd stuck to her side of the bargain, perhaps she'd with him now. Perhaps – but probably not. The bottle of Moet, his high spirits, that bundle of ten pound notes: *the kiss-off*. No sooner has she acknowledged it than her mind veers away. All is not lost. Yes, she made a mistake or two, but *the path of true love* and all that. She always knew she would have to play the long game. It could yet come right, if she holds her nerve and carries on writing her funny, sexy letters. She heard from him the other day. A postcard of the Forth Bridge in an envelope with a second-class stamp. The sight of her name in his handwriting went through her like a thousand volts. Rosie had died! Or he'd walked out! But when she turned the card over, there was no message, just three kisses on the back.

Deep in these thoughts, she doesn't hear the Land Rover until it brakes alongside her.

'*You've been up the top field?*'

Jake. He doesn't cut the engine, preferring to address her at the top of his lungs through the open window.

'*You think that gate's there for decoration? When you open it, you shut it behind you—*'

He has caught her leaving the door of the black barn unlatched a couple of times recently, so she knows why he would blame her. She has no idea whether he is right. She remembers stepping around the S-H-one-T on her way across the field, but the moment she passed through the gate is a blank.

'*There's stirks all over. Munro's had them in his tatties. I've just had the police on, they're on the fucking road—*'

Even if it is her fault, what gives him the right to shout like this, flecks of spittle flying from his lips? For Lili, anger is an intimate privilege. She could no more lose her temper with a stranger than she could take one into her bed.

'*We're trying to make a living here, it's not a holiday camp for us. By the time you're up I've been at it four hours: you think I've nothing better to do than follow you round shutting gates after you?*'

'*I DIDN'T LEAVE YOUR GATE OPEN!*'

He blinks in surprise.

They see each other every day, at least from a distance, but it doesn't get any easier. Nothing she does escapes his notice. Brushing her hand across a seat as she sits down. Pushing the gristle to the side of her plate before feeding it to the spaniel under the table. She thinks of the rabbits transfixed in the headlight's beam while he picks them off with the shotgun. Do they, too, detect a sort of homage in his attention? So much animosity, and all for her.

'If you want me to leave, just tell me.'

He wasn't expecting this either.

Seeing that she has the advantage, she says, 'I didn't deliberately seek you out.'

'But you stayed.'

It's true. And her presence will be a constant reminder to him.

'It must be a hard thing to live with,' she says, 'afterwards.'

Such a naked look on his face. Like pulling off a mask. 'Not when you've no choice.'

'But there's always a choice,' she meets his eye, 'isn't there?'

'Maybe for folk like you.'

'You have no idea of the price I'm paying.'

Now she, too, is exposed, in all her self-pity. She waits for some sardonic remark. He pushes up his sleeve to scratch his

102

arm. Where it has been screened from the sun, his melanous skin is the colour of brambles in milk.

She says, 'I'll pack tonight and leave first thing tomorrow—'

His face shows nothing.

'That's what you want, isn't it?'

'It's my mother's house. It's up to her who stays here.'

'But you want me out.'

'I don't care.'

She laughs softly. 'Oh, I think you do.'

She is turning away when he blurts out, 'She's got used to having the extra money.'

And who knows, perhaps she has.

The border collie comes around the corner, head down, tail wagging. She crouches to stroke the soft fur under his muzzle. His master watches disapprovingly through the open window. Sam's a working dog, not a pet. Foreman, herdman, pig man, sheepdog: everyone here has a job to do. Lili feels the sudden lowering of spirits that comes and goes these days. The summer half-over. Kisses on a card. Sam's doggy ecstasy at every pat and stroke. And the other reason, of course.

'If I stay,' she says, 'it's on one condition. You don't tell your mother I'm pregnant.'

Barley

I turned into the farmyard, braking just in time to spare the foxhound that charged under my wheels, barking. A farmhand emerged from the barn and shouted at the dog but did not wait to see me safely out of the car, so I stayed put, sweltering in the glare through the windscreen. I wasn't sure I could spend six weeks here, even to make Frankie eat his words. When it was this hot in Glasgow I swam a few laps or strolled down the supermarket chilled goods aisle. Here, all I could do was open the window.

The foxhound leapt at the gap, its snapping teeth heart-stoppingly close to my face.

A woman's voice bellowed, '*Get down!*'

That evening I would turn this scene into a story (leaving out the claws skittering over the BMW's paintwork), making a punch-line of the moment when I emerged from the car and the dog licked my toes. The woman who'd come out of the farmhouse stood five feet eleven in her wellingtons. Her upper arms suggested white pudding vacuum-packed in its sheep-gut sleeve. Her wrists had the heft of honey-glazed hams. Everything about her was outsize: that meaty face under its greying fringe, the brown plait as thick as my arm, her oddly square front teeth. The wolf dressed up as grandmama, I thought, and had to remind myself I was no Little Red Riding Hood. We both qualified for the label 'middle-aged'.

'Can I help you?'

She sounded like Edith Evans as Lady Bracknell. I wondered what she was doing befriending someone like Nikki.

'You must be Margo.'

'And you are?'

'Freya.' I smiled. 'Freya Cavalle.'

'Pleased to meet you Freya,' she said as if she'd never heard the name before. 'I suppose you're wanting a look round.'

Since I knew nothing of farming, most of what she told me over the next thirty minutes was so much wasted breath, but I learned a lot about Margo. Her scorn for supermarket buyers, government paper-pushers and 'organic fanatics'. Her scepticism about nut allergies and wheat intolerance. Her disgust at the proliferation of play barns and petting sheds. As a visitor, I was helpless in the torrent of her opinions, but I foresaw no problem as a paying guest. I would be civil at the table and spend the rest of my time alone, walking leafy lanes, cooling my feet in babbling burns, whatever it was people did in the country. As we crossed the farmyard she pointed out the grain store, the hay barns, the silage clamp (which I'd taken for a tyre dump), the milking parlour, tractor shed and byre. These would be my landmarks. Only the Georgian farmhouse had any appeal. I could see it stripped of its various off-shoots and lean-tos, its stone lintels picked out in Farrow and Ball paint. Beyond the silage clamp was an unfenced patch of grass. We were almost upon it when I noticed the sheep lying on its side. Its fleece recalled those knitted dishcloths, dotted with tea leaves and toast crumbs, found beside the sink in a certain kind of theatrical boarding house. Flies pulsed on the jellied camber of each eye. I wasn't used to dead things and my *oh* was tinged with shock.

'It was perfectly all right last night. I get up this morning, and...' Margo gestured exasperatedly at the corpse. 'Wretched animals, more trouble than they're worth. The first sign of illness is sudden death. And that's after you've vaccinated them, trimmed their hooves, sprayed them for fly strike and three kinds of foot rot. I wouldn't bother with them, only *something's* got to eat the grass.'

I nearly lost my nerve then. It was a farm: a place of blood and excrement and a million strains of bacteria that could harm a growing foetus. But farmers had children, and they seemed to survive.

Margo flapped the hem of her shirt, wafting air towards her breasts. 'You'll be from the city, I suppose.'

'If you mean *do I know one end of a sheep from the other*, I don't,' I admitted.

'No shame in ignorance, if you know you're ignorant. It's the goons who expect the country to be just like the town who get my goat. Turning up with their clipboards and their twenty-page forms. Terrified we're going to track dirt into the grain store on our wellies. No good telling them it grows in a bloody field. In Canada, they harvest it and keep it in a pile on the side of the road.' She looked me in the eye. 'What do you do, Freya?'

Something about her brought out the tease in me. 'I'm a civil service paper-pusher.'

'For the Min of Ag?'

It was called Rural Affairs these days but I bit back the impulse to correct her.

'No, I'm working on a cross-departmental project to make government more transparent.'

'Transparently incompetent, if you ask me.'

'Well, that's a start.'

She didn't smile.

Over-revving engines were the soundtrack of my daily life, along with taxi horns and the bleep of reversing trucks. At first I hardly noticed the noise. Then it struck me that we were in rural Perthshire and the throaty roar was getting louder. I turned to see an electric-blue sports saloon with pram-handle spoiler and stainless-steel exhausts disappearing around the side of the barn, where the driver cut the engine.

106

'So what brings you here?' Margo asked.

'Did Nikki not tell you?'

'She may have mentioned something.' For the first time those big teeth showed in amusement. 'I don't always listen.'

It was obvious Nikki had not warned her to expect me, had not mentioned our meeting at the clinic, for all I knew had not told Margo she was attending the clinic at all. Part of what had made this visit possible was the relief of not having to explain. Nikki would have put her in the picture, she would understand. But she understood nothing.

'I'm having treatment at the fertility clinic down the road.'

I knew exactly what she would be thinking. I'd had my fun and left it too late. Perhaps too much fun. There were all sorts of streptococcal reprisals for women too generous with their favours. Or else I was one of those spinsters who'd snared someone else's man, now his children were grown, and was determined to put him through nappies and night feeds all over again. Mostly people squeaked politely, but from time to time I would be told how hard it was on a kid having a mother the age of every other kid's granny. Frankie said I should tell them to mind their own business, but the continuation of the species was everybody's business, and from the perspective of the species I was selfish. What could I say? Objectively I agreed with them, but I wasn't feeling very objective in those days.

There was a hummock on the other side of the patch of grass. It had the look of a Stone Age barrow. On its summit grew seven Scots pines, each with a fat foreshortened shadow at the base of its trunk. I climbed this hill with Margo.

'My mother had me when she was forty-six,' she said.

We were barely five metres above the surrounding land. I wasn't expecting such a view. Blue sky, yellow fields, a bright green combine in a cloud of biscuit-coloured dust. Further off, a tractor was ploughing, trailing a long black-and-white streamer. I guessed there would be some bloodthirsty explanation but, at this distance, the crows and gulls seemed to be braiding in an intricate airborn dance. My eyes returned to the barley, all the millions of seeds brought to this single state of ripeness.

'Forty-*six*?' I said.

'And I wasn't the last.'

'How much for full board?'

'I usually just do bed and breakfast.' She wafted her shirt again and I glimpsed her barrel belly, white as lard. 'Shall we say forty pounds a day?'

Behind me, a voice said, 'Better make it fifty.'

It was the cocky boy from the clinic, Nikki's husband. I recognised his tricksy tuft of beard.

He joined us on the hill top. 'Might as well make a profit out of something this year.'

Margo turned to me. 'This is Christopher, my son, a position he holds for life. Unlike his tenure as farm manager, which is on a very shaky nail.'

I can't fully explain what happened next. There were so many reasons for it not to happen. What I knew about the boy, what the boy knew about me, the embarrassing question of money, being caught in the middle of a family spat. Despite all this, he dipped his head and I raised mine and somewhere in the middle our eyes met.

'And you are?' he said.

'Three hundred and fifty quid a week, cash in hand.'

It had been a long time since anyone had grinned at me like that. 'How soon can you move in?'

Margo looked between us with narrowed eyes. She was no fool. 'I suppose forty-five's not unreasonable.'

'Wendy charges fifty,' he said, 'and you can't swing a cat in her place.'

'That'll be why she's empty nine weeks out of ten.'

'Fifty's fine,' I cut in.

She gave me a severe look. 'I suppose it's the taxpayer who's footing the bill, in the end.'

And that was how I became a lodger at Margo's farm.

He called himself Kit, I remembered on the drive home. He seemed subtly different from my first sight of him in the clinic, or perhaps it was just the presence of his mother, the way she behaved as if she were the only woman in his life.

Bull

The hall was vast as an aircraft hangar, its acoustics playing havoc with the incantatory gabble of the auctioneer. For a moment I wanted Lilias beside me. She would have loved the spectacle. And I would have found myself hating it, so, on second thoughts, I was glad she wasn't there. I filed past the stalls, inspecting the sleepy merchandise bedded down in the yellowest straw I had ever seen. Who would have thought a shed full of beef could look so glamorous, pelts back-combed into a blond tousle, a tufted end brushed into each platinum tail? Aisle after aisle of these beauties, their cloven hooves buffed to oyster, the puckered arsehole washed baby-doll pink, a fetching tartan ribbon around the wattled neck, and still the sellers fussed with water spray and curry comb.

We had come to buy a replacement for Virgil, who after ten years' rutting to order showed more interest in a good scratch. Margo was dressed to kill in a new pair of corduroys, her iron-grey plait brushed loose. Kit had swapped the T-shirt and denims that flattered his lanky grace for a tweed jacket I guessed had belonged to his father. I too had made the effort, with a cream sweater that rendered me almost as radiant as the bulls. Not that anyone noticed. Any appreciative glances were kept for the Charolais, who did seem almost womanish, with their huge hind quarters and indolent swaying walk, peering at the world with a moistly myopic gaze. Only the weighted sacks between their back legs hinted at another story.

I was surprised it wasn't all done by artificial insemination.

'With pigs it is,' Margo said. 'With sheep and cattle, you can't beat humping for results.'

Kit and I shared an expressionless glance.

When she bumped into a breeder she knew, we both took the chance to escape. I continued along the same row of stalls, while he veered down a cross-aisle. There must have been five hundred bulls, each attended by a team of cowhands wearing liveried overalls like pit-stop mechanics. Above each stall was pinned a chart bearing a name and a sequence of numbers.

'*Oh.*'

We stopped just short of collision, faces centimetres apart. We had been walking in parallel down adjacent aisles, I'd turned left, he'd turned right. It wasn't the first time this sort of thing had happened. There had been other near-misses, barging into the kitchen just as he was on his way out; rounding a blind corner of byre or barn; turning on my heel to find him just behind me. It was as if our bodies were navigating autonomously, like aircraft on intersecting flight paths.

'Sorry,' I said.

'Any time.'

I had been at the farm almost two weeks by then, long enough to have had my first impressions of Kit confirmed. He was a shoulder-roller and knuckle-cracker, a drinker of milk straight from the bottle, a yawner who opened his mouth a fraction too wide to show off his strong square teeth. A couple of days before, in the kitchen, I had watched him scribble a reminder on a sticky label and slap it to his denim-clad thigh. Had the boys I'd known in my twenties displayed like this to women twice their age? I made a mental note to ask Frankie when we talked on the phone that night.

The tiered seats around the auction ring were packed. We ended up among the overspill of buyers in the cattle hall, under the dead man's stare of the Tic Tac boy, until he shocked into life with the spasm that signalled a bid. When

111

the time came Margo would deal with the auctioneer, it was her son's job to monitor the prices. I left him scribbling in his catalogue with a chewed pencil, while I made a circuit of the hall. The sawdust had been trodden to an orange paste, what with the buyers milling around, and the sellers queuing for the ring, and the cowhands criss-crossing through the crowd leading bulls inexorable as oncoming trains. I stared at the leathery faces and fashion-free haircuts, the acres of Barbour green and Harris tweed, trying to guess who was yeoman and who was gentry, then eavesdropping on their accents to find out if I was right.

'Be easier if you could do it like this, eh—'

Kit had crept up behind me.

'Go down to the market and pick up a stud?

I supposed we had to have the assisted conception conversation sometime.

'That's more or less how it works in some parts of Glasgow,' I said.

'But not round your way.'

'No.'

A granite-faced farmer, eighty if he was a day, nodded at us on his way past. I was used to the old men I saw in Glasgow: seven-stone flotsam with appeasers' smiles.

'You don't go for studs, then,' Kit said. 'You prefer the romantic type—?'

I gave him a discouraging look. He flashed his naughty-boy grin.

'They need to do the business, but you want a bit of versatility. Like a Charolais: good for beef and dairy. I'd say Frankie's more your Aberdeen Angus.'

I have to admit I laughed.

While they lunched on pie and chips in the café, Margo and Kit bickered over how much they should pay for which bull. I finished my bowl of tinned broth and left them to it, making

112

my way to the narrow corridor used by the beasts on their return from the ring. It was a popular spot, with spectators lining one side of the passage and a few reckless individuals loitering in the path of the bulls. Whenever a newly sold lot was led through, these dare-devils would merge with the crowd along the wall. After a while Kit turned up, choosing to slot into a gap a few feet away rather than play chicken with the bulls. It was obvious somebody's luck would run out sooner or later. The victim was an elderly farmer, standing chatting with his back to the ring. He had no inkling that the beast was behind him. I watched it happen, his little legs tripping in a futile attempt to keep up as he was dragged along between the bull and a stretch of breeze-block wall. The farmers around me found it hilarious.

I heard Kit ask, 'What number was that last lot?'

Someone told him.

The auctioneer was moving the sale along at impressive speed. Forty lots had been despatched in little more than an hour and still he had time for jokes. Vesuvius drew the inevitable comment; Valentine, a pun about calf love. Only eight months old and already he had seven heifers in the family way.

'I was the same at that age,' said the farmer to my left.

Kit joined in the laughter.

'*Do I hear five thousand, gentlemen? Four? Three? Two? Fifteen hundred...*'

Somewhere in the hall a finger was raised, or a catalogue twitched. With a bidder committed, the price began to climb.

'*...Sixteen. Eighteen. Two thousand. Two thousand two. Four. Six. Eight.*' The bidding stalled. '*A fine bull, gentlemen, high on the saddle, seven cows in calf.*'

'Is he sedated?' I wondered.

The man on my left turned towards me. He was as tall as Kit but much older, with a spade-shaped jaw and a checked cap pulled down low over his eyes. His waxed jacket gave

113

off a smell that a fortnight before I would have described as 'stables' but was now able to identify as sheep.

I nodded at the bull in the ring. 'He's so placid.'

The sheep man looked doubtful. 'You don't want him too quiet, he's got to give twenty-five heifers a good seeing-to. The more raised they are the better they are on the job.'

Kit called to me, 'We've got him!'

I saw Margo slip out of her seat above the ring. The bull came towards us, a fur-covered sideboard on legs.

'Is that Margo Oliphant's laddie?' my neighbour asked, when Kit had led it away.

'That's right.'

'He's the spit of his father.'

My imagination conjured an older version of Kit, a man I could flirt with and not feel like a cradle-snatcher. More suitable, if less desirable.

'Bad business, that,' he said, 'hard on the laddie—'

I looked up, a proper look that took in the whiskers breaking through his weathered skin, the hair in his nostrils, those long flaccid ears, and in spite of all this, the impression of, not youth exactly, but some quality that closes off with age. He still wanted something from the world.

'Harder on her, mind. He was just a bairn: they dinnae miss what they never had.'

'I'm not so sure about that,' I said.

On the other side of the hall, Margo had taken possession of her prize. She saw me, and beckoned.

'No?' he said. 'You think it's marked him?'

'I don't know him well enough to say.'

'But if it was you?'

All at once I was uneasy with the conversation. It had a peculiar tone, inconsequential and pointed at the same time. We seemed to have moved from the candour of strangers to a more personal exchange, the sort where I might choose not to be so candid. I glanced at his Tattersall shirt and high-waisted

114

trousers. The body inside them was lean, spare even, but still somehow substantial, reminiscent of someone I couldn't place. What was a sheep man doing at a bull sale, anyway?

'Is the father still alive?' I asked.

'Last I heard.'

'I don't understand men like that,' I said, 'to have a son and never get in touch.'

'Ach, the laddie's doing all right for himself, from what I've seen.'

I know now that, in trying to put a normal social distance between us, I had stepped away from the wall, but I had no sense of it then. All I knew was that he was pulling me towards him. His strength was astonishing. No chance to resist: I was weightless in his grip. The next instant I felt myself crushed against his chest by the heft of the bull at my back. And then the beast passed by, and he released me, and everything was the same as it had been ten seconds before, except that I felt unaccountably tearful.

'Thank you,' I said.

Margo was beckoning me more emphatically now. I told him I had to go.

He nodded. 'I'll see you again.'

It was an odd thing to say but, who knew, perhaps he would, at some sheep dog trials or tractor rally.

I was halfway across the hall before the suspicion surfaced. It wasn't only his eyes the cap had concealed: it was his hair, the flop of charcoal hair that had been so conspicuous in Edinburgh, and the long, bony insistence of his face that, with the cap pulled so low, had gained the illusion of breadth. The accent, too, was broader, with a rural quaver mid-throat. The more I thought about it, the more certain I became that the man who smelled of sheep was my fraudulent interview candidate, Mr Smith. But by the time I looked round to double-check, he had melted into the crowd.

Bath

That Saturday, when I woke in my attic room, I streaked across the landing for a bath. The water pressure was so high that the hot tap ran cloudy, like seltzer, but the tank was small. The plastic tub creaked when I rolled onto my stomach, making the most of the six inches of water. Blue sky through the steamed-up window, jackdaws quarrelling on the roof above my head. I pulled the plug, wiped the fog from the mirror over the sink, and studied my reflection. Perhaps it was right, what they said about country air. There was a new bloom on my skin, a sparkle in my eyes. My breasts, slick with water, were white as a young girl's. Unless it was just the hormone injections. Turning from the mirror, I noticed the water was still in the bath. Usually it drained quickly, with a rattling gurgle.

I found the plunger in the downstairs loo, and decided to have breakfast before going back up. The farmhands had milked the cows and gone and Margo would be out all morning. After the shadowy hall, the kitchen was dazzling. Sunlight blazed from the window over the sink. Lifting a hand to shield my eyes, I found a black shape in the afterburn on my retina.

Kit was sitting, elbows on the table, shovelling bacon into his mouth. At the sight of me in my towel he almost choked.

'Good morning,' I said.

He wiped his mouth with the back of his hand.

I wanted to turn around and walk back out, but if

there was one thing worse than showing my middle-aged flesh to a twenty-four-year-old, it was letting him see my embarrassment.

He sliced a corner off his fried bread and speared it to a strip of bacon.

'I thought...'

'I'm waiting...'

We began simultaneously. Broke off.

I saw him looking at the plunger.

'The bath's not draining.'

'It should be.'

'Yes, I'd worked that out for myself.'

He gave me the once-over, slowly, wet hair to toenail polish and back. 'I thought you'd be in Glasgow.'

'Frankie works most Saturdays.'

'Watching football?'

'That's the one.'

The fork knocked against his teeth as he put the bacon in his mouth. 'Is this your weekend look?'

'I don't take baths fully clothed.' Neither of us smiled. 'Does it bother you?'

'Not at all.'

We held the moment: him at the table, overalled in the Aga's heat, me underdressed and on my feet, the air between us with its perfect balance of levity and weight, and then it dawned on me. He was playing with me, or I was playing with him.

His cutlery clattered onto the plate. 'I'd better have a swatch at that bath.'

He removed his boots at the bottom of the stairs and stood aside, letting me go first. The towel barely skimmed the tops of my thighs, but I climbed the staircase as carelessly as a teenager. Do a job for twenty-odd years and your career becomes your identity. I was always the responsible party, the one to cut through the flannel: *let's get real*. But on Margo's

117

farm, the Transparency Unit felt about as real as another galaxy. Who was I, stripped of my bureaucratic status? I was only just beginning to find out. Today's discovery: in a game of bluff, I wasn't going to be the one to back down.

The bathroom was too small for two people. The mirror had misted over again. The bath seemed filled with lemon barley water, only it was soap scum, not lemon, floating on the surface, along with a couple of pubic hairs.

He dropped to his knees, shrugging out of the top half of his overalls. Underneath he was wearing one of his many tight jumpers, worn at the elbows where his skin glimmered through the fishnet of wool.

He pushed up the sleeves and immersed one arm in my dirty water. I had already checked: there was no nest of hairs blocking the drain. He replaced the plug, took out a penknife and began to unscrew the bath panel.

'I'll be sleeping here tonight.' He raised his eyes to mine.

'Margo didn't mention it.'

'Margo doesn't know.'

'Trouble at home?'

'Ovary madness. An incontrollable urge to rip the dick off any man in a fifty-mile radius.' He pocketed the loose screws. 'Especially mine.'

'It's like being injected with plutonium,' I said.

'Yeah, yeah, and it's not my body, and she's not even twenty-one, and it'd be nice to have a bit of fun before she's stuck pushing a buggy...'

'She's got a point.'

'If you know what you want, why wait?'

The panel came away revealing the rough outer skin of the tub and, underneath, amid the dust-clogged cobwebs, the mummified body of a mouse.

'Oh good,' I said, 'wildlife.'

In the cupboard concealing the hot-water tank was a plumber's wrench and a blackened roasting pan shallow enough to ease under the pipes to catch any escaping water. He fitted the wrench around the copper joint, but the angle was awkward and the jaws kept slipping. Downstairs, Margo's grandfather clock chimed the half hour, and then the three-quarters. The morning sun beat on the roof above us. When he took off his beanie, damp strands of hair were stuck to his forehead. He had a firm grip on the coupler by now, but it wouldn't move. He tried a new technique, levering the wrench up and down. Abruptly he dropped it and took off his jumper. I blushed. It wasn't the shock of exposed flesh, so much as the intimate act of undressing: the arm reaching over his head, the clumsy tug on the knitted collar, the same heedless gesture Frankie made night after night.

'That's better,' he said, sitting back on his haunches.

Though I told myself not to look, some third eye saw the graceful lines of his body: the camber of his biceps, those long-muscled forearms, the narrowing from shoulders to waist. Lean as he was, every inch of him was sleek with youth's cushioned flesh.

The jackdaws had fallen silent. I could hear the drone of a tractor in the field across the burn. Kit's sweat was a faint tang on the roof of my mouth.

'I'll sleep next door, if it's all right with you.'

A couple of seconds too late, I said, 'Why wouldn't it be?'

He leaned in under the bath again. A grunt of effort and the metal surrendered.

'*Yes!*'

But the job was not finished. He remained on the floor, his face hidden from me, his right hand working at something. After a while he took up the wrench again. Curiosity got the better of me. I hunkered down on the lino beside him.

He pulled the plug out and, with a violent sucking sound, the water started to drain. He handed me the roasting pan, half-filled with a sort of delta mud, fibred, rank-smelling. I set it down on the floor.

119

He saw my revulsion. Grinning, he scooped up a fistful of slops.

'Forget it,' I said.

He weighed it in his palm, deliberating.

'I mean it.'

He brought it to his nose. *'Mmm.'*

'Kit.'

'What's the matter? It's just skin, scurf, hair,' a moment's hesitation before he added, 'spunk.'

I shoved his hand and the black slime splattered over his chin. It was worth it to see the amazement in his face. He caught my hand, the remains of the stuff squelching between our fingers. When he scooped up more with his free hand, I grabbed his wrist and fought him off like the giggling girl I hadn't been for twenty years. And perhaps hadn't been even then.

Downstairs the front door banged. A voice hallooed. Margo was back from her shopping.

Poker

At five years old I loved my mother infatuatedly. The oily-sweet smell of her lipstick, her blue-white cleavage in its square décolletage of cream chiffon Ossie Clark. I watch Ruth's kids now, stroking their cheeks with the velvet curtain, cuddling the sausage-dog draught excluder when Mummy and Daddy go out, and I'm amazed my love survived so many separations, along with the constant change of fixtures and fittings, all those newly-stale sets of smells. It even survived each new Lilias, each time she took a new role.

She spoke beautiful RP, as all Scottish actresses must. Her tall, fine-boned body and sculpted face made her the obvious choice as Beatrice, Rosalind, Amanda (she was born to wear bias-cut satin and drawl Coward's lines), various thigh-slapping principal boys, and Ibsen's neurotic wives. The week rehearsals began she would throw a tea party, a jolly gathering around the gas fire, rolling joints and toasting crumpets. Before I circled the room with my plate of buttered bannock she would introduce me to the backstage staff, who could be relied on to amuse me with endless games of Pontoon and Stop the Bus should the other childminding options let her down. The only time I recall her touching me, apart from hand-holding on busy roads, was at those tea parties. It helped if the object of this affection were herself a little performer, and for a long time I obliged, but over the years I began to notice something. The delirious gaiety of the occasion, the sucking and blowing on burned fingers, the gleam of melted butter on chin, the clashing perfumes and tinkling bangles, the twinkle in the eyes of the rude mechanicals, the hoots of mirth... all this caused a hollow feeling in me.

As I moved through adolescence I became increasingly allergic to showbusiness. The shrieking camp, the promiscuous endearments, the personality cults, and the phrase that cropped up in every magazine interview, every drunken heart-to-heart. *One day they're going to find me out.* What did it mean: one day they'll realise I'm no good as an actor? Surely the ability to conceal their professional shortcomings *was* acting. Or was the 'me' at issue their very self – one day they'll realise there is no me, it's *all* acting? Either way, it seemed like a boast. Some of them (never Lilias) babbled of neurosis and self-doubt, but they all agreed it was much finer to be a performer. To run the gamut of emotions in perpetual catharsis, not helplessly as others did, but for art. To be at once exemplarily human, and hardly human at all.

Lilias and her actress friends were always falling in love. With their leading men, as often as not. Though falling isn't quite the verb. Taking a running jump at love. Hurling themselves over the cliff of love. Telling everyone they spoke to, including themselves, this was it: the head-over-heels, out-of-control, once-in-a-lifetime Real Thing. I read enough novels to know what they meant. I'd seen love depicted on screen (by actors), and I witnessed it at second-hand, between Lilias and a succession of minor soap stars and provincial matinee idols. Three weeks of burning intensity, a blizzard of talk, electricity that lifted the hairs on my neck across a room, the moans and cries lasting almost until dawn. And then the day-long silences, the visceral revulsion.

By thirteen, I was an expert in love's shamanic chemicals, its inevitable progress from trance to disillusion. By fourteen, I knew that loving someone didn't mean they loved you in return. Love was a kind of applause, an effusion generated by narcissistic display. In the days when I still went to the theatre I'd come across actors who took the curtain call with arms at full stretch, applauding the audience whose receptive genius had brought forth their performance. One thing I'll say for Lilias, she never went in for that sort of cant. In love, as in life, some were born to do the clapping, and others to be clapped.

These were the thoughts I had too much time to dwell on now I was living at Margo's farm.

The hospital canteen smelled of battered haddock and a greasily spicy something the whiteboard menu identified as 'Sausage Surprise'. A queue of porters batted grinning insults across the servery at the woman with the ladle and the dermatitis gloves. Lilias would be in with the consultant by now, saying she had an audition at four and how strange it was to be sitting here without the cameras. The last time she'd seen the inside of a hospital she'd been playing the neurosurgeon's mother in *Casualty* – just a cameo, but pivotal to the story. Oh, he'd seen that one? How funny. She'd always assumed men like him would avoid medical dramas like the plague. Of course, he couldn't be expected to recognise her. She'd spent an hour in Make-Up, being aged for the part...

I checked my watch. I didn't like to think of her coming out of the consultant's office with no one to meet her. Another ten minutes and I'd go up to Oncology. The door from the lobby swung open and there she was, walking towards me, cheeks flushed, coat buttoned. In the anxiety of the moment I gave it no thought.

'Shall I get you a cup of tea?'

She sat down, glancing over her shoulder towards the servery. 'No thank you, darling.'

I looked her over. She seemed keyed-up but not, as far as I could tell, distressed.

'Well?' I said.

She unbuttoned her coat and I saw she was wearing a

123

turtleneck jumper. I had expected Jaeger and pearls, or Boho Theatrical Dame.

I tried again. 'What did he say?'

'They should get away with just snipping it out.'

'A lumpectomy?' I knew she hated the jargon, but I needed to be clear. 'With the option of calling you back once they have the histology results?'

'He has a feeling I'll be lucky.'

I wondered how this translated into medical language. 'Will you have to have radiotherapy?'

'Oh no, darling, nothing like that.'

'Tamoxifen?'

She looked vague for a moment. 'I might have to take some drugs, but really it's good news.'

There was a sensation in my chest, as if a block of concrete had started to crumble. I thought I might laugh, or burst into tears.

'*Thank God*,' I croaked.

She said nothing.

I realised a part of me had her dead and buried, but she was going to live! Then I was on my knees with my arms around her. I felt her pull back from the surface of her skin to somewhere unreachable inside her, but I held on, my face pressed to that precious breast, wanting her to know how frightened I'd been, how glad I was, hoping the moment would come right.

When it didn't, I released her and returned to my chair.

'It must be an incredible relief,' I said.

Her eyes stared back at me, hard and bright.

She touched the corner of her mouth. 'It'll make filming a lot easier, that's for sure.'

'It'll make living a lot easier,' I said.

'Three weeks in Mexico and a fortnight in Boston. I've always wanted to see New England in the fall.'

'It'll make seeing anything a lot easier,' I said.

'It's all very last minute. Maggie Buckley's broken her hip. You only have to look at her to see she's as brittle as a cheese straw. Of course, nothing's definite yet, but the audition went very well.'

'So when are you going in?'

She looked at me uncomprehendingly.

'For the lumpectomy.'

Her lips tightened. 'Soon.' She anticipated my next question. 'I'm not going to tell you when, because I don't want you there. I know you're trying to be kind, darling, but it doesn't help. I have to do this in my own way.'

'By pretending it's not happening.'

Her eyes widened. 'Exactly.'

She looked around the cafeteria, dismissing everyone but five junior doctors playing poker, watched by a table of nurses lunching on Diet Coke and chips. When she turned back to me I could see the subject was closed.

'It was very good of you to do this, darling, but I don't want to keep you from your rural idyll.'

'You've done me a favour, giving me an excuse to see Frankie and eat a decent veggie lunch. Margo did me stuffed peppers the other day – stuffed with mince.'

'Oh dear,' she said tonelessly.

I took my phone out and found a picture of Margo and Kit in front of the farmhouse. She tilted the screen to see better and laughed the way she might have laughed if I'd pinched her unexpectedly, and hard.

'What?'

'Nothing,' she said. Her eyes burned into the screen. 'It's just... Nothing.'

She lifted her head and gave me a penetrating look.

'It's obviously not nothing,' I said.

Her glance returned to the phone. 'He looks like someone I used to know.'

'Who?'

'Actually, now I've had a proper look it's not such a like-ness.' She found a better shot of the farmhouse. 'What's it like inside? Open fires, original features, or wet rooms and laminate floors?'

I shrugged. 'It feels like a place things could happen.'

'An unread script, an untrod stage.'

'I meant I might conceive.'

'Of course. How's all that going? You must have had your thingamijig by now.'

I stood up. 'Do you fancy going out for tea? I think we should celebrate. Smoked salmon sandwiches, cream scones. What d'you say? We could try the hotel up the road.'

She glanced down at her turtleneck. 'I might have a black coffee, if they do Italian.'

'You sybarite you.'

She gave me an ironic look. We didn't go in for affectionate talk. Unless you count 'darling', which I did not.

Just then the table of card players exploded into laughter. The grinning victor checked his pager. I picked up my bag. Lilias was still seated. With that instinct for tragedy that may have been her greatest gift as an actress, she reached out and lifted the hem of my shirt.

'Oh, *darling*.'

Despite all the assurances that laparoscopy was a discreet procedure, the surgeon had botched the job. He had taken three stabs at it: two in my navel, the third in the hitherto-blemishless curve of my belly. It was beginning to heal at last, but the wound was still an out-take from a slasher movie.

'Your lovely tummy.'

Lilias had never expressed any admiration for my tummy until it was spoiled beyond remedy.

'It looks worse than it is,' I said, 'they stitch it loosely so it knits from the inside.'

'But what about the *outside*?'

I arranged my shirt over the gash. To add insult to injury,

the surgeon had found nothing. My tubes were clear. No cyst to remove, no blockage to fix, no obvious reason why my womb should still be empty.

'It looks *sore*, darling.'

Lilias had not spoken to me like this in thirty years. Not since the summer I caught chicken pox, when she'd risen to the occasion with thermometer and cold compress. The memory of her cooing over me in that mellifluous voice makes me itchy even now.

She let go of the shirt. 'Sorry, darling, I forgot. You never liked being touched, even as a little girl.'

Had Lilias starved me of a mother's love, or had I cheated her of a lovable child? There would never be a definitive answer, since neither of us was prepared to accept the role of monster. I could have told her the rarity of her touch made it unbearable, but she would only have dredged up memories of me as a baby, screaming to be taken from her by every passer-by.

I sighed. 'Or I could just drive you home.'

'If you'd rather, darling.'

Out of the corner of my eye I saw two women, one about my age, the other much older, presumably her mother, and completely bald. The old woman had managed to fasten her raincoat with an extra button at the top and an extra button-hole at the bottom. Patiently the daughter rectified this. They didn't speak to each other, but there was a tenderness in the mother's submission to the efficiency of her daughter's fingers. I stared at that pallid, hairless skull and thought how differently the afternoon might have gone.

'You really have the luck of the devil,' I said.

Lilias looked at me blankly.

I shook my head. 'What is it they say: only the good die young?'

She stood up. 'I think perhaps I will go straight home, darling.'

1972

Heart thudding, Lili surfaces from a dream. The clock at her bedside shows a little after two, but her wakefulness has the sharp-edged quality of morning. She gets up to close the curtains against the moonlight, then changes her mind and unlatches the window. The casement bucks in her grasp, letting in a blast of night. Down below, the collie's tin bowl rattles across the yard. A loose triangle of tarpaulin flaps crazily over the seed drill. A flickering light in the pig shed catches her eye. *Flames*, she thinks, the word bringing back a flavour of her dream. She pulls on the flannel dressing gown Mrs S has loaned her while her own is in the wash and goes downstairs, groping her way along the darkened hall into the kitchen, stepping into the nearest pair of wellingtons, grimacing at their clammy touch on her bare legs. The wind fights her as she opens the back door. The dressing gown balloons in a gust of wind. She knots the tasselled cord and crosses the farmyard to the shed.

Not flames but a Tilley lamp. She flicks the electric switch by the door. The fuse must have blown. Jake is pacing up and down, his shadow flaring on the rubble-built wall. He nods towards the corner pen. In the barely diluted darkness she makes out the most heavily pregnant of the sows.

'I've no tobacco.' He sounds exhausted. 'Can you wait here till I get back?'

'From where?'

He gestures in the direction of the road, too tired to explain, too tired to remember his dislike of her.

128

'All right,' she says.

The sow is on her feet, nosing through the straw, shaping it into a nest. Below the swag of belly, twelve swollen teats hang just shy of the floor.

He takes the Land Rover keys out of the pocket of his jeans. 'Ever delivered a pig before?'

'Not that I recall.'

'Aye, well, there's a first time...' The rest is lost in an enormous yawn.

'For everything,' she finishes. 'Are you all right to drive?'

He rubs his face. 'I'm only going to Alan's.'

The sow backs into the furthest corner of the pen, pressing her hindquarters against the wall. Swinging his long legs over the barrier, he stoops to squeeze one of those womanly teats between finger and thumb. A bead of milk appears. He crosses to the darkened end of the shed and returns with a tin tub half-filled with straw.

'If she farrows, put them in here. Break the cord her end, or they'll bleed. There's clips in the box if you need them.' He misreads the horror on her face for a sentimental objection. 'If you leave them with her, she'll lie on them, or eat them.'

He frowns, distracted. She points to the pocket in which he has just replaced the keys.

'You'll be fine.' He recognises his mother's dressing gown and a sardonic humour stirs in his eyes. 'A wee rehearsal for you.'

Within minutes of his departure the sow is pawing the ground.

'Hold on, piggy,' she murmurs.

But piggy can't hold on. Something compulsive about her movements suggests the business has begun.

'He won't be long.'

The sow's raisin eye stares back at her.

Lili goes outside. It starts to rain. The wind lashes the dressing gown against her legs. She holds the flannel lapels

129

closed across her chest. Better a soaking than the inexorable event underway in the shed. And yet, not so long ago, she would have made the most of it.

Did I ever tell you about the night I played midwife to a litter of pigs?

Pull the other one!

Brownie's honour.

And was it disgusting?

No worse than a Saturday at the Blackpool Grand.

Brod phoned late last night. All these weeks she's been longing to hear his voice, and it was awful. Worse than awful: stilted, unnatural, with long uncomfortable silences. How was she keeping? Did she need any moolah? She told him about Alasdair's ram turning out to be queer. It was the sort of thing he found funny as a rule, but he was barely listening. Had anyone in Edinburgh been in touch? When she said no, she could feel his relief down the line. He pretended somebody had walked into the room, as if she wouldn't recognise bad acting. 'TTFN,' he said, hanging up.

He has played her like a fool – and why not? She is a bloody fool. He was never going to marry her or get a divorce. He hasn't given her a second thought since she left Edinburgh. Or he hadn't until someone made him nervous. *Old smoothy-chops* Oliver used to call him. Of course he was a liar: that was part of his charm. It was a game between them: could he get away with it, would she catch him out? But she never dreamed he would tell so many of her friends *she's going to be Mrs Broderick* with absolutely no intention of bringing it about.

She remembers the day she went to Glasgow. It was almost six o'clock when she got back. The van was still parked outside the vintners. She waited at the corner. At last he came out.

'Hel-*lo*.'

He thought he was free of her. It was all there in his voice: that reflexively flirtatious note, as if she were a pretty stranger. And she was flattered. Bloody fool.

She blurted it out: 'I couldn't do it.'

'*Get in.*'

The exact words he used are gone. Oh, she remembers 'devious little slut' amid the furious torrent, but he went on and on, some of it reasonable, or at least understandable, some of it vicious and, frankly, paranoid. She had planned the whole thing, coming off the pill without telling him. (That bit was true: the hormones made her fat.) For all he knew, it wasn't even his. If she thought she was going to trick him into playing happy families with someone else's brat, she could think again. If she wanted to keep it: fine, go ahead. But she could count him out. She screamed at him to stop the van. He was driving like a madman. He could have killed them both. For the first time she felt sorry for Rosie, being married to someone like that.

In the end she offered to leave Edinburgh and keep a low profile until it was all over, and he calmed down. They drove to the flat and had one last screw to see them through the separation. It would be funny if it wasn't so tragic. She is tempted to write him a letter: *Dear Brod, here's a tip. Don't propose to women you don't intend to marry. It might seem rude to you not to, and of course you like to know we're all head over heels in love with you, but it's not terribly kind. Yours no longer, Lili.* Or she could deliver the message in person, turn up at the house. *How do you do – I'm carrying your husband's child.* Though it might be sweeter just to move back, find herself a muscled stagehand to walk around Edinburgh with his hand on her rump. It wouldn't take more than a week for Brod to find out.

She won't do it, of course. Her clothes still fit, just about, but every time she looks in the mirror she's a pound or two heavier. Breasts, bottom, her thickening waist. She can't afford to let anyone see her like this. Word would spread like wildfire. *Lili's got fat!* And then who'd want to sleep with her? (Which, being honest, is half the secret of swinging a part – that and getting to the end of the audition without stopping to throw up.) Instead she is going to do the *sensible thing*, like any convent schoolgirl skewered on a first date. Brod will never have to see it, or even know its sex. The adoption people will whisk it away, and Lili will stay at the farm, living on grapefruit and hard-boiled eggs until she fits into her cheongsam again. And then, all bets are off!

By now the borrowed dressing gown is wet through. Reluctantly she returns to the shed. The gorgonzola smell of pig is stronger. The sow lies on her side in the straw, belly rising and falling. The clump of flesh under her tail is raspberry-red, engorged and glistening. She breaks wind, her back legs kick, and something slides out in a slick of amniotic juice. Greyish-pink and boiled-looking, but unmistakeably a pig. Stunned by transition, it lies on the straw, steaming gently. For several seconds it doesn't move, then a shake of the head expels a light froth from its jaws. The skinny legs splay, trying to stand. It goes down, tries again. At the third attempt it manages a stagger and within moments it is walking, shivery with life, slippery with the mucus gelling on its body, already questing for the nipple. The sow lies facing the wall, oblivious to the drama at her hindquarters. A fat, twisting, purple ribbon stretches from the birth canal to the piglet's midriff. Gritting her teeth, Lili takes hold of this warm ribbon at the maternal end. When she pulls, it pays out like a never-ending rope: twelve inches, eighteen, twenty-four. Finally it breaks and she scoops the piglet between her hands. It keeps up a guttural squealing until deposited in the tub, where it burrows under the straw, making little quacking sounds to comfort itself. By the time she turns back to the pen, the second of the litter has been born.

By the fourth birth she's relaxed, by the eleventh she feels like an old hand. They come at regular intervals, head first, tail first, turn and turn about, the seventh arriving so hard on the heels of the sixth that both are straining to outrun their umbilical cords simultaneously, like dancers attached to a maypole. Her palms are stained with blood and brown slime but she doesn't care. She's as shivery as the piglets, carried along on a racing tide, eager for the next slippery birth, the next squealing handful of flesh. Later, remembering, she will dwell on the white velvet nap on each rosy back, the miniature trotters, the pinned-back ears, but right now she's indifferent to their sweetness. It's the repetition she craves, the careless abundance of new life.

Until her luck runs out.

The twelfth piglet lies where it landed on expulsion from the birth canal, its tiny wrinkled body small as a child's fist and pale as tripe, the eye a blueish shadow under closed lids. She touches it again, less tentatively this time, more of a prod. Nothing. It seems cooler than its siblings, less definitely formed. Revulsion thickens in her throat, like the feeling she gets when she cracks open an under-boiled egg. She thinks of the thing she nearly did, so nearly that her second thoughts count for nothing. In her heart, the deed was done.

Jake brings the smell of tobacco with him into the shed. The nicotine has woken him up. He nods approvingly at the pink huddle in the tub before glancing over the side of the pen at the runt.

'It's dead,' she says.

He gives her a sideways look. 'Better that way—'

She keeps her eyes on the floor.

'See the colour?'

Still she says nothing. Perhaps he reads her thoughts. He passes a hand over his groin.

'It's not meant to live,' he insists. But now, with a sharp tug, he frees the umbilical cord. Picking up the runt by its back legs, he swings the lifeless body in an arc, head first, slack jaws open to the air, then – to her horror – he slaps it. Another swing, another slap. He brings the lardy corpse up to his mouth.

133

'Wake up, wee man,' he croons, blowing into its snout.

Hooking his pinkie inside the unresisting jaws, he dislodges a little viscous fluid, then repeats the swinging and slapping routine. The tender brutality of it seems a sort of madness, but now the impossible happens. A bubble of amniotic fluid emerges from the side of the open mouth. Weakly, the piglet coughs.

Lili looks at Jake in wonder.

He tosses the scrap of precarious life into her hands and returns the other piglets to the sow. They nudge and butt and climb over one another, rooting at the mountainous belly. Finding a teat, they suckle fervently, as if this is what they were born for. The pig cradled between her palms remains motionless, translucently pale, its eyes seamed shut, but she can just detect the rhythmic rise and fall of its breathing.

Loan

So many things tasted better at the farm. The strong tea Margo mixed half-and-half with full-cream milk to blunt its bitter edge, her home-made crab apple jelly, even toast, which was done on the Aga using a contraption like two tennis rackets soldered together. The food, the air, the light, the way I slept all through the night, the complete freedom from responsibility. All I had to do was pay my daily visit to the clinic.

Now I was off the carousel, I saw my enviable life with Frankie rather differently. All those opening nights and gallery private views, the witty haggis canapés and champagne flutes (filled with cava), the semi-famous faces I knew, if not to speak to then to smile hello. It was all so *tiring*. The newspaper skimmed and recycled every day, the YouTube clips watched, the Facebook posts liked, the trending tweet retweeted, the rave-reviewed restaurant tried, the Booker-shortlisted novel read, the season's fashion diktat obeyed. There was hardly time to pick up the latest slang before it became obsolete, but we had to do it, along with everything else we had to cram into the day: the two litres of water we had to drink, the five portions of veg to keep cancer at bay, the six miles on the treadmill I ran to stand still, the eight hours we were advised to sleep, the love we made three times a week – well, I admit I did miss that.

But then, there was another advantage to living at the farm.

I was sitting on the back step with a dog-eared copy of *Women in Love* I'd found in Margo's bookcase when a shadow fell across my shirt.

'Have you got five minutes?'

Kit was standing over me. I lowered my sunglasses and saw his lips plump in a furtive smirk.

'I need to sound like a guy you'd lend ten grand to.'

'Is that "you" as in someone – or "you" as in me?'

'What a woman! Thanks very much...'

'Because if you mean me, two thousand quid a minute seems a bit steep.'

He unsheathed his slow grin. 'How long do you want?'

We talked like this all the time. While Margo was around we were her paying guest and grown-up son, but the minute she left we slipped into a routine of teasing insults and wide-eyed innuendo. Then, once in a while, he'd surprise me by treating me as a friend.

He dug into the back pocket of his jeans and handed me a wad of paper which, unfolded, turned out to be a bank manager's letter. Addressed to him, not Margo or the farm. The money wasn't for the business.

'What do you think?'

I made an equivocal face. (*No chance* would have been my honest answer.) 'I thought you were funded by the NHS.'

'They gave us two free shots at it. After that it's pay-up or piss off.'

'And you can't ask anyone else?'

'Who do I know with a spare ten grand? Anyway, you and Frankie got a loan—'

I could have told him we'd paid it ourselves, but there was something so middle-aged about having savings.

'You can teach me the magic words.'

In a professional voice, I said, 'Good afternoon, Mr Oliphant...'

'I need you to be a man.' He saw my reaction. 'If it's a woman I'll be fine.'

'She'll take one look at you and hand over the keys to the safe?'

'Wouldn't you?'

He stood there looking down at me, the tall shape of him against the sky, with this feeling coming off him, a sort of *brightness*, and I was struck, as I was often struck in those months, by the doubleness of bodies: their dandruff and sebum, the prosaic fact of flesh, and the one-in-a-million miracle of its fascination. It was then I had the idea. A well-meaning thought that turned in my mind, becoming something more anarchic.

'There's no point rehearsing what you're going to say until we've done some work on the way you look.'

'What's wrong with the way I look?'

Now it was my turn to smile.

It was four years since Kit had moved into the cottage with Nikki, and at least another five since anything had been changed in his teenage bedroom. Christopher Eccleston as Doctor Who stood guard over the single bed, along with Franz Ferdinand, Green Day, Destiny's Child and a *Big Brother* winner I could no longer name. The CDs on the shelf (along with several Neil Gaimans and a full set of *Harry Potter*) were as precious to him as the twelve-inch singles I had stashed away in Glasgow. Aztec Camera, Hue and Cry: music that, for a long hot adolescent summer, had told me everything I needed to know about the world.

I checked the chest of drawers and the press beside the boarded-up fireplace. There was nothing I could use.

'I don't suppose you own a suit?'

His eyes bulged at the very idea.

'You can't turn up in that tweed jacket you wore to the bull sale.'

'Why not?'

'It makes you look like a packing crate.'

For a moment he was disconcerted. Teasing insults were

137

one thing, to suggest he'd made a fool of himself in public quite another. 'That's my dad's wardrobe off to Oxfam tomorrow morning.'

'How much has she kept?'

He crooked his finger to lead me out of the room.

The clothes were stored in the attic bedroom next to mine, where he slept the odd night when he fell out with Nikki. I sorted through the wardrobe, breathing in the smell of old tobacco and dry-cleaning fluid. Padded shoulders, slim lapels, a double-breasted power suit, an off-white linen jacket. I didn't need a photograph to tell me the owner of these garments had been a looker, which solved the riddle of how a woman as functionally put-together as Margo had managed to produce a son like Kit. I envied him this treasure trove, and at the same time I could see how the company of so many things his father had had no use for might hurt. I wondered when he had grown too big to burrow between the hangers and pull the door shut after him.

'I'll be staying here tonight,' he said.

Sometimes I varied the game by blocking his attempts to flirt.

'"Ovary madness"?'

Was that a flicker of shame in his glance?

'Are you sure…' *it's the only way? That you and Nikki will last? That it wouldn't be easier to wait till you split up and try again with somebody else?* I managed not to say any of this, but perhaps he heard it anyway.

'Am I sure *what*?'

'Arms out,' I said.

I loaded him up with his father's clothes and sent him downstairs.

He laughed at the bundle I brought down.

'There are vintage shops in Glasgow that'd kill for this stuff,' I said.

'So let me get this straight. There's this bank manager in

138

Perth. Next suit, Volkswagen Bora. I walk in there looking like Roger Moore, the *Octopussy* years, and he hands over ten grand?'

'*Octopussy* was the early eighties,' I said. 'These are Timothy Dalton, maybe even Pierce Brosnan.' For a moment the unmentionable reared its head. I had been out with men who dressed like this, Frankie among them. We had had our first snog under the mirrorball before Kit was born.

'You're the boss.' He hauled his T-shirt over his head.

I went to get my make-up bag.

When I got back he was dressed. The leg length was right, and the pinstriped cloth fine enough to be gathered in graceful folds by his belt. The jacket could have doubled as a tent. He took it off, and I was startled by how much less boyish he looked in a crisp white shirt.

I pointed to the tuft on his chin. 'That has to go.'

To my surprise, he did as he was told.

I sat him in a chair facing away from the mirror. 'No keeking before I'm finished.'

He closed his eyes. 'I'm in your hands.'

He looked wrong clean-shaven, his face larger, like a room cleared of furniture, until I worked a little green into the base I applied to take off his youthful bloom. I flattened his cheeks, added five years around his eyes, thinned the provocation of his lower lip, wetted and tamed the hair back from his face. It was odd, having this licence to lay hands on him, touching his soft skin, breathing in the faint acridity of his scalp and a meaty whiff of armpit and that indefinable scent I recognised from Ruth's children, wholesome as newly baked bread. Of course we flirted, how could it be otherwise: a boy barely out of adolescence, brain and balls on the same seven-second loop? Even he must have known he couldn't have us all. But he could play with the idea, and where was the harm in that?

'D'you do this for Frankie?'

'No, they do it at the studios.'

139

'And you're not jealous?'

'Of what?'

'Other women touching him. Like you're touching me.' He opened his eyes to gauge the effect of this.

'Why?' I said. 'Is it unbearably exciting?'

'I can take it. If you can.'

We were silent for a minute or two while I reapplied the fine brush to his lower lip.

'Are you two getting on?'

I looked at him. He wasn't joking.

'I thought you might be splitting up.'

Frankie had yet to set foot on the farm. Problems at work, he said. It was a battle of wills now: if he couldn't make the effort to come up here, why should I go home?

'We'll be spending the rest of our lives together. We can survive a few weeks without seeing each other.'

'Or shagging.'

Or waking up together, or cooking Sunday brunch, or taking a picnic into the hills, or just sitting on the sofa talking about nothing. He said he missed me, when we spoke on the phone, but obviously not enough to drive seventy miles to see me.

'Is that what it's like, being married ten years?'

'Nine years.' I reached for the eyebrow pencil.

'You can't be arsed being jealous any more?'

'Not when there's nothing to be jealous of.'

'He's not that bad. A wee bit Gerard Butler, but some women must go for that.'

A good fifty per cent of Kit's taunts ricocheted off Frankie. If he expected me to take a swipe at Nikki, I never obliged. I liked her, in so far as liking was compatible with forgetting she existed much of the time.

'You grow up,' I told him. 'You don't sleep with other people, but you accept you're not the beginning and end of your partner's interest in the world.'

'And that's monogamy? Doing it with each other when you're thinking about somebody else?'

'You can't control their libido any more than you can control anything else that goes on in their head. The sooner you realise that the less unhappy you're going to be.'

'You don't need to control them, if they love you.' He smiled to himself. 'I get it—'

I began working on the sleepless night I'd sketched under his eyes.

'He loves you more than you love him. That's why you're not jealous. You're the one with the libido he can't control.' He caught my hand. 'You're blushing, Mrs MacKewon.'

He was stronger than Frankie. Or at least, it had been a long time since Frankie had demonstrated his strength to me.

He let go. 'Are you done?'

'Nearly.'

I thumb-smudged the frown lines I'd drawn between his eyebrows, then let him out of the chair.

'*Fuck's sake.*'

For a moment I thought he was upset. He approached the mirror as if a stranger were trapped behind the glass. Outside, a cloud slid over the sun, cutting the golden reflections on the wall, turning the light in the room a sombre grey. He turned towards me. He looked like a man with make-up on, of course. But the effect, at a distance, was very different from when I'd fussed over him at close range.

He said, 'How long have you known—?'

The hairs lifted on my arms.

'Did she show you a picture?'

I laughed, a brief nervous cough.

'*Did she?*'

'It's fluke,' I said, 'coincidence.'

I had given him the intelligent, ironic face of my imaginary father.

He turned back to the mirror. 'How did you do it?'

141

'I've spent a lot of time in theatre dressing rooms.'

He shook his head as if I were wilfully misunderstanding. 'Have you met him?'

I knew we were talking at cross purposes, we couldn't be reminded of the same man, but the conversation was unnerving all the same. 'I'll clean it off.'

'No.' He took out his phone. 'I want a photo.'

I collected my bits and pieces while he pored over the screen. I was about to leave him to it when he spoke.

'She burned all his pictures. I remember sitting on my grandad's knee, and being pushed around in my buggy, and my first day at school, but my dad's the invisible man. Four years in the same house – nothing. Till now.' He touched the screen to enlarge the image. 'It's weird. All these years thinking I couldn't remember him, and he was in here,' he tapped his head, 'all the time.'

I walked over to the window and pushed the sash up as high as it would go. The turbulent air held the smell of approaching rain. Gulls wheeled and cried, white against the grey, while just beyond the sill, close enough to touch, a net of flies traced careering figures of eight.

'Why'd you leave it so late?' he asked.

I could have said *so late for what*, but really we'd been talking about it all along. Fatherlessness and childlessness were two sides of the same coin for him, as they were for me.

'I suppose I never felt old enough to do it.'

'But if you don't do it…'

'…you never grow up.'

He spoke with sudden vehemence. 'I hate that fucking place. Frankenstein's lab. Raking in the cash, no promises. And what if it happens, what're we meant to tell him? Mummy and Daddy had you *manufactured*. What's that going to do to the little fucker's head?'

Such a relief to hear it said, to abandon the relentless positivity I had to show with Frankie. The day before, they had

142

transferred an embryo to my womb. It would be another fortnight before I could take the test, but I was absolutely sure it
hadn't worked. However desolate I felt (and what was I doing
with Kit if not trying to distract myself from the misery?) there
was one consolation. I hated the idea of having a child by
unnatural means, my body made over by the pharmaceutical
industry, the spark of life kindled by strangers in an empty
room. I wanted magic, the original everyday miracle: a new
person created from the secret power inside me. Frankie was
right, for as long as I could remember I had considered myself
a technocrat. But I turned out to be someone else.

The floor creaked as Kit approached the window. 'And
you don't love him, so that was another reason to put it off.'

He was standing beside me. I watched the flies' zigzagging
frenzy in the electric air. The single bed behind us felt less
innocent now.

'You don't know what you're talking about,' I said.

'No? All right then, tell me. Tell me how you feel about this
guy you haven't seen for weeks. I'm asking Freya Cavalle here,
not the Weegie WAG or Mrs silver BMW Gran Turismo—'

He was bluffing, boundary-testing, as all young men do,
but the words he didn't necessarily mean still had power in
his mouth.

'You want to know what it's like to love someone, but
you've not got the guts to break his heart, so you're going to
have a baby.'

Outside the open window it began to rain.

'Are we talking about me or about you?' I said.

When I got back with the Vaseline and tissues he was sitting
on the bed. I had to scrub quite hard, one hand clamped on
his head to hold him steady. It took a while, but gradually the
boy I knew re-emerged through the grease.

'Kit, if the bank manager says no tomorrow...'

He opened his eyes.

'I might be able to help you out.'

143

Baby

What was different about that day? A part of me says nothing. It was a day like any other, when the potential became actual in its inevitable way. And yet the air was so warm and the gale so wild, bludgeoning the windows when I awoke, scrawling a queasy excitement on the blank canvas of the sky. Margo had been up before first light. Wet sheets and towels thrashed on the line.

Frankie was early. There was a split-second's awkwardness before we kissed, and another when he noticed my jeans: fine for the farmyard, but not to sit in a chintz armchair surrounded by women in Hobbs and Jigsaw. I reminded him that I went every day, and never wore anything else. There was no point hanging around the clinic for an extra half hour, so I gave him a tour of the farm. The milking parlour. The churchy hush of the grainstore. The kitchen, where Margo challenged him to explain why there was nothing but rubbish on telly these days. After ten minutes, I put on my coat, tipping his half-drunk tea down the sink, rattling the crockery in the cupboard as I slammed the back door behind us. I was no calmer in the yard, snatching the keys out of his hand, stalling the car, doing a passable impression of someone fleeing the scene of a crime.

The receptionist did a double-take when we walked in. I was old news, but Frankie hadn't shown his face in weeks. So then they all looked: the Glasgow blonde and her pony-tailed escort, the Sinhalese couple with the Mercedes convertible, the husband and wife who'd given me a card for their country house hotel. The door from the car park opened. A man and a woman came in: mid-thirties, good-looking, moneyed. Even before I saw what they were carrying I recognised the glamour of an Event.

The baby was knobble-headed with skin the colour of a household candle and the prognathous jaw of Early Man. His mouth shaped itself around the absent nipple, his toes curling and uncurling as his feet, held at right angles to his puffy ankles, kicked their slow spasmodic jig. At the sight of his beauty, the women in the waiting room uttered a collective 'aah', our gym-toned hips spreading, the strain on our faces dissolving. The receptionist held him first, over her shoulder. He watched us with unblinking eyes while she whispered in his ear. A smiling delegation of pyjama girls came through from the medical wing. The father basked in their questions, while the mother's vigilant gaze followed her son around the room. One of the doctors planted him on her knee, cupping his neck between forefinger and thumb, rubbing his back till she became drowsy with her own caresses and lacked a free hand to cover her yawn. The Glaswegian hoisted him in the air and made pop-eyed faces. The hotel manageress winded him until he burped. The Sinhalese woman rocked him in her arms like a plaster Madonna and surveyed the room with a heart-breaking smile. My turn. He was lighter than his swaddling suggested, but so solid between my hands. There is a stretch of me from throat to breast that has one too few protective layers. I held him there. His head with its silky weave of colourless hair was warm against my cheek, his drool soft on my neck, his fontanelle pulsed, our heart-beats kept time. I breathed him in, strolling away from the cluster of people, making the low crooning that was my secret language with babies. I knew there was someone in my path, but was so caught up with the life against my chest I gave the obstacle no thought until I looked up into Kit's face. The baby gave a little stutter of referred shock and I cuddled him quiet as Kit reached out to take him. For a moment, we held him between us.

The receptionist was taking a call on her mobile. The hoteliers discussed a staffing problem in lowered tones. Beside me, Frankie keyed some interminable email into his phone. Kit was back in his usual corner with Nikki. They were going through a rocky patch. I never knew when I was going to walk into the bathroom and meet the scroll of his naked back, his eyes in the mirror. I always said sorry, though he was the one who left the door unlocked.

When Nikki and I had consecutive appointments I could stare at him without apology, and he could return my stare, like the strangers everyone supposed us to be. That's if anyone noticed amid the comings and goings, new patients filling out paperwork, deliveries of surgical supplies, girls in blue pyjamas popping through to use the vending machine. He'd ogle when they bent to retrieve the goodies from the slot and I'd watch his gaze moving over their curves, knowing my watching was part of his pleasure. That day, Frankie's presence ruled out staring, but I sneaked a glance. He was slumped low in the chair, his long legs stretching across the carpet. There was a *crump* from outside as a wheelie bin blew over. I was suddenly, shamingly, aware of our geometry, the straight line through my body to the apex of the triangle formed by his legs. I shifted position, but every nerve was aware of him, turning the aftertaste of coffee and the glossy weight of *Vogue*'s thickened pages into ciphers for the signals I was jamming.

When Frankie touched my wrist I jumped.

'What goes *clip-clop clip-clop bang*?' He only told jokes in the presence of other men.

'I don't know. What?'

'A drive-by shooting in Perth.'

The pony-tailed Glaswegian laughed.

Kit got up and walked over to the vending machine. He was wearing the low-riding jeans that showed the waistband of his boxers.

Frankie waited till his back was turned. 'Funny, me forgetting you were staying with a fellow-customer.'

'It's his mother's farm. His wife fixed me up there.'

'Did I know that?'

'I don't know, did you?'

Before Frankie could say anything more, Kit collected his Coke and crossed the room towards us.

Nikki closed her magazine and walked out.

He watched her go, then took the chair positioned as a companion to our seats. 'Some weather,' he remarked.

Frankie put his phone away.

'Haven't seen you here for a while.'

'We're two men down at work.' Frankie glanced pointedly at my midriff and the inadvertently exposed pucker of the laparoscopy scar.

'Who d'you fancy for the Champions League?'

My husband's gaze circled the faces in the waiting room. They weren't even pretending not to listen. 'Ladbrokes are offering seven to four on Inter Milan.'

'But you think?'

'The French are in with a chance.'

'FC Lyon's looking good.'

'Or Bordeaux. They've picked up some strong players. Huysman, Bradjek.'

Football. The lingua franca of masculinity. What was a wife compared with a stoater of a goal?

Frankie gave my navel another meaningful glance. The day I took Lilias to the hospital, he'd shouted *Jesus!* and looked away. He could never stand the sight of blood. But now the wound was fully healed, and still it turned his stomach. Funnily enough, I resented this.

147

I undid another button.

'Makes a change, you feeling too warm,' Kit said.

I returned my shortest smile.

He grinned, man to man. 'It's been a shock for her, finding out Perthshire doesn't have a thermostat. I lent her a jumper a couple of weeks back, this is the first day she's had it off.'

We each decided to overlook this unfortunate phrase.

'She doesn't like the cold, or mud, or getting wet. Or cows. Farting all day, melting the ice cap. But she doesn't want them slaughtered, they've to die of natural causes. Still, we're making progress.' He paused, his eyes wide. I had felt the flattery of this look, as my husband was feeling it now. 'Yesterday I caught her getting wired-in to a ham sandwich.'

Frankie looked me in the eye. 'Did you now?'

Kit pulled the ring on his can of fizz. 'It wasn't the first time either.' He leaned in confidentially. 'Chicken drumstick, two weeks ago, when she thought I wasn't looking.'

As it happens, I hadn't eaten chicken or ham, any more than I had borrowed his jumper, or ventured an opinion on the cows' carbon footprint, but to have denied any of it would have confirmed to my husband that Kit and I were habitual flirts.

Frankie wrapped an arm around my neck. It might have looked like a cuddle but it felt like a wrestling hold. 'The thing about Freya is she's selective. She'll rescue baby birds from next door's cat, but you should see her battering seven shades of shite out of a wasp with a rolled-up newspaper.'

'Only if it stings me.'

Kit shrugged at Frankie. 'Self-defence.'

'A couple of years back she thought we had mice. We needed a licence from the UN for all the poison she bought.'

'What is this,' I said, 'gang up on Freya day?'

Dr Ross appeared, escorting the Sinhalese woman to the door. It was our turn next. I stood up.

'Could I have a word, Mr MacKewon?'

Frankie gestured for me to go first.

The consultant's glance shuttled between us. 'Just yourself for the moment, if you don't mind.'

I sat down again, while Frankie followed her through to the consulting room. I imagined his face as she told him – what? That she could use a couple of tickets to the next Old Firm game? That his wife and another patient's husband had been eyeing each other up in the waiting room? Just then a pyjama girl arrived to show the Glaswegians out and collect the hotel manageress. The husband withdrew to the carpark for a cigarette. The Sinhalese couple had gone by then. The receptionist opened a drawer and took out a laminated card asking visitors to ring the bell for attention. 'I'm away for my lunch,' she said, pulling on her coat and stepping out into the wind.

Kit and I were left alone in the waiting room.

There was no trace of the joker he had been a moment before. The phone on the reception desk rang twice, then stopped. He pushed himself out of his chair to kneel on the carpet in front of me. His hands slid between my thighs. For one dizzying moment I thought the unthinkable, then I real-ised he was lifting the unbuttoned flaps of my shirt. I watched my hand remove his beanie. His hair crackled with static. I wove my fingers into its flossy mass. He dipped towards my navel and I felt the scratch of soft bristle as his lips fastened on my scar.

His hearing was more acute than mine. He was up off the floor and back in his chair before my husband emerged from the medical wing. I caught the look on Frankie's face and my stomach lurched, but it was as if he didn't see me. He made for the door to the car park.

'Frankie?'

His head turned. 'I have to go.'

'What about our appointment?'

'It's postponed.'

149

I scrambled up from my chair.

He put out a hand to ward me off. 'I need to get back.'

A problem at the studios, I thought bitterly, a thirty-second clip they needed him to redub. But generally he relished a crisis. The man in front of me showed every sign of falling apart.

'Is somebody hurt?' I asked.

'No, it's fine.' He pulled at the door, which refused to yield. 'I'll talk to you tonight.'

He couldn't get away from me quickly enough.

'I'm walking back to the farm then, am I?'

'What?' Finally he worked out the door had to be pushed open.

'I'll see she's all right.' Kit was on his feet behind me. I felt the pressure of a finger on my spine.

'Thanks, son,' my husband said.

Banana

The Sunday after I slept with Kit dawned cloudless. Women in gilt-monogrammed shades drank iced frappuccino at the pavement tables along Byres Road. The fruit shop smelled of chrysanthemums and vegetables newly pulled from the earth. Wasps hovered above the Victoria plums. The pineapples flown in from Brazil, the Israeli avocados and Chilean grapes were upstaged by greengages and damsons with a mouth-puckering bloom, football-sized cauliflowers, carmine-stemmed beets, the plums' baroque tumble of rose and gold.

Frankie passed me a yellow courgette. I was stuck with the basket while he took the role of hunter-gatherer. Next came a plantain, and a carrot that could have doubled as a police baton.

'Are you around this week?'

I stiffened. Why would he ask me this unless the clinic had phoned to tell him I had not been back? On the other hand, if he knew, why hadn't we had a row about it?

'I wasn't planning to be,' I said. 'Why?'

He parted the stringy leaves of a sweetcorn cob to check the plumply snaggled kernels. 'I'm away to Sicily Tuesday morning, coming back Friday.'

His work continued undisturbed, while I had used all my holiday and was now on unpaid leave. My belly was bloated from the daily hormones, my skull was bursting, my blood roiling, my heart beating nineteen to the dozen. 'Like PMT,' the nurse had warned before the first injection, but my cycle had always been tension-free. I had felt like this for *six weeks*. I couldn't put myself through another six (or I couldn't without the sweetener of sleeping with Kit). I had come back to have the conversation with Frankie. Not an easy thing to do. All our hopes, all that money. But when I thought about the despair I felt every time I crossed the clinic threshold, every cell in my body told me I was right.

'I thought I'd make bouillabaisse tonight,' he said.

My favourite, a terrible fiddle to prepare.

'What have I done to deserve this?'

He brought his lips to my ear. 'Have you forgotten already?'

We had made love that morning. The first time in six weeks, unless I counted the mingling of bodily fluids in the lab.

This was my chance. *If I came home, we could make love any time*. I would have said it, only he spoke first.

'There's something I need to tell you.'

I recognised our neighbour Johann at the other end of the shop and stepped away from him. Lilias had left me squeamish about displaying intimacy in public places. 'Oh, yes?' I said.

'Never mind, it'll keep—'

If he'd given any sign that it was important, I would have pressed him.

'D'you fancy some Jerusalem artichokes?'

I picked one up. It was flaccid to the touch. I made a face and dropped it back on the display.

He leaned across to feel for himself. 'Like an old feller's balls.'

'I hope that's not the voice of experience, big man.'

We turned. A fleshy, appealing, puppyish face. The football shorts showed off his muscular legs, scumbled by mud and glinting gold hairs.

'You're out of luck, chum,' Frankie said, 'Gordon's picked his squad for Spain.'

The stranger flashed a set of very white teeth in very pink

152

gums. 'He could do worse. Man of the match, scored four minutes in. First of three.'

'Whose goal?'

'Funny guy!' He struck Frankie in the solar plexus, a playful blow too soft to wind him but too quick for him to tense his abdominal wall. 'You should give it a shot. Mens sana in corpus etcetera. Blooter the ball up the park, wee foul when the ref's not looking, volley over the keeper into the back of the net. Cannae whack it, man. It'd tone up the middle-aged spread.'

'That's solid muscle, pal.'

'Scott,' he said suddenly, putting out his hand.

I took it. 'Freya.'

'Scott's on the Saturday panel,' Frankie said in a neutral tone I understood perfectly. He turned to Scott. 'I need to keep her up to speed. She's got better things to do than watch the old man on telly.'

Scott took a grape from the display and popped it in his mouth. 'So you're a pitch widow Saturday nights?'

'Get your own bird,' Frankie growled. We all laughed.

'See me, doll, I'd get you into Hospitality, take you out after the show.' He ran a hand through his gelled hair. 'What're you doing next Saturday?'

'I've got a date with a duvet.'

'Bring it along.'

'I'm warning you, she snores.'

I gave Frankie a look to say the joke had run its course.

A woman pushed between us to get to the tomatoes. I sidled a couple of steps nearer the till.

'Well...' I said concludingly.

Scott shifted into the space I had left, keeping the triangle equilateral. 'I was gonnae call you about this midweek thing.'

I felt the kick in Frankie's stomach from three feet away.

'What thing's this?' I said, so he didn't have to.

'A two-hander. Something different. Stevie Connell's idea.

A wee bit of banter, youth and, eh,' he grinned, letting us fill in the gap before he finished the sentence with 'experience.'

'First I've heard of it,' my husband said.

'Stevie reckons it'll widen the demographic. Cheeky young thruster takes on the Grand Old Man. You never know, might get your missus watching again.'

'Oh I always watch *Midweek Round-Up*.'

'They tried a two-hander before I took over,' Frankie said, 'it didn't work.'

Two old farts in pastel Pringle sweaters. Frankie had been the young thruster then. I could tell he was remembering the taste of priapic contempt. Frankie and Scott: it sounded better that way round, which was something. I tried to see them as a viewer would, or rather, the station controller's idea of a viewer. What Frankie didn't know about the game wasn't worth knowing, but he couldn't deliver the skinny on the striker and the bulimic weather girl, or tell you what the team was worth in sponsorship if you counted the cars, the suits, the double glazing, the probiotic yoghurt and the butch cosmetics. It would be easy enough to find out, but could he bring himself to do it? Scott was the type who would care about these things. He was still young enough to covet a silver Ferrari and lust after glamour models. He wasn't stupid, even on two minutes' acquaintance I could see that, but he could get inside the empty head of Kevin Ferguson or Jojo Damer and feel thoroughly at home

'I see you with more of a reporter's role,' Frankie said.

I took the basket to the checkout.

The youth behind the till had served me dozens of times: a gentle boy with greasy hair falling into his faraway eyes, one hand reaching across to boost the volume on the boom box while the other rang up my shopping. The purchases I had made from him in the past had been accomplished heedlessly, my thoughts following their own course, his trained on the monotony of the task in hand, but recently I had started

154

noticing youths his age. The sort of boys who could have been my sons and yet were old enough. His eyes were on the till and the foodstuffs he was arranging in the bag, root vegetables at the bottom, the bruisable apples and tomatoes on top. I knew he knew I was looking.

'Six forty-six.'

I put the coins in his grimy palm, then took one of the fives back, to replace it with a discoloured penny. His skin was warm to the touch, soft under its layer of dirt. We both looked at the money. I had given him the exact sum, the cash drawer was open, but the game – if that's what it was – was not over. He sifted through the coins, picking out one of the ten-pence pieces, leaving me with no choice but to put out my hand and have him press it into my palm.

'When you've finished, there's a queue of us wanting served.'

My head whipped round, looking for Frankie. (Still halfway down the shop, chatting to Johann.)

Scott was greatly amused by my reaction. He set his basket on the counter. 'By the way, if you watch *Midweek Round-Up*, I'm a one-legged black lesbian.'

'What do you mean by that?'

His white teeth flashed in a smile. 'Tune in next week. You'll find out.'

Turning away to collect Frankie, I stubbed my toe on a crate of blackened bananas reduced for quick sale. Last week they'd been ripe, next week they'd be rotten. For now they were still sweet, with a winy aftertaste.

Misdial

My mobile rang.

'Hi,' I said.

'Hello?' Not Lilias's usual telephone voice.

'Are you OK?'

'Very well thank you. How are you?'

'Fine.'

'I've not caught you at a bad moment, have I?'

'No.'

'So… what are you up to?'

A suspicion struck me. 'You do know who I am?'

There was a pause. 'It's not a *terribly* good connection.'

The line was crystal-clear.

'I'll give you a clue, you've known me all my life.'

She laughed. 'I'm sorry, darling, you must think I'm awful. I meant to dial Julia. I just couldn't think… If *you'd* rung *me* I'd've known straightaway.'

'So you do know—?'

More laughter. She understood why it was funny. I felt lightened, almost giddy, to be sharing the joke.

'You can hang up and call her, it's OK.'

'Don't be silly, darling. I'm glad to have a chance to talk to you. I tried you the other night, in fact. Thought I'd rung the barracks and got through to the company sergeant major.'

'That would be Margo.'

'She said you'd gone up to bed. I'd have asked her to call

156

you down but I was worried it was after lights-out. I wouldn't want you to forfeit any privileges.'

I was standing outside the village shop. The postman drove past. I waved.

Lilias's voice dropped to a conspiratorial whisper. 'Is she there?'

'No, I'm not at the farm.'

'But she's had you electronically tagged?'

We got the giggles again.

'She's about four times the size of Rosa Klebb,' I said, 'if that's what you're thinking.'

'All the more to be frightened of, my dear.'

A fragment from my childhood came back to me. 'She looks a bit like that woman who ran the digs in Sheffield.'

'Mrs Gerritetten,' Lilias supplied, in her most gracious RP.

This time my laughter came out as a snort. Encouraged, she dropped into a Yorkshire accent. *'If you think I'm wasting good food because you're not hungry you've got another think comin'. Geritetten, now, or you'll feel the rough end of my tongue.'*

I was ten years old again, in that brick-built terrace with the smell of the budgie's cage and the television on all day.

'I was terrified of her,' I said.

'You weren't the only one, darling.'

'What – *you*?' This was a new take on the past: Lilias daunted by one of the *little people*.

'She was completely insane, darling. You must remember. Furious about everything, and so thrilled to be furious. One felt obliged to offend her as a matter of courtesy. The way she treated her poor son, positively frothing at the mouth, then she'd talk to that revolting bird with a voice like honey.'

'There must have been somewhere else we could have stayed?'

'Oh, probably. But by the time I realised how barking mad

157

she was, she'd done for me. I barely had the smeddum to get out to rehearsals.'

Margo's friend Alison passed me on her way into the shop. I echoed her *hi*.

'What was that?'

'Just someone I know. I'm in the village.'

I regretted letting this slip. Telephoning in the street belonged to the same category of taboo as eating, smoking and singing there.

'I should let you go, darling.'

She always said this when she wanted me off the phone, but this time I thought I detected genuine regret.

'Make sure you get Julia this time.'

We laughed again, not because it was still funny, just for another snatch of shared laughter.

'Well,' she said, 'it's been nice talking to you like this.'

Out of the blue, she meant. Without the mutual entrenchment we went in for when we knew we were going to speak.

'Yes,' I said, 'it's been nice.'

1972

Summer's long swansong is over. Rosehips and brambles crush under Lili's shoes when she takes her evening stroll down Halfhorn Lane. There are dewy cobwebs in the hedgerows, toadstools like teacakes buttered-side-down in the fields. The rowan berries glow electrically bright. Mrs S says it means an icy winter. Her son rolls his eyes.

With the harvest finished, he has more time to loiter indoors. His mother makes chutney. There's plenty of work for a second pair of hands, peeling apples, stoning damsons. It's helpful to have something to do when he is around. He drinks stewed tea with his feet up on the table (one sock is navy, the other brown), waiting for his mother to flick him with the dish towel. If she doesn't, he'll take out his cigarette papers, or belch, or prise the dirt from under his fingernails with the point of the chopping knife until Mrs S looks up from her pan and roars. It's obvious they both enjoy the game, while Lili sits between them, chopping fruit, glancing from the mother's broken capillaries to the sooty pigment of the son. She is becoming an observer, the sort of woman who can assume invisibility at will, withdrawing from the surface of her skin to the watery cave where the incubus is growing. Her Edinburgh friends think of her as vivacious, all quickfire aperçus and breathless laughter, but now she has the trick of it, she finds this torpor strangely addictive. The sluggish flow of her thickened blood. The slow, open-mouthed pant of her breathing.

One evening she phones Oliver at the flat. What's the point of cutting herself off when Brod has no intention of keeping his promise? And anyway, her disappearance has only fuelled the gossip. 'Are you preggers, darling?' '*Olly*, what sort of girl do you think I am?' There's a pile of post for her. He opens it while she waits on the line. The most recent letter is from the casting director who turned her down for *Please, Sir!* He's offering a day's filming at Elstree.

The wardrobe in Mrs S's bedroom has a full-length mirror. She has to force herself to look. The cameras add at least ten pounds. She could be playing the same scenes as Nyree Dawn Porter, who weighs all of seven-and-a-half stones. But it's money, and it'll keep her face out there until she's ready to come back. Her legs are still good, thank God. She can wear a roll-on girdle under the white lab coat.

She takes the sleeper down to London. The director hates her on sight. Robert Vaughn is sweet to her, but the scenes they play together are a disaster. Four months since her last job. When she opens her mouth she sounds like an amateur. The shame of it like acid in her blood. The journey back to Scotland takes for ever. The train breaks down. An hour's wait in Perth for the bus. When she arrives at the farm, the kitchen windows are steamy. Mother and son are sitting at the table.

'It was definitely her.'

He shrugs. 'Be embarrassing if it wasn't.'

His mother's voice shrills. 'She was seen in broad daylight.'

'Aye, well.'

'There's only one reason folk go to twenty-eight Skinner Street.'

He looks up and spots her standing in the doorway.

Without moving from her chair Mrs S becomes bustling, slathering butter on an up-ended loaf. 'Still raining is it? For goodness sake. The bottom field'll be into a bog. Come away in and have a heat at the Rayburn, get yourself dried off.'

The room is so warm the butter is melting in its dish. Twelve jam tarts are cooling on a wire tray. Before his mother can tell him not to, he takes one. The jam burns his mouth, and he spits it out.

His mother's look says *serves you right*. She drops into the chivvying tone she uses to address him. 'Make yourself useful, dry a couple of plates.'

He stands up. Lili can smell the last cigarette he smoked, along with a trace of tractor fuel.

She takes off her raincoat. The kettle is boiling. While he dries the dishes, she makes the tea. Although neither glances at the other, she feels the pull of his gravitational field. They barely speak to each other, his mother has taken to prompting him to *say good morning*, but there is no moment of the day when their bodies are not in dialogue.

'Will you look at those socks,' Mrs S grumbles, 'not even a year old—'

All three of them glance down at his big toe poking through the knit.

'But never mind, Ma'll mend them. More fool Ma.'

'You know you like doing it,' he says.

Even as he teases his mother, Lili feels his attention fixed on her. They stand fifteen inches apart, she at the Rayburn, he by the sink. After so many years spent trying to please, she is surprised to find his dislike a relief. Knowing nothing she does will make any difference: he needs to find everything about her so inimical that what *he* did must have been right. His stockinged foot taps her ankle. A warning. With every second that passes their proximity grows more conspicuous. He passes his mother a jar of peanut butter. Lili fills the teapot and returns to the table.

Mrs S makes him a sandwich, rapping his hand with the blunt side of the bread knife as he reaches to take it. '*Wait*, will you.' He waits until it has been cut in half, and the two halves put on a plate. Watching him chew, Lili can taste the

161

way peanut butter is never quite as peanutty as it promises to be, the way it cleaves to the roof of his mouth.

His mother brushes the crumbs from the table into her cupped hand, then straightens with sudden purpose. 'I'll need to ask you to leave.'

Lili laughs, though it's hardly a situation to be improved by laughter. 'Can I ask why?'

'Rhoda Spiers saw you walking in that place. You know fine well what I'm talking about.'

Damn Rhoda Spiers, whoever she is. Not that there is anyone to blame but herself. What was she thinking of, wearing that coat? In Edinburgh, she has had women approach her on the street to run covetous fingers over the red leather. That day in Glasgow it drew a different kind of attention. Instant infamy. Even before she passed through the door of twenty-eight Skinner Street.

'Nothing to say for yourself?' Mrs S sounds disappointed. 'I don't know how you've got the nerve to stand there—'

Jake is watching this – watching *Lili* – with the look he might give an unexploded bomb.

'It might not be against the law any more, but it's still murder in my book.'

Lili opens her mouth to defend herself. Across the other side of the table, in his mother's blindspot, he moves his head in a quick, curt shake. He is afraid she will give him away. And why not, she thinks? *Half an hour earlier and Rhoda Spiers would have seen your son walking his ex-girlfriend in there.*

Instead she says, 'Do you mean the abortion clinic?'

She glances from mother to son. He dislikes her all the more for being able to say the words aloud, not caring what Rhoda Spiers thinks, or the minister, or the sweetie wives in the village shop. The notoriety he dreads is nothing to her. His purlieu is her back of beyond. And anyway, her shame was redeemed by that last-minute change of heart.

162

'I did walk in, you're right, but then I walked out again. I was desperate. I saw the address on a lavatory wall…'

Here come the tears, bang on cue. Pitilessly he watches her weep. He knows she is lying. Not about the turmoil – that was real enough – but about its resolution, her sudden flash of moral conviction. She doesn't know why she couldn't do away with the child inside her. It might have been the disinfectant-and-sour-milk smell of the clinic curdling in the back of her throat, or the hideous carpet, or the yellow stain on the empty chair, or arriving early and being made to wait, having to sit there with a boy who smelled of cows while his girlfriend sobbed on the other side of the door. Or none of these reasons. The most significant decision of her life seems the whim of a moment, as random as tossing a coin. Is he any different? In that instant it seemed to him easier to see the thing through, and to her, easier to mutter an excuse and bolt for the street, but who knows how it would have gone another day? They tossed the coin and neither knows who called the winning side. That's what binds them, and divides them: the fact that it's still not finished. She fills the idle hours with all kinds of fantasies. Sometimes he holds her baby and weeps bitter, restorative tears. Sometimes she is the one who walked through the door while his girlfriend ran away. Sometimes the child she is carrying is his.

Mrs S hands her a tea towel from the rail across the Rayburn. 'Wheesht, wheesht now, don't be getting yourself into a state.'

The warm cloth smells of week-old gravy.

Mrs S shrieks.

The opened oven door brings an almighty smell of charred sugar and an engulfing wave of heat. Jake's upper lip shows a light film of sweat. He really thought she'd tell on him, and now the danger is past he feels not gratitude, or obligation, but a need to redress the balance of power. Their eyes lock. The possibility hangs in the heat shimmer, closer than ever, and it has been close for weeks now. They both know it's coming. Inevitability has made its deferral, too, a pleasure, but the time for waiting is over. All that remains is for one of them to decide. No need for words, she'll see it in his eyes, or he'll see it in hers. How hard can it be, to think *I want this*, to embrace your mirror image, your backwards self?

'Just caught it in time.' His mother turns around, offering the well-fired fruit cake for inspection, and finds she is addressing an empty room.

Kilt

You spend ten years with someone. You know chocolate gives him spots, and donuts make him fart, and he snores less with his arms above the duvet. You know the voice he uses to answer when he's not listening. You can predict which women he'll look at on the street. And then one day you catch a glimpse of the stranger he is when he's away from you, the man other women see all the time.

I nearly didn't bother to watch *Midweek Round-Up*, but I'd read the newspaper and finished my book, so when Margo went to bed I picked up the remote.

I wasn't surprised to find Scott anchoring the show from Glasgow. That was how it worked in television, by the time you heard the rumour it was a done deal. The cameras were kind to one man in fifty, I was glad to see that Scott was among the forty-nine. Introducing the report from 'sunny Sicily', he pulled the same smirk I'd seen in the shop.

The film opened with a long shot of a traffic-choked street. Palermo was in the sticky grip of the same unseasonal heat wave as Scotland. Sunlight bounced off car bonnets with a headachy glare. A black-swathed crone fanned herself in a doorway. Frankie's voice-over spoke of the ravages of Mediterranean sun on pasty celtic skin and withdrawal symptoms caused by a lack of Irn Bru and fish suppers. Despite this, the Tartan Army was doing Scotland proud. Cut to the inside of a bus, the locals smiling at a strap-hanging diplomat with a saltire painted across his face. His pal lifted a Jimmy wig and scratched. Two young women boarded. A third Scotsman stood to offer them his seat. The camera made the most of him, starting at his boots, moving up over the furry calves, the pleated kilt, the hair on his bare chest, those muscled shoulders. I saw him through the eyes of the women on the bus: a courteous savage in a skirt that was far from sissy. At last the camera reached his face. I waited in vain for the raised eyebrow that would say *blame the director*. As far as I knew, the first and last time he'd worn a kilt had been at our wedding.

When he got off the bus, the camera followed his progress up the street. The sea of pedestrians parted before him, children laughed and pointed. Still he didn't crack. No smile, no complicit glance at the lens. I was worried for him, embarrassed by the cheesiness of the stunt, afraid he'd been set up by Scott. So far so wifely. But was it wifely to notice the pornographic gleam of sweat on his skin, to experience his deadpan look as a delectable threat? The man striding down that Sicilian street had been hidden from me for a decade, and had to be hidden: around me, he could not exist. You couldn't share a home with such a man, or divvy up domestic tasks, or undress together and just fall asleep.

Not that Frankie and I were really bedmates by then.

If I couldn't feel grateful, it was nonetheless a wake-up call. Somehow, amid his obsession with work, my resentment about it, the stand-off over who was going to travel to whom, my failure to come clean about quitting the clinic, and my flirting with Kit, I had failed to see what was happening to us.

By the following Wednesday Frankie was growing a hipster beard and wearing a skinny fit, peacock-blue suit.

'God no,' I said.

Margo was dozing in the other chair. She opened her eyes and, not recognising him, snorted with cheerful malice, 'Where do they get them?'

Surprisingly, the show worked as a two-hander. An

on-screen partner gave him licence to ad lib. Scott was quick on the draw but Frankie was funnier. Apart from having two presenters, the format was much the same: a panel discussion of the night's match highlights followed by a location report on Inverness Caley Thistle. I did the crossword with half an eye on the screen, until a woman walked on set babbling in Italian. I recognised her straightaway. Christina Agostino, the production assistant, born and bred in Shawlands. She was dressed in a short skirt and tight top instead of her usual jeans and T-shirt. I'd never noticed she had a figure before. She was pretending to have travelled from Palermo to convey her city's gratitude for the exemplary conduct of the Scottish fans, and who better to thank in person than my husband, tottering on her silly heels as she closed in for an enthusiastic sequence of cheek-kissing? The credits rolled over Frankie's face covered in scarlet lip-prints as he touched a steadying hand to her waist.

A smell of burned toast reached us from the kitchen. Back from an evening at the Drover's, Kit poked his head around the door.

Shout

The Indian summer gave way to an early cold snap. The days grew shorter. Without street lamps and shop windows, teatime felt like dead of night. After the table was cleared, Margo and I sat on in the kitchen, talking over the complacent murmur of Radio 4. One moonless night she surprised me by suggesting a walk. From indoors, the darkness appeared blank as an unplugged screen but, leaving the house with her, I discovered a new world. There was a solidity to the sweetened air with its scents of rotting leaves, baled hay, the yeasty breath of cattle, the spoor of deer or fox. Groping for a wall, I touched shadow. Unnerved by my own footsteps, I stopped to find the quiet rushing in my ears. Crossing the farmyard on our way back, I heard a sound like a hundred sweaty fingertips squeaking against a window pane and, looking up, saw nothing, even as my blood felt the skein of geese flying south.

Those night-time walks became a habit. Soon I was going out before breakfast too, the moon in the blue-black sky bright enough to blind me, the concrete yard glittering with rime. While the foxhound slept in his kennel, dreaming of the chase, rabbits foraged around the barn. I had never seen ice crystals on a spider's web, never felt the cold freeze the tears in my watering eyes. It was fierce, but exhilarating too: I knew I had breath in my gasping lungs and blood in my searing fingers. And it was wonderful to come into the warmth of the kitchen just as Margo was lifting the bacon from the pan, to sit at the table and coat my chapped lips with that salty grease.

Kit told me I was paranoid, Nikki suspected nothing, but I locked myself in the bathroom whenever her Fiat pulled up in the yard. The strangest thing was, the clinic never rang to ask why I'd stopped coming. Nor, as far as I could tell, had they contacted Frankie. He phoned most nights, but we had less and less to say to each other. I told myself the one subject of burning interest to us both was best avoided until we could discuss it face-to-face. The whole situation was unreal. Every night I swore tomorrow I'd book an appointment with the consultant or go back to my old responsible life, but another week would pass and still I'd done nothing.

Kit and I didn't make love again. Not that we hadn't had a good time – quite the opposite. We'd taken it slowly, touching, watching, nuzzling, smiling, stopping to share a distracting thought, starting again, stopping again, looking into each other's eyes, to arrive at that unmappable place I'd only ever been with Frankie. Afterwards we were our ordinary selves – what else? I thought, *It's just that we've been married too long, we've lost the knack of casual sex*, but remembering it scared me, and I had the feeling it scared Kit. There was a week of mutual uncertainty and another of injured vanity, before we settled back into our old routine. We still flirted, only now what went unspoken was not the inevitability of our coupling but its status as a one-off. He was the only friend I had within a radius of seventy miles. Who else was I going to talk to?

Every couple of days we'd trump up some errand and disappear for an hour or two. Sometimes to the pint-size swimming bath in Crieff, driving between threadbare fields strewn with turnip halves to feed the porridge-coloured sheep. A perilous diet. One afternoon he explained how to skewer a ewe's distended guts with a knitting needle to relieve a life-threatening case of wind, while I squirmed in the passenger seat with my hands over my ears. Often we'd walk in the pine wood, looking up through the sepia-tinted spaces between the branches, gloating at the pattering of rain high above us and the magical dryness beneath. There was a stone circle in the thick of the forest, if you knew where to look, a modestly proportioned ring that reminded me of a gloomy boarding-house parlour I'd been forbidden to enter as a child. The stones were small and mossily domestic. Always a bobbin-shaped cone and a crow's feather resting on the dominant boulder. Kit might mention some snippet he'd gleaned about his father – the keenness of his eyesight, his sentimental insist-ence on bringing the cattle in at Christmas – and we'd stand awhile, breathing in the resiny perfume of the trees, listening to the creak of a loosening trunk, until we were spooked by the clatter of a wood pigeon's wings. Once we allowed ourselves a hungry kiss, before drawing apart as if nothing had happened. I would lean into the biggest stone, my belly pressed to the cushioning moss, and feel myself part of the long chain stretching between the bodies who had dragged that rock there five thousand years before and the bodies who would lean against it five thousand years' hence. And always, underneath those afternoons, more poignant than our vanished fathers or our superseded lust, was our shared longing for a child.

Of all our expeditions, I remember best the trek to the Roman watchtower. We drove for miles without seeing another soul. No estate workers' cottages, not even the tumbled stones of an abandoned shieling, only the shaggy-tailed hill sheep crop-ping at the sapless grass. We abandoned the Subaru by the side of the road and climbed a slope of rusted heather. The ground was a hybrid of pasture and moorland, littered with the clustered liquorice of sheep droppings. The watery sun lit the hills to the north and, beyond them, a line of peaks capped with early snow. Kit pointed to a barely perceptible mound in the heather. 'We've come all this way to see *that*?'

I said, yet there was something in the timeless landscape that justified the walk. I had never been anywhere more remote. As soon as we stopped moving, the cold got its teeth into us. We hunkered down on the heather to avoid the worst of the wind, and Kit told me Pontius Pilate had been born to a girl in the next glen who'd slept with a Roman legionary. I knew of this legend, and had always counted it among the more laughably self-aggrandising Scottish myths, but it was credible that day, in that place. That a forgotten woman could carry history in her belly over those godforsaken hills.

The day was fading. I packed him off ahead of me, wanting a last unhurried look at the lonely view. I had not long begun my descent – Kit already far below, eager for the shelter of the car – when he turned, looking up at something. On the summit, hundreds of metres above us, a speck was silhouetted against the sky. I strained my eyes to make it out, and for a moment thought I saw a face. The next moment it was a speck again. Then I heard what Kit had heard: a sound so faint I almost doubted my ears. It came again, more distinctly, carried on a gust of wind.

I had grown up without a father, married Frankie and spent my working life in the fork-tongued but never less than civil service. I could count on the fingers of one hand all the men who had ever shouted – really shouted – at me.

'*What*?' I bawled, spreading my arms in a semaphore of incomprehension.

The shouting grew louder, as if goaded by my failure to understand. Kit had started walking again. I didn't want to be left behind, but I couldn't move. The hillside was huge around me, the now-sunless summit dark against a sky bleaching into dusk. I had seen birds swooping over the heather minutes before, now there were none.

'What do you *want*?' I yelled.

I knew the law, I had every right to be there, so why this uncertainty, this feeling of shame? The light was almost gone, the wind had chilled me to the bone, and still that Old Testament prophet cursed me from his mountain. It made no sense, but my sensible self was not in control: I believed he could hear me, see the expression on my face, even read my thoughts.

I was glad to get into the car, out of the buffeting air. We reversed over the grass onto the estate road.

'Some pair of lungs,' Kit remarked.

'Is he dangerous? Or does no one get close enough to find out?'

He grinned as if I had said something funny.

'What?' I asked.

He still had a boy's laugh, a four-note arpeggio that reminded me it was only six years since he had left school. The joke grew on him, his laughter ripening into a full-throated guffaw. By which time I had seen the sheep stampeding down the hillside, a couple of hundred fleeces converging, while a black-and-white dog traced a sweeping arc on the long leash of his master's voice.

Test

There was sun that morning. Its white drill, levelled at my eyes, turned them to slits, turned the High Street shoppers to silhouettes and the spaces between them to chalk – though when I turned to peer after the faceless shape that had said hello, the sky was a perfect blue. I hadn't had a proper period for two months. They had messed up my cycle with all those drugs. I told myself there was no reason to hope, but still I drove past the village where the chemist greeted his customers by name, and headed for Perth. Taking my money, the girl behind the counter barely drew breath from chatting with her friend.

A rhombus of light from the high window splashed warm across my naked thigh. I listened to the flushing cisterns, the drone of hand driers, the swing and slam of the door out to the shop. Someone broke wind, tentatively, as women do in such public-private places. A mother chivvied her young son into washing his hands. I looked down at the knickers nesting in the jeans around my ankles, the cardboard packet dropped on the floor, the white stick with its blue plus sign.

I felt like a woman I might notice on the other side of the road and think *she just sails through life,* a woman I would envy too much to make my friend. I felt solid, as if every cell in me had weight; and hefted, as sheep are to their estate; and full, as the sky is full of air. I felt inevitable. Unpreventable. Like a plumb line of honey twisting from a spoon, or the

173

nanosecond before a mind-blanking sneeze. I felt ordinary, blissfully, magnificently run-of-the-mill, for what may have been the first time in my life.

I felt pregnant with the future.

PART II

The past is never dead. It's not even past.

Requiem for a Nun, William Faulkner

Nudge

There was standing room only in the bar. Holly along the gantry, mistletoe by the door, the inglenook heaped with glowing peats. Kit sat in the circle of musicians, watching his fingers on the frets, with so many buttons of his father's shirt undone he was virtually undressed. His cuffs flapped loose, exposing the strip of leather I had knotted around his wrist.

In all those months I had seen nothing to counter my prejudices about this corner of the country: a backwater, the last market for winceyette nighties, where the gastro-pubs still served cod in parsley sauce. How had it taken me so long to discover this village with its ruined abbey and rushing river and eighteenth-century bridge? A hundred and one kinds of oatcake in the deli, designer hand-knits, celebrity cookware, and this bar: a spit-and-sawdust country pub with a Friday-night scratch band that could have sold tickets in Glasgow. My eyes travelled from the sweating fiddler to the white-haired pensioner on squeezebox, the curly-headed laird's son on sax, the bodhran player in his black stetsun, the stockman coaxing liquid honey from the uillean pipes. Only Kit played like a hick, and still my blood reared at the sight of him in that sleazy nineties dress shirt, hamfisting his guitar.

The umpteenth chorus of 'Sweet Home Alabama' petered out, and the piper started a traditional reel. Knowing his limits, Kit switched to beating out the rhythm on his sound box. I scanned the room. Nikki was at her sister's in Livingston, but there was no guaranteeing the whereabouts of her pals. Kit had introduced me around – as a friend of his mother's – so there were people I could talk to. I knew the barman's name was Donald and that he worked online as an ethical fundraiser. Greig maintained the log cabins in the tourist camp. Niall was the fencer, having been a librarian in Edinburgh before he downsized. Hamish was something in the City Monday to Friday, and dressed his rosy-cheeked twins in miniature versions of the Barbour and tweed cap he wore himself. The fat girl whose grizzled lurcher slunk through the forest of legs sniffing out packets of crisps was Becca. Her sister Lindsey was the bar's teenage mother, sinking a pint of lager while jiggling a podgy infant on her hip. When I caught her eye accidentally we smiled like old friends.

Why shouldn't I belong? I knew the songs, and I knew why they sang them, the thread of self-definition running through the medley of Rabbie Burns, Ry Cooder and Steve Earle. I could parse the grammar of their hiking boots and leather waistcoats, the modish-mythic territory they claimed somewhere between Loch Tummel and the American south. Why shouldn't I make a life here? Quit the government, cash in my share of the house, buy a three-roomed bothy and live off the rest, topped-up with the odd day of fencing or cabin-painting. A nightly visit from Uncle Kit, source of tickling and tractor rides and all-round over-excitement. Or I'd amble down to the bar, teach myself guitar and jam with the boys. Lindsey and I could go halves on a babysitter.

It was cold by the river, away from the beery fug. An owl screeched as it flew overhead. Kit was sitting on one of the picnic tables with his feet on the bench, smoking. I lay across the neighbouring table. All I could see were stars and black sky. I heard him walk down to the river, toss his roll-up into the water, and walk back, his boots crunching on the frozen ground.

'How d'you do that?' he said.

'Do what?'

He brought his face down to mine. 'Make me want to touch you.'

His skin was pale in the moonlight, the soft plum of his underlip almost within reach. He jerked back just in time.

'There's nobody here to see us,' I said.

'I've snogged in warmer places.'

'Ach well,' I shrugged, 'if it was only going to be a snog...'

'That's me missed my chance of an *al fresco* shag, is it?'

'It has been known.'

He grinned. 'Like when?'

'Every once in a while.'

'In the park?'

'The park's full of gay guys doing it.'

'Not up a close?'

'In Glasgow, up a close counts as inside.'

He climbed onto the table and crouched above me. 'So old Frankie likes it out in the open, does he?' His jaw jutted in a crude impersonation which nevertheless held some echo of my husband. 'With the wind on his hairy balls?'

'Don't push it.'

There was just enough light to see the transgressive glint in his eye. 'Do you two still do it?'

'Why, did I seem out of practice?'

It should have been sad, this business of talking as if we were lovers, but somehow it was not. Love had always been problematic for me: was it too much of the body, or too much in the head, was it selfless enough yet *invested* enough, was it there at all? Kit and I bypassed these anxieties. Our love was a running joke. But a joke that kept surprising me with its sweet stabs of feeling.

I moved over and he lay alongside me on the table.

'The passion must be gone by now,' he said.

'It must, must it?'

We listened to the fiddle notes leaking from the bar. I was

179

glad of his warmth against my side. A breeze rustled the saplings that had seeded in the rich soil by the river. I could smell the white water gushing over the weir.

'What are we?' he asked.

'I don't know – what?' The minute I said it I knew there was no punchline. 'You mean...'

'I mean you and me. Us.'

A few seconds before I might have told him, but asking the question had changed the answer. I was his cradle-snatcher, his Mrs Robinson, his rich-bitch bored wife. He was my Oedipus, my Benjamin Braddock, my toyboy, my Tithonus. But what were *we*?

'A good time,' I said, 'in a dull world.'

A possibility occurred to me – a fantastical possibility, but just then I couldn't think of a more plausible alternative. I turned to look at him.

Something snuffed at the crown of my head.

Kit sprang back and fell off the table.

The lurcher barked.

'Oh my God, I didn't know you were there!' It was Becca from the bar, a hand spread across her chest in shock. Behind her embarrassment, I could see her looking forward to the story she would tell when she went back inside.

Kit had retreated a couple of metres from the table. She asked him for a light. She was one of those unlucky fat girls whose surplus weight doesn't translate into a cleavage, which ruled her out as a former girlfriend. I wondered if she was a friend of Nikki's. Or an enemy, which could prove just as dangerous. I was sitting up by then, trying to look unconcerned. The lurcher planted his front paws on the bench beneath me and raised his shameless-soulful eyes in entreaty. I opened my hands – 'No crisps' – and the dog lifted his grizzled muzzle to nudge at my breast.

'*Mungo!*' His mistress laughed. 'Not on a first date!'

The dog went over to try his luck with Kit.

180

Becca assumed that sociable smoker's pose, hip cocked, one arm folded across her midriff. 'He used to do that to Lindsey when she was expecting Kyle. He knew before she did. Mum says they can smell it.'

Perhaps it really was a guileless remark, but I wasn't about to give her the benefit of the doubt. She looked away, flustered by my stare. Rebuffed by Kit, the lurcher was making a circuit of the beer garden, sniffing and cocking his leg. She ground out her cigarette and clicked her tongue to call him to heel.

'Sorry if I...' She let the sentence hang unfinished. 'I, eh... I didn't see anything.'

For a long time after she was gone neither of us spoke. A lorry clanked over the bridge. My left nipple, the one nudged by the dog, throbbed as if from a human touch.

'We should go back in,' I said, 'you'll be missed.'

He walked up to the table, reaching through my open coat to place the flat of his hand against my belly. I closed my eyes. As a young woman I had been wary of young men, their spunked-up noise and violence. It was Frankie who taught me to see the vulnerability underneath. They all yearned for something. A football team, a cause, a woman, a child.

'You got what you came for, then,' he said.

'You came too, as I recall.'

The eyes he turned on me were dark-rimmed in the pallor of his face, a look I'd seen in Ruth's children just before they cried. 'When were you going to tell me?'

I massaged my neck, which had started to ache. 'When I knew what to do.'

His look hardened. 'What's to know?' He took his hand away. 'Congratulations, Mrs MacKewon.'

'It's yours,' I said.

I saw the eager light flare in his eyes, and as quickly go out. 'What makes you think that?'

'I just know.'

181

The leakage from the bar grew louder. The customers were singing along to a tune I almost recognised.

He rolled himself another cigarette. 'You'll be off, then,' he said, 'back to Glasgow.'

I couldn't deny it. What were we? *Married to other people.*

'We don't have to lose touch,' I said.

'No? What do you have in mind: a quickie in your lunch hour in the back of the Subaru?'

It was exactly the sort of thing he would have said before, only now there was a bitter edge to the innuendo.

'Course, you won't be working, with a baby.' He lit the roll-up and exhaled, narrowing his eyes as the breeze blew the smoke back against his face.

A cloud covered the moon, leaving the glowing end of his cigarette the only source of light.

'I should have got him to slip Nikki one while he was at it.'

I stared into the darkness. 'What d'you mean?'

He dropped the cigarette, crushing it underfoot. 'What d'you think I mean?' I had never heard cruelty in his voice before. 'I fire blanks. Billions of the fuckers. Every one a dud.'

It wasn't a lie any man I knew would tell.

'Why didn't you say?'

'I wanted to shag you. You weren't complaining.'

The moon came out from behind its cloud.

'Tell you what,' he said, 'I'll do you a deal. You let me keep that ten grand you lent me, and I'll make sure Frankie doesn't get to hear about our afternoon in bed—'

I had been so sure Kit was the father.

'You get your brains shagged out and go home to play happy families, Frankie gets his son and heir, Nikki and I get a free shot at the Miracle. Sounds fair to me.'

I was about to say I didn't care about the money (it was only going to sit in my savings account earning 0.25 per cent interest). But then he would have had to find another way of getting back at me.

'I'm sorry you had to find out like this.'

'Don't mention it. Glad to be of service.' He stuck out his hand like a salesman clinching a deal.

'Stop it.'

He looked at the hand I refused to shake, shrugged and went back through the garden to the bar.

I sat listening to the river. For a while I thought I was going to cry. I would never get to untie that strip of leather from his wrist, never feel again the surprising softness of his skin. Ahead of me stretched all the years when I would look back on us. If I remembered him at ninety, he would not be more irretrievably gone than he was then.

Champagne

Lilias paused just inside the restaurant, taking a long, conspicuous look around. Her eyelids were frosted silver, her white-gold hair sparkled with its thousand lights. She was wearing the rabbit-fur tippet she insisted was winter mountain hare, over her floor-length, lapis blue coat. She might as well have carried a sign, *I am an actress*.

I reminded myself that being an actress was not a capital offence.

'You are clever, darling, to have found this place.'

A waiter approached us and nodded at the far side of the room. I watched her lips purse at not being shown personally to our table.

She sat down, draping the fur over the back of her chair. 'Well, this is a treat.'

We smiled at each other.

'You're looking rather… '

'Yes?' I said, too eager.

'Peelie-wallie,' she said. 'Or perhaps it's just that colour on you.'

I glanced down at my green empire-line dress. 'So. What have you been doing with yourself?'

'Oh you know, the usual.'

'Shopping, socialising, breaking hearts?'

She gave me a narrow look. 'Reading a couple of scripts actually.'

'Anything interesting?' I was burning to share my news, but I wanted her to guess.

'Actually there is something. A one-woman show by a new writer, an Irishman. Very talented.' She smiled, lowering her lashes, showing the frosted silver. 'It's called *Dinner with the Contessa*. The part's a wee bit old for me, but I'm sure,' another smile, 'Dermot can be persuaded. It'll be quite exciting, holding the audience for ninety minutes all by myself.'

She hadn't done anything longer than a five-minute take in years. 'What sort of run?' I asked.

'An eleven-week tour.'

I shrugged. 'If your consultant's OK with it.'

'You mean my agent.'

'I mean you're recovering from cancer.'

She seemed to shrink before my eyes. I had shot her down in her moment of triumph, but if I wasn't going to point out the potential hazards of this venture, who was?

The waiter arrived with a bottle of water and hovered until it was clear we weren't yet ready to order.

'This is a treat,' she said again.

'We can still go somewhere else.'

'Don't be silly, darling.' She ran her eye down the menu. The waiter had left a taint of perspiration in his wake. The calendula on our table had been placed over a ghostly stain that laundering had failed to remove from the cloth. As soon as I saw it, I knew she had noticed.

'There's chicken and chorizo stew. You could leave the chorizo. I'm going to have the lamb.' I smiled at her surprise. 'I'm a carnivore these days.'

'Darling! When did this happen?'

'A few weeks ago. I got sick of macaroni cheese.' But I didn't want to talk about my diet, I had something more important to say. 'Ma, I thought this lunch could be a new start for us—'

She assumed a pleasantly quizzical expression.

185

'I've been thinking about what you said back in the summer, about you not being a good mother. I realised when I got home you were trying to open things up between us, and I just shut the conversation down…'

I stared at her suddenly sparkling eyes, the flush in her cheeks, the slight jut of her chin to correct her overbite. She stood up, waving at someone on the far side of the high counter that separated the tables from the kitchen. Turning, I saw a tall, heavily built, handsome man whose silver quiff and billowing white shirt were pitched somewhere between camp and piratical machismo. I had never seen him before, but I knew he was an actor. He would have played Antony to her Cleopatra, or Sky Masterson to her Sister Sarah, and was now supplementing his income frying tapas. He cut a path through the tables with such energy that our fellow lunchers paused their forks to watch.

They kissed cheeks – once, twice, thrice, four times – laughing and exclaiming, pulling back to take a proper look. She teased him about going grey. He pulled a face: wasn't it *awful*? Oh *no*, it suited him. Very *distingué*. But look at her! Not changed a bit: she had to have a portrait up in the attic! He turned his attention to me. I was afraid he was trying to flirt, but when I met his eye it was pity I read there, mixed with a sort of superstitious thrill. He touched me on the shoulder, as people will bring their hand to a kettle to check if it's still hot. 'And this was…?' Lilias nodded, a rapid, dismissive nod, almost a warning, and all at once he was boisterous again, pulling out a chair and shouting for wine, clasping Lilias's hand and mine with the sort of spontaneous exhibitionism I had dreaded all my life.

It turned out to be Benedick he'd played to her Beatrice, how many years ago? Oh, too many. In Manchester. And they hadn't met since. Apart from that time… Anyway. It was *wonderful* to see her.

His name was Xavier and he was French by birth, though

186

you wouldn't have known it from his Lancashire accent. On the back of his success in *Much Ado*, he'd done a couple of seasons at Stratford and a Hampton revival off Broadway. After that he'd returned to France and been a mainstay of some interminable serial which was death to the soul but allowed him long liquid lunches with the week's guest actress. Here Lilias shot him a reproachful look and he mugged like a naughty schoolboy. I wondered if they'd ever tasted each other's sweat, or just teased the cast with their simulated foreplay. Twenty years of brunettes, he sighed. The casting director had a thing about them. In the end, boredom and too many long-lens shots in *Paris Match* had pushed him into a *crise*. *De conscience?* she wondered. *De foie*, he said.

He was out of the business now, an old dog learning new tricks. She might remember he'd always loved to cook. Oh how could she forget! Those omelettes whipped up on the coal fire in his digs – fit for the Gods! The *boeuf bourgignon* he made for the cast party! But behind this gush I could see her mind working, weighing his status as a failed actor against the admiration he had to offer and his possible future as an entrepreneurial success. It was tough, he said, realising he'd spent forty years on the wrong path. Cooking was so much more creative. Or at least – with a gallant nod at her – more so than the fist he'd made of acting. *Oh no:* she'd never forgotten the way he'd played Benedick as a sort of South Ken Peter Cook – or was Peter Cook actually *from* Kensington? She knew what he meant about cooking, though. She had once eaten a *baccala con carciofi* at a little place in Chichester that was like standing by a driftwood fire on a stormy night under the spray of crashing breakers.

Xavier was watching me again. I could feel the burn of his eyes (rogueish for Lilias, doggy for me) searching my face for something that wasn't there.

'What do you do when you're being creative, Freya?'

I was on the verge of replying *I don't*, but what law decreed I had to spend my life as Lilias's other?

'I'm pregnant,' I said.

When I saw the tenderness bloom in his gaze I thought of Frankie.

'Darling!' Lilias exclaimed.

Xavier beckoned a waiter. 'Bugger the *verdejo*, we need a bottle of champagne,' his arm froze in mid-air, 'unless you're not drinking?'

'A glass won't do any harm.'

'Darling,' Lilias said again, 'that's marvellous.'

The words rang hollow. She was a better actress than this. She wanted me to see she wasn't pleased. Over forty-odd years, I had learned to anticipate Lilias's rebuffs, but every once in a while she got past my defences and I was a child again, blinking back the hurt.

Meanwhile Xavier was pressing me for details. How many weeks gone was I? Did I want a boy or a girl this time? On hearing it was my first pregnancy, he became even more solicitous, ordering me the mildest dish on the menu, assuring me it went well with champagne. He approved of me drinking. It wasn't only nutrients a child absorbed from its mother, but *joie de vivre*. He had memories, not faces or events of course, but feelings and associations he was sure dated back to the womb. The smile died on his lips, his eyes suddenly furtive. By the time I'd turned to check Lilias's expression, the waiter was opening our bottle of champagne. She squealed at the *pop*, making Xavier laugh.

'You're lucky you can drink.' She touched my forearm but kept her face angled towards Xavier. 'When I was carrying you I was *so sick*. I couldn't keep anything down. I was getting thinner and thinner. I was afraid you wouldn't grow. There was a nest in the eaves outside my window. So I used to...' she gave a breathy laugh, 'I suppose you'd call it a sort of spell. I used to lie in bed listening to the nestlings calling for food. I'd go down to the kitchen and cut myself a slice of bread, tear the middle into pieces and leave them out on the sill. Then I'd go back to bed and suck on the crusts and imagine I was feeding the baby bird inside me.'

Xavier regarded her with melting eyes.

'And from that day I started to put on weight?'

I kept the mockery light, and she pretended not to hear it. 'We didn't have scans back then, darling, so I can't be sure, but I rather think you did. It *is* a sort of magic, being two people. I hardly knew myself. I was ticklish all over, and smelled of geraniums.'

Xavier looked suitably enchanted.

'Apart from my feet, which were more like *brie de Meaux*.' Her voice became huskier. 'I've always thought the true changelings are pregnant women. Having these feelings you've never had before, dreaming someone else's dreams. It's hard to explain if you've never experienced it. Do you feel it, darling?'

'No,' I said.

'It didn't end with the birth, either. Even after I went back to work it was as if they hadn't cut the umbilical cord. I'd go through the motions on stage, but you were always at the back of my mind. Poor Xavier, having to convince eight houses a week you were falling in love with this woman who was only half there.'

'Half of you was twice any other woman,' he said, 'and I wasn't really acting.'

She stretched her hand across the table and he brought it to his lips.

'*Get us, duckie*,' he said in a camp drawl.

I looked away. The dates were almost right, the genetics not impossible, but the more I saw of him the less likely it seemed. He was not a man to father a child and move on without a backward glance. Even if Lilias had transferred her affections, he would have turned up once a year with his camera and his gift-wrapped doll. The postman would have brought birthday cards with French stamps, and Easter dragées, and a bottle of scent when I passed my exams. I had liked him at first, despite his affectations. Now all I could see was his unsatisfactoriness, like a jigsaw piece the right colour but the wrong shape.

The food arrived. Xavier had ordered himself a starter portion of risotto to keep us company. Between mouthfuls, they exchanged gossip about old friends. The pretty girls who'd married well, that dancer who was on the game. He began to explain why he'd left acting. The creative satisfaction of cooking was only half the story. He'd had a heart attack not long after his sixtieth birthday.

'…the quack read me the riot act, no more stress. I told him: if you don't get stage fright, you're not worth watching. He said in that case the next theatre I played was going to be the operating theatre—'

Lilias's glance settled on a part of the restaurant visible over his shoulder.

'I guess once you get to our age, if it's not one thing, it's another.' He could tell he'd lost her. Then he guessed why. 'Oh God, Lili, I'm a tactless oaf.'

Her blue eyes turned to ice.

'Is it serious?' He touched her fingers, which she instantly retracted. I knew she would never forgive him this note of human sympathy, its complete lack of chivalric awe.

'It was cancer,' I said.

'*Darling!*'

What else was I to do? If she was going to freeze him out, at least he would know why.

He reached across the table to trap her hand beneath his. 'I'm sorry to hear that, Lili.'

She looked at him with little short of loathing, but he held on.

'She's been very lucky,' I said. 'No chemo, no radiotherapy, no adverse reaction to the drugs.'

Was it his expression, or hers, that told me?

'No,' I said, '*no*.'

She met my eye. 'Darling.' It was a plea, and simultaneously an admission.

My voice shook. 'Tell me they've done *something*.'

'Later,' she said.

Being angry with Lilias was hardly new to me, you could call it my default position, but I'd never felt anger like this before. 'I went to the hospital with you.'

Her face became a mask.

'How could you be so stupid?'

She turned the full power of her stage presence on me, the resonant voice, the imperious gaze. 'I said, we'll discuss it later.'

'How much later? A day? A week? You'd better make it soon. Who knows how much longer you'll be around?'

Xavier flinched.

She let the silence grow. Then, very softly, she said, 'Has it not occurred to you I might have had all the life I want?'

My face must have reflected the absurdity of this statement.

'I'm perfectly serious, darling.'

'I've never met anyone as greedy for life as you.'

'We're talking about the life available to a cancer patient, which is rather different.'

'You won't be a patient for ever. You'll come out the other side.'

'If there's anything left of me.'

I had been dealing with the fallout from Lilias's choices all my life. The stage career she preferred to the craftless trade of television, even if it meant not seeing me for nine months of the year. The suitcases she lived out of rather than end up in some domestic trap. The string of affairs that precluded a life with the father of her child. But this time, she would be the one to suffer the consequences.

'It's not a battle of wills,' I said, 'you can't dominate a

191

cancer by force of personality. If you don't get treatment, you're going to die.' I turned to Xavier for support but he avoided my gaze. 'What – you think it'll be a magnificent death, is that it? You'll make a beautiful corpse? *Nobody's watching*. In six months, a year, who's going to remember you?'

'I rather thought you might,' she said.

'I'll remember you chose to kill yourself rather than admit you're like everybody else.'

She was beyond embarrassment now, her only hope of saving face a show-stopping performance. Defiantly – magnificently, I suppose – she squared her shoulders.

'Well obviously I'm not like *you*. I'm sure you'll squeeze a few more years out of your body than I manage out of mine, flogging yourself on those machines at the gym, eating like a Bangladeshi peasant so your stools are up to scratch. But what are you going to do with those extra years? You're so keen on the gift of life – what's it for? An earthworm is alive. Is that so very marvellous? You seem to think the purpose of life is to get to the end and hand it back as clean as the day you received it, like a blank sheet of paper.' Her voice switched from scorn to an intense vibrato. 'I've *lived* my life. Dying isn't a tragedy for me. It's you I worry about, you and your clean sheet. Sometimes I think I should have brought you up a Catholic, at least then you'd have sin. What are you: just a collection of cells, a more sophisticated earthworm. My cells may be cancerous, but they're not *me*. I've made a self out of art, and poetry, and imagination, I've nothing to regret. But you? When it's your turn, what will you be, darling, apart from your dying cells?'

She was finished. She sat back in her chair.

What happens to love, where does it go? How many times had I thought *we're practically strangers*, only to be astonished by everything I felt for her? I knew I'd never have exploded with such rage had I not cared, but that didn't explain why it had to be rage I felt. Why not wordless shock, or garment-rending grief, or a hell-or-highwater resolve to change her mind? Why was I so angry with her, when all I wanted was a place in her heart?

The waiter came by and we declined a second round of coffees. Xavier was pretending to monitor what was happening in the kitchen. Outside the window, light leached from the afternoon. Table by table, our fellow customers put on their coats.

'Have you thought about names?' Xavier asked me.

'Isobel. I have a feeling it's a girl.' I took a last sip of champagne. 'If it turns out to be a boy, I'd like to name him for my father.'

Lilias flexed her lips in a brisk smile. 'Freya thinks if she knew her father's name the sun would shine every day and the world would be full of happiness.'

I could see Xavier wishing he hadn't asked.

'She thinks it would turn the clock back forty years and he'd be overjoyed to have a daughter.'

Xavier looked startled. 'Doesn't she…?'

'No,' she snapped, perhaps startling herself, for she added sweetly, 'whatever you were going to say.'

I had never competed with Lilias for male attention, but then I'd never had such pressing cause. I made my voice low and intimate. 'Did you ever meet my father, Xavier?'

The question seemed to alarm him. 'No, I met Lilias after…' He broke off. 'No.'

'Do you know his name?'

'His name, no.'

'Is there something else you know about him?'

He looked from me to Lilias, his fleshy, handsome face raddled with anxiety. 'I think you should trust your mother.'

Lilias's coffee cup clinked as she replaced it in the saucer. 'For heaven's sake, is that the time? I have to be at Andrea's

193

in ten minutes. We should get the bill.' She treated Xavier to her most winning smile. 'Unless it's on the house?'

As if things weren't bad enough, I bumped into Scott on my way home.

'The big man not with you today?'

'No, I've only just…' Got back, I had been about to say, but what sort of husband wasn't glued to his wife's side the instant she returned from months away? The sort whose wife hadn't told him what time she would arrive. 'I was having lunch with my mother.'

'Where's Frankie-boy, then?' He raised an eyebrow. 'Getting his beard trimmed? Buying more of those funky duds?'

'The thing about Frankie is he's forgotten more about football than you'll ever know. He could present that show in a pink tutu and still pull in a million viewers.'

'*Two* million in a pink tutu,' Scott said, but the smirk was gone. 'Have you got time for a quick coffee?'

'Sorry, no.'

Our eyes met in a moment of candid dislike.

In a new voice, he said, 'See this heartbreak-hotel number? You need to tell him, it's freaking people out.'

I tried to look as if I knew what he was talking about.

'He needs to put a lid on it, or he can kiss his career ta-ta.'

'That must be keeping you awake at night.'

An old man was coming down the street. Something about us made him cross the road. Scott waited until he was on the other side.

'See Frankie and me, it's like a heavyweight title fight. No one wants to watch the champ take a dive in the first round. You need to give people their money's worth.'

'You want him standing up so you can knock him down?'

'That's about the size of it.' He lowered his voice. 'Tell him to keep it in his keks on air. The mid-life crisis threads – aye, OK, if he has to. But this is too much information.'

194

'I don't really think it's any of your business.'

He let his mouth fall open, revealing his (I now realised) professionally whitened teeth. 'It's *everybody's* business, man. Frankie's seen to that.'

I met his glance, which was a mistake. He looked at me as if I'd just handed him the most marvellous present.

'You've not been watching.'

'I saw it last week.'

'Right to the end?'

'It's nice to see you again, Scott,' I said, 'but I'm running late.'

He stared at me. 'I *told* you. *Jeez*. You don't know when somebody's doing you a favour.'

I flagged down a cab.

Soup

The MacKewons were Sligo Irish transplanted to a council house on Glasgow's south side, a systems-built semi littered with half-drunk mugs of tea and squeezed-out tubes of Deep Heat muscle rub. Mr MacKewon worked on the buildings, a balding man whose looks I found unremarkable until the night I saw him without a shirt. Six of us had trailed back to the house after an evening's under-age drinking and were sprawled around the lounge, the couples sharing armchairs, Frankie and I on the pouffes, the other four MacKewon boys on the three-seater sofa. We were watching *On the Waterfront* with the sound turned down. Paul MacKewon had a record on repeat on the stereo. I wasn't paying much attention until Kevin MacKewon dragged the needle across the vinyl, and Mickey MacKewon knocked him to the floor. The next I knew, coffee cups were smashing and table lamps were flying and Mrs MacKewon was in the doorway in her quilted dressing gown wailing about the shame of it all with guests in the house. Her husband thundered downstairs in his striped pyjama bottoms, calling on Jesus, Mary and Joseph. He was well into his fifties then, but his back was still a solid slab of muscle. My teenage years were crowded with epiphanies, and this was one: the father as Yahweh, forcing himself between the fists and feet of his strapping sons.

The MacKewons were famous pub brawlers. Picking a fight with one meant taking on all five, but there was always someone spilling a MacKewon pint or eyeing a MacKewon girlfriend or doing nothing very much in a way a MacKewon could take exception to. Frankie explained that these rammies were recreational, all parties rose from their beds next morning none the worse for wear, but I was glad when he outgrew them. They were a likeable family: quick to throw a punch and as quick to throw their arms around you, downing a skinful Saturday night but always scrubbed and sober for Mass on Sunday. Ravenously hungry, even by the standards of teenage boys. Always a couple of them in the kitchen frying gipsy toast or slathering golden syrup over slices of pan bread. There was something about them that was not quite of the late-twentieth century. They had their Celtic season tickets, their muddy trainers, their second-hand electric guitars, the old banger that spent more time in bits in the front garden than it did on the road, but not one of them was going to complain that his childhood fucked him up. You could smell the love on them, even when they were throwing table lamps at each other. Why else, at an age when our classmates skulked alone in their bedrooms, were the MacKewon boys still crammed into that three-seater settee?

'He does *what*?' Lilias said, when I told her Frankie's father was a steel erector. She couldn't quite believe a television journalist with a degree from Glasgow University could come from the same stock as an electrician, a plumber, a plasterer, a carpenter, and a scaffolder with what she termed a 'bog-trotter accent'. Never mind the seventeen uncles and aunts and the sixty-eight cousins. But even she succumbed to the MacKewon charm in the end. For me, the MacKewons were one of my husband's great attractions: an off-the-shelf family, gloriously ordinary, the least neurotic people I knew. Of course Frankie wasn't quite the same as his brothers, and even as I was marrying into his family he was marrying out of it, but when I pictured the child I would deliver to the world

– her freckled nose, her clear green stare – it was MacKewon genes I gave her, even when I'd believed the seed was Kit's.

I rang the bell to see his face light up when he realised it was me, but he wasn't in, so I took out my keys.

The door slammed shut behind me. Too late, I remembered the fragility of the stained glass, closing my eyes for a second before turning around to check. It had survived. The newel post caught my shoulder as I walked past. The kitchen was spotless. No crumbs on the countertops, no dishes by the sink. Had he finally learned to clean up after himself?

There was a note on the table:
Ruth in labour! gone to watch the kids till K gets back
Soup in the pan
I lit the gas and went upstairs to unpack.

The broth steamed like molten lava, more solid than liquid. I bent over the bowl and felt its fierce heat on my face. Leeks, peas, lentils, pearl barley, carrots sliced fine as two-pence pieces, dissolving cubes of potato. I disturbed the smoking surface with a spoon, wondering if the metal would bend, if a fingertip dipped for a second would blister. I wanted punishment, tissue damage to the roof of my mouth, the secondary burn of the pepper. What I got was the comfort of starch, a lump in my throat as if an arm had been wrapped around my shoulders, or a tartan blanket on a chilly day. As if someone I had done an immeasurable wrong were saying *there there, never mind, have a good cry*.

Ruth's baby was a girl, ejected into the world around the time Frankie was scribbling his note to me. They called her Mhairi, pronounced the Gaelic way. Kenny floated home a few hours later, clutching a bottle of Laphroaig and the obligatory cigars. By the time Frankie rolled in I was asleep. We drove to the hospital next morning, and he gave the new arrival his pinkie to hold while Ruth and I dusted off the old jokes. ('I always knew you had it in you.') We didn't feel properly alone until we left the car park.

'Can I drop you somewhere?'

He was driving.

'I thought we could have lunch.'

'I told Stevie I'd go in to the studios.'

'On your day off?'

'It's a heavy week.'

So began the civil period of our marriage. The bathroom floor had never been so clean, the dishwasher so promptly stacked. The chores were a blessing, keeping us busy: the drone of the washing machine, the Dyson, the fan oven, a welcome cover for our lack of talk. It was palpable, his longing to be out of my sight, to escape the enervating stasis of our hours together. After a day or two, I was just as eager to have him gone.

It crossed my mind that he was having an affair. *Tell him to keep it in his keks*, Scott had said. Plus his lack of interest in meeting up at weekends, all those nights his phone had been switched off, the 'something' he'd been about to tell me in the fruit shop that I'd never followed up. I remembered his hand on Christina Agostino's waist. There was a type of woman who loved the idea of hanging out with the guys in the locker room. Half pin-up, half tomboy: the sort who always knew a filthier joke, who bought her round and didn't switch to mineral water halfway through the night, who could take a man to ecstasy *and* understand the offside rule. There were a dozen Christinas in his office, he could have been sleeping with any of them. But I knew he wasn't.

On Wednesday I stayed up to watch *Midweek Round-Up*. It was his turn to chair the ex-players' panel, paraphrasing their wittering into semi-coherent analysis. His shirt was too tight, but it wasn't the worst thing I'd seen him wear on screen. He made a joke about Jan Rensburg's match fitness and the latest red-top kiss-and-tell, scored a couple of good-natured hits against Scott, and the final credits rolled over a collage of the week's best goals. A typical show. I was about to switch off when I realised that, instead of the usual trailer for some soap opera or comedy-drama, Frankie was still on camera. Despite the semi-darkened set, I knew it was no technical hitch.

He leaned in to the lens, his face filling the screen. 'You still here? Good stuff, I was wanting a wee word.'

I had a bad feeling about this.

'Now maybe you're thinking it's going to be a word like "rat", or "skunk", or maybe a bigger word like "betrayal". I'm hearing those words in one or two bars on London Road, after a wee refreshment, but let's keep the heid and talk about loyalty. Fidelity. I know, I know: it's the twenty-first century, the world's moved on. Everybody wants to do that wee bit better for themselves. More money. Bigger league. Aye, there's better squads than Celtic if you go looking, but the magic combo, that chemistry together: that's something else.'

It didn't take long to find out what he was talking about, the story was all over the net. Liam McVay had fined Jojo Damer two months' wages for a nightclub brawl. Damer had got himself signed off sick. Ajax and Bayern Munich were sniffing around. There were grown men and women in the west of Scotland weeping actual tears, but everything there was to say had already been said twenty times over, so Frankie had come up with this.

'I'm not going to try and tell you what to do. It's your call. There's not a team in Europe's going to turn you down. Spain, Italy, France. Great food, decent weather. There's a cost, but. I'm not talking about eleven million, I mean the human cost, people's feelings. People who've stuck by you for years. *Fidelity*. And aye, OK, maybe it wasnae always perfect, but it was *good*.'

No, I thought, *he wouldn't do that*, but it wasn't just the words. There was the green of his eyes like lasers in the gloom, the intimate business of muttering in the dark.

'You fancied something different. Who doesnae? Same old same old, week in, week out. I've been tempted, I'd be a liar if I said I hadn't. But I never did anything about it, and I had plenty chances. *Loyalty*. I wouldnae put a dog through what I'm going through the now. Not sleeping. Nae appetite. I get up, go to work,' he shook his head, 'cannae concentrate. I've got this pain, here,' he clapped his chest, 'I thought it was just something they put in songs – aye, I know: you heard it last week, I'm like a cracked record,' his voice was barely a whisper, 'you've broken my heart.'

I remembered sitting in Margo's kitchen with the phone to my ear the night I told him I was pregnant, listening to him sobbing. I'd thought it was relief after wanting a child for so long. I had to admit Scott was right: it was everybody's business now.

Fungus

The meals we had eaten with Kenny and Ruth spanned two decades of culinary fashion. The false dawn of fresh pasta, the stir-fry years, warm salads, seared tuna, sashimi, polenta. The miraculous discovery that any old muck tasted better with enough olive oil. Ten years ago we had sat into the small hours of the morning talking politics or music or films. Now we did lunch at ours, or early supper at Kenny and Ruth's. She'd be up with Mhairi half the night, and the other two woke at six.

I started the conversation, drawing attention to the way Frankie kept looking at the sleeping baby on the settee.

'He can't help it,' Ruth said, 'it's his paternal instinct.'

'It's his instinct to be the centre of attention,' I said. 'Asleep! In the same room as big Frankie MacKewon! God forbid, she might grow up watching the competition.'

Frankie studied his plate. I had lost the knack of wifely teasing. I sounded like the sort of second division club manager who punched his arm and laughed hysterically when their paths crossed in John Lewis.

I wondered aloud why no one ever talked about paternal instinct.

'Because it's called wanting a shag?' Kenny suggested.

Ruth rolled her eyes. 'Because they won't admit to it in front of other men.'

Kenny winked at Frankie. 'This touchy-feely business has gone too far. They'll have us in frocks and Manolo yokema-bobs if we don't watch it.'

'Even Torcuil,' Ruth said, 'he's dying for a shot with Meaghan's dolls, but he won't let himself.'

'She ties them up and plays hostages with them,' Kenny told us. 'She'll make someone a great mammy one day.'

I topped up my glass of water. 'It's not a million miles from Lilias's idea of mothering.'

'She never beheaded you on the Internet,' Frankie said.

'That *is* a difference,' I conceded.

But Ruth hadn't finished with paternal instinct. 'I suppose boys are slower to develop the nurturing urge.' She looked at Frankie. 'What age were you?'

'Thirty-nine.'

She gave him the look I'd seen her use with Torquil when he was showing off. 'They have to get mating out of their systems first, all that displaying and competition.'

'You've turned into a right wee biological determinist,' he said.

'It's having kids. All that guff about nurture goes out the window. Animals have two basic drives: reproduction and survival.'

'What about football,' Kenny said, with another wink at Frankie, 'is that not a basic drive?'

'More basic than reproduction these days,' I said, in another attempt at conjugal teasing.

There was a silence.

'I'll get the pudding,' Ruth said.

'How are you?'

We were by the sink, site of a hundred feminine confidences, only that night it was Kenny washing, and me drying, while Ruth sought Frankie's opinion on the fungus that had appeared in the garage.

'Blooming,' I said, 'does it not show? Still, I'll pay for it in the end.'

This was Ruth's joke. You got a good pregnancy or a

203

speedy labour, not both. She had suffered from indigestion every day of her nine months to deliver Mhairi in just fifty-three minutes. Kenny called her the human cannon.

He was running hot water into a pan. 'I meant the both of you.'

I could have told him Frankie was baking brownies to appease my breeder's sweet tooth and swimming shotgun at the public pool lest a passing breaststroker kick my bump, but if I walked into a room he happened to be in, within ten seconds he'd walk out.

'We get by,' I said.

He nodded. 'How long is it you were away, four months?'

'About that.'

'Long enough to get used to it.'

I liked the combination of ungainliness and grace in Kenny's six-foot-seven-inch frame. I liked the bulk of him looming over me as we worked at the sink. Despite his smoker's skin and stringy hair and yellow nails, around him the world was a more wholesome place. But we didn't do personal conversation.

He handed me the saucepan. 'Ruth says you haven't been back to the clinic.'

'I've never felt so well in my life.'

'Good for you,' he said in a tone that told me exactly what it was like to be a patient of his, 'but we don't know about the little fella.'

'The baby's fine.'

'Ah, he'll be grand, but you'd want to be sure of that. Have you even had a blood test?'

I glanced down, past my newly magnificent breasts.

'It'd be a fecking big tumour, so,' he admitted.

We laughed.

'I'm a bloke,' he said, 'pity on us: watching it all happen. Remember Wonderwoman out there, eight months gone with Torcuil, dragging thirteen-and-a-half stone up and down

204

stairs with trays of Bovril and dry toast? I had myself tested for glandular fever, hepatitis.' He laughed shamefacedly. 'Couvade syndrome. She knew what it was all along, but she didn't go on and on about it.'

'She did to me,' I said.

'Ah, shur, that's what friends are for.'

A wail rose from the settee at the far end of the long room. The baby quietened as soon as he picked her up. He brought her back to the kitchen, and I thought: why not be honest?

'I don't know him any more.'

Preoccupied with the baby, Kenny frowned.

'I see more of him on screen than I do at home. If he's not flashing his pecs in Sicily, he's prancing around in satin shorts sparring with Amir Khan. Do you watch *Midweek Round-Up*?'

'Most weeks.'

'So you caught his little chat to camera after the credits?'

'Oh,' he shifted the baby to his other shoulder, 'Ruth said you wouldn't like it.'

'Maybe she should have a word.' Something occurred to me. I had noticed it countless times and yet it had never really registered until then. 'He's always looking for her approval lately. Everything he says, he checks her reaction.'

Kenny ducked his head into his shoulders. 'She's been counselling him.'

I nodded as if this were a minor piece of news. 'About what?'

'I can't say.'

But I could see he knew.

'I don't know what to do,' I said, 'it's like I'm sharing the house with a stranger.'

'Jaysus, Freya, have you looked at yourself? I mean, it's great and all, but you aren't the woman you were.'

'So what am I?'

His mouth slackened into an expression that, on any other

man but Kenny, I would have described as a leer. The hand not holding his daughter shaped the air. 'You're softer.'

I felt a stab of disappointment, he was talking about my figure.

'You've slowed down – no, it's good, it's good. You're more instinctive, not so,' he tapped his forehead, 'all up here.'

'If you're trying to say my brain's shrunk, it happens to all pregnant women.'

'No, no, no, no, no. I'm not talking about intelligence.' He squinted. 'Or am I, now? A different kind of intelligence, maybe. Like a cat. Or a…. a lioness. The way you walk – you've a lovely sway on you now.' He put his hand over the baby's head as if to shield her from what he was about to say. 'He's good for you, anyone can see that, but it's hard on the big man.'

'It's finished,' I said. 'It hardly started.'

'Ah, well, I won't pretend I'm sorry about that.'

Having been shared with a million viewers of *Midweek Round-Up*, my infidelity was hardly a secret, but the shame I felt then was scalding, corrosive.

'*I* didn't want to be stuck out in the boondocks. I didn't see him for weeks on end. I was lonely. All right: I was his first love, he's never looked at another woman – when did he last take a proper look at *me*?' The baby was watching me, fascinated. 'Of course it's a demanding job, and they pay him very well, and I worked long hours too, but… I just wish he'd told the studios to *fuck off* once in a while. I know what you're thinking, and Ruth: he adored me. Yes, he did. But he was quite happy not seeing me for weeks on end. Well, it turned out there was somebody up there who actually enjoyed my company, who was prepared to *make time* to be with me—'

I could hear how I sounded. Better the unvarnished truth than this whining self-justification.

'Look, when you both want something that much and it doesn't happen, month after month after month, it drives a

206

wedge between you. I'd look at his face and all I saw was unhappiness. You love each other, but it's *so painful*. We had all the tests: nothing wrong with him, nothing wrong with me. It still wasn't happening. Was the clinic going to make any difference? I couldn't see it. We couldn't go on like that. Another six months, a year, and we'd have forgotten why we got together in the first place. We needed to get past this. I *needed* to get pregnant—'

I'd said so much, was there any point in not admitting it?

'And I thought it might happen with a younger man.'

In his tactful, doctor's voice, Kenny said, 'Does Frankie know it's over with this bloke?'

'Yesterday we had a discussion about the funny noise the Dyson's been making. That's about as meaningful as it gets.'

'He's having a tough time of it, Freya. Cut him some slack.'

Another wave of resistance rose in my chest. 'And what slack's he cutting me?'

'Don't you know?'

Just then the CD, having fallen silent twenty minutes before, reached its hidden bonus track, a cacophonous Rolling Stones cover. Mhairi began to cry. Kenny paced between cooker and fridge, murmuring into her scalp. This time it didn't work. Her face grew red, her brow compacting to make room for the furious oval of her mouth. Touching my belly to reassure the child inside me, I turned the music off.

'What slack is Frankie cutting me?'

At the peremptory note in my voice Mhairi stopped crying. Kenny tipped his head back in relief, or perhaps it was resignation.

'He knows the little fella isn't his.'

The back door opened. Frankie walked across to the radiator. Ruth followed him in.

'Is there any more coffee?' She answered herself, 'No, but I know where the kettle is.' She flicked the switch and relieved Kenny of their daughter.

There was a pause filled only by her sing-song to the baby and the asthmatic grumble of the warming kettle. Kenny's eyes strayed to the ventilation grille above the cooker.

I didn't really need to ask. 'You heard us, didn't you?'

Ruth's glance intersected with mine but she carried on fussing the baby.

'Aye,' Frankie said.

I saw he was angry with Kenny, and humiliated in front of Ruth. I didn't want to think about how he was feeling towards me. I went over to the sink and washed the cafetière. He took it from me. I watched him set out the cups and fetch the milk from the fridge. He seemed familiar to me in a way he hadn't for a long time. Not like the menopausal last-chancer who stripped off on camera, or the poker-faced stranger who shared my home and bed, but like the old Frankie. My husband. And so I placed my hands on my belly and told him. 'There's no question, she's yours.'

The kettle came to the boil and switched itself off. The baby mewed against Ruth's breast.

For the first time since coming in from the garage, Frankie looked at me. 'That's not what the second sperm count said. There was a cock-up at the lab, it was some other guy's sample first time round. Mine are fucking useless.'

We got into the car. I didn't start the engine. We sat there, staring through the windscreen at the Mini parked ahead of us.

I said, 'Why didn't you tell me—?'

He laughed under his breath. I supposed I deserved it.

'It's not his child either—'

He held up his hands as if he couldn't bear to hear any more. 'That *fucking* clinic.'

He shook his head. 'It doesn't matter.'

'Of course it matters. If it's not yours, and it's not his, whose is it?'

'I don't care, Freya.'

208

I sighed. 'Thank you.'

He turned to look at me. 'No,' he said, more distinctly. 'I. Don't. Care.'

The pain was so sudden, I thought I was having a heart attack.

He turned back to the windscreen.

'Frankie, listen, I know I haven't behaved well—'

'*Shut it!*'

I couldn't have been more shocked if he'd hit me. We called the sort of men who told their wives to *shut it* 'sexist shitheads'. But then, what would we call the sort of wife who slept with another man because he had younger sperm?

'This isn't us,' I said. 'You and me, we've always – we *talk*—'

He laughed under his breath again, shaking his head in disbelief.

'It happened *once*. I know that's one time too many, but it was only once, and I felt – I *feel* bad about it...'

He talked over me. 'I've had it up to here, Freya. I can't take any more. I thought I could, but I can't.'

'No,' I said, pleading now.

He looked at me.

'Frankie...'

'You can keep the house.'

'You love me!'

'I did, aye. It's a pity you never noticed until now.'

'We'll start again – you, me and the baby.'

'You just don't get it, do you?'

I had to admit it. 'Not really.'

He closed his eyes as if to summon new reserves of strength. 'I don't care who the father is. Your farmer, Barack Obama, Mickey fucking Mouse: *it's not mine*. I thought if I kept my mouth shut, if I didn't say anything I'd regret later, I'd get used to the idea, but I'm not a saint. I'm sorry, but I can't watch you giving birth to another man's child.'

209

Even now a part of me refused to accept it. This was Frankie, who had loved me, man and boy. There had to be something I could say to change his mind. And perhaps there was. *I'll give her up for adoption.* But I was never going to say that.

'I'll move out tomorrow,' he said.

'No,' I turned the key in the ignition. 'I'll go.'

Blood

I moved into a Travelodge. It was just what I needed: an empty room where I could tidy away every trace of myself. To minimise the risk of miscarriage, I decided not to go back to work. After so many weeks I was inured to what others called my life of leisure. Early to bed. A long lie in the morning. Hours whiled away in bookshops and cafés and galleries. The odd lazy afternoon at Ruth's, holding the new baby. She knew I'd moved out, but after a couple of rebuffs she stopped trying to discuss it. I told myself it was better not to think about it, to blank my desperate feelings so they didn't poison the baby.

I kept the news from Lilias, as did Frankie. Or at least, she never referred to it. She was making a point of ignoring the pregnancy. I wasn't sure why, but because I would never ask for anything withheld, I followed her lead. It became a sort of game between us: who was going to crack and mention it first. I suppose I won. We were queueing at the box office to collect tickets for *Andromache* when, *apropos* of nothing, she cast a jaundiced eye over my dress, and said, 'I'm not sure about the wisdom of horizontal stripes, darling.' After that, it was open season. She was *not sure* about me wearing low-waisted jeans, and snacking between meals, and resting my hands on my bump ('It's not going to go away if you stop touching it, you know'). Was I absolutely certain of my dates? I really shouldn't be that big. She hadn't shown until her fifth month, and never had to buy a maternity dress. She hoped I

211

was using oil of evening primrose, although at my age I'd be left with a kangaroo's pouch whatever I did. I'd be lucky not to get piles, the size it'd be by the time it was ready to come out. Frankie would feel the difference too, unless I begged them for the husband's stitch, and she didn't think they did it these days – the feminists had spoiled things for everyone else. I could look forward to constipation, indigestion, loosening teeth, postnatal hair loss. My breasts would go south, if they hadn't already. And I wasn't to believe the propaganda about pelvic floor exercises: I'd never cough off the lavatory again.

Then one day she phoned asking me to meet her at the hospital.

The nurse was young and overweight, with a swag of flesh joining her chin to the place where her collarbone should have been. Lovely skin, like Galloway milk, except where she'd smeared herself in sand-coloured foundation. I got this eye for detail from Lilias, it was part of who I was, but recently I had been making an effort to switch it off. It wasn't a trait I wanted to pass on to my daughter. The knack of walking into a diamond shop and instantly seeing the flaws makes no one any happier.

'You should have come through,' the nurse said, ushering me down the corridor.

'The sign said to wait.'

She wrinkled her nose indulgently. Evidently the rules were not made for relatives of Lilias. 'You can keep an eye on her for me, see she doesn't overdo it.'

'Which of her many overdoings do you have in mind?'

She flashed me a disconcerted glance. 'My gran was the same. Never had a day in bed. If you needed a hand, she was there for you, but when *she* needed help, would she ask?' We walked a few steps in silence. 'It's Freya, isn't it?' she said. I glanced at the laminated badge pinned to her uniform. Someone had christened her Grace.

'The thing is, Freya, she needs everything she's got to fight the cancer. She can't be running your life *and* hers.'

Nurse Grace wanted my mother to move in with me. It would be useful with the baby coming, having someone there if I wanted to get out to the shops. And it would make all the difference to her. But she wouldn't be running after me. Those days were gone. It was my turn to hold everything together.

After a lifetime of being ambushed by Lilias's scripts, I didn't even blink.

'I know it's scary, she's your mum, she's always been there for you, but she's got enough to worry about without you in bits.'

We pushed through a set of double doors into a large room lined with examination cubicles. The nurse pulled back a curtain. 'Here we are.'

I was reminded of uncooked chicken wings on cold-cabinet shelves. Meatless sinew, those scaly wrists. Stick legs stuck out below the paper gown. I felt a sudden fury at the blinking striplight, the scuffed plastic chair, the handwashing instructions on the wall.

'Hello, Freya,' Lilias said in an accent located somewhere north of Inverness.

Behind the hospital smell of bedpans and disinfectant, I caught another, more troubling scent.

Addressing my mother, the nurse's voice gained a note of affectionate reproach. 'I was just saying, Missus, we'll need to get you on CCTV, make sure you're not putting the ward to rights the minute my back's turned.'

Lilias twinkled at her.

'Don't give me that butter-wouldn't-melt look, I know what like you are. The tea trolley'll be along in a minute. You'll have a cup of tea and two biscuits.' She wagged a finger. 'And no giving them to *you know who* when you think I'm not looking.'

'What did you tell her?' I murmured, when the nurse left us alone.

'Nothing, darling.'

'Then why does she think you've spent your life waiting on me hand and foot?'

'Does she?' Lilias examined her painted toenails.

'Apparently I'm falling apart at the thought of life without you.'

She looked up. 'And aren't you?'

It was rare for Lilias to take me so completely by surprise.

'You're indestructible,' I said.

The nurse returned with a dressing gown that had once been white but was now semolina grey. The name of the hospital was embroidered across one pocket. She draped it over her patient's shoulders, tucking the collar around her neck, while Lilias snuggled in to the towelling.

'Can't have you catching your death in hospital, can we, Missus?'

'No, Grace.'

There it was again: that Highland lilt. I was used to vocal leakage when she was working, but she hadn't had a sniff of a part since the one-woman show fell through.

The nurse touched her cheek with the back of one hand. I watched Lilias move towards the caress, as a cat will rise to meet stroking fingers.

'No wonder you feel the cold, Missus. There's not a pick of flesh on you.'

'Oh I've always been slender, even when I was pregnant with Freya. I wore a mini-skirt till the day I gave birth. It caused endless misunderstandings with men who saw me from behind. Of course I had to be slim for the cameras.'

Nurse Grace looked confused.

'My mother is an actress,' I said.

The girl's face lit up in the usual way. 'Were you famous?'

Lilias gave a shrug that came across as charming modesty.

214

'I suppose I was. It seems such a long time ago now. Another lifetime. Of course acting was completely different then, you really had to learn your craft. Slave labour they'd call it now, but you knew Larry and Rex and Dickie had done their time, so it was a badge of honour.'

There was a routine Lilias used with star-struck civilians, a summary of her career that glossed over all those matinees playing to the half-price nodders from the council retirement home. She gave Nurse Grace the edited highlights. The day she voice-coached Vanessa to say 'a pint of mulk'. Beating Judi at ping-pong dressed in crinoline and stays. Rescuing Ralphie when he dried. There was an art to doing it so they couldn't tell in the stalls.

'Forty years ago being a stage actress meant something. It wasn't a sideline for resting soap stars then.'

'You've done your share of TV work,' I said, 'even then. You just said, you had to be slim for the cameras.'

'Oh *that*. It was only a cameo in *The Protectors*. Everyone did them. Charlotte, Donald, Christopher, all the character actors. They cast me as a Parisian *parfumeuse*. I had to flirt with Robert Vaughn and meet a sticky end, blown up by my own distillery. I could have had some fun with it, playing against type, but the director was rather a literalist. "*Come on lovey, put a bit of oo-la-la into it.*" I told him, if he wanted that sort of sexy he should have hired Babs Windsor. He got his own back in the end, of course.' She made a scissoring motion with her fingers. 'I could spit when I think of the repeat fees.'

'He cut you out?' The nurse was shocked. I knew such things happened, but I too felt a dislocation at the news.

'He was very lucky the script still worked. The shooting schedule was unbelievably tight, virtually as live. I suppose I shouldn't say it was him – I don't *really* know. It might have been Nyree Dawn Porter. I was lovely in those days, all the more so with being...' Delicately she touched the flat of her hand to her stomach. 'You know that glow pregnant women have.' For an eloquent second they both looked at me. 'Well, sometimes.'

The nurse was sitting in a vacant cubicle eating a Kit Kat, tucked away behind the half-drawn curtain.

'She's asleep in the chair,' I said. 'I'll be off.'

Nurse Grace nodded. 'Did you ask her, about moving in?'

'I don't think it'd be good for her.'

'It's just what she needs.'

'Not if I stab her with a bread knife in the first twenty-four hours.'

She flapped a hand at me. 'You'll be fine.'

'Your grandmother,' I said, 'was she a Highlander by any chance?'

She looked at me in astonishment. 'From Dornoch, aye. How did you know?'

I couldn't tell her. To explain Lilias was to be implicated in her tricks, or suspected of making them up.

'She'd rather sleep in a cardboard box than live with me, whatever she's told you.'

The nurse's face turned grave. 'She's your mum. You only get one. Talk to her about it.' She chewed her lip. 'I shouldn't be saying this but, do it today. It'd mean the world to her. Mr McCaul's a brilliant surgeon, but you never know. It's a big operation for a woman your mum's age.'

'Operation,' I repeated dully.

'The mastectomies, tomorrow.' I saw realisation dawning in her eyes, just as she must have seen it dawn in mine. 'Did she not…'

'She told me she was in for tests.'

The canteen was empty of customers, the serving hatches shuttered. I sat down. The woman pushing the floor polisher gave me an odd look. After a minute or two I realised I was cradling my breasts. *Mine look just like yours*. Pale nipples, a girlish upward tilt. Mine were bigger now, but it was reasonable to assume hers, too, had once been this size. Ruth only had to kiss Kenny to spurt with milk, a party trick I longed to ask them to demonstrate (but for Kenny's sake could not). I thought of Lilias aching, holding out until the source ran dry, seeping those precious antibodies every time I cried. There are women who bottle-feed out of embarrassment, but I couldn't believe she was among them. One of my earliest memories was Lilias in a see-through shirt. White organza, stiff and a little scratchy to the touch, fastened with oddly formal covered buttons. Young as I was, I grasped the mixed messages: the invitation to look but not touch, the way its weave caught the light so you had to stare to make out the rosy snub of nipple and the crescent-shaped shadow on the underside of each breast. One night, teased beyond endurance by this garment, a bearded stage manager poured a pint of lager down her chest and she slapped his face so ringingly that the party stopped, until her laughter turned it into a joke.

I found them together when I got back from the canteen. Lilias was staring at the floor while the nurse wrote in a blue cardboard folder.

'Ma,' I said.

The nurse looked up, startled, but Lilias already knew I was there. 'Yes, darling?'

Love me.

The words were so loud in my head I half-believed I'd said them, but the nurse's expression did not change.

'You're doing the right thing,' I said.

She frowned. 'I'm not sure I...'

I moved my eyes towards Nurse Grace.

'Oh.' A throwaway syllable, unabashed by her failure to keep me informed. 'Well it's nice to know you approve, darling.'

The nurse sent me an encouraging glance.

'You're getting rid of it,' I said, 'that's the main thing.'

'You mean my breasts?' The word had never been so perfectly enunciated. 'I'm getting rid of my *breasts*?'

I met her eye. She wasn't being fair, and she knew it, but I understood the impulse to pass the misery on.

'Once the plastic surgeon's finished with you, you won't know the difference,' I said.

The nurse's eyes showed alarm. 'Reconstruction's not usual with someone your mum's age.'

'She's not your usual seventy-year-old.'

'Actually, darling, I don't think I'll bother.'

I looked at her, the hideous towelling robe, the defeated slope of her shoulders. Yet still I sensed some fight in her. Those scarlet toenails. The tension in her neck. And then I grasped what Lilias's consent to surgery actually meant. Not the wish to enjoy a long life, not that at all. Her body had betrayed her so to Hell with it, let the surgeon butcher it. The more bloodily the better, as far as she was concerned.

I grasped this, but was sufficiently frightened to pretend I had not. 'Think about it, Ma. You won't go to an audition with a spot on your chin, it's a major tragedy if you break a nail. Anything less than perfection, and your life's...'

Not worth living, I managed not to say.

She shrugged. 'I just find the whole idea too vulgar.'

'They're not going to turn you into Dolly Parton. I'm sure they'll do you a refined pair, if you ask.'

Mindful of the patients in the other cubicles, the nurse put a finger to her lips.

Lilias said, 'It's all right, darling.'

'How can it possibly be *all right*?'

There was a blanched pause. She looked down at the floor again. 'Of course it's not all right.' Her voice was a whisper. 'But do you mind if we don't talk about it?'

The nurse placed a hand on my upper arm, her chocolate-breath sticky in my ear. 'Be *nice* to her.'

218

Lie to her, she meant. Play it any way she wants it. The truth's no good to her now.

Above me, the faulty striplight stuttered on and off. The stink I'd noticed when I first walked in was stronger now. 'What's that smell?'

Nurse Grace frowned.

'Sort of bitter, gets you in the back of the throat.'

'I think you'll find it's me, darling,' Lilias said, and we laughed, my mother and I, crammed into that cubicle with her small-but-oh-so-vividly-present breasts, and my neediness, and my counter-need to succour her, and her refusal to be succoured, and her self-destructive rage, and the plump, well-meaning nurse who had no inkling of any of this. Gallows humour was one of the things Lilias and I had in common, along with our lethal eye for detail. Not much to set against our differences – her faith in display and my mistrust of it; my need for a truth beyond manipulation, and her panic at the very thought; the endearments she used so casually, and the feelings I could never name – yet it struck me then, we were like nothing so much as an old photographic print and its negative: complete opposites and, in some awful way, the same.

The nurse finished writing in her folder and rolled up the patient's sleeve. Lilias shut her eyes as the syringe was stripped of its wrapper.

'You're not going to make a fuss about a wee needle, are you, Missus?'

'It's the sight of blood,' I explained, 'she likes to believe her veins run with Chanel No. 5.'

The nurse's finger flicked at the crook of Lilias's elbow. The hypodermic pierced her arm, digging around for a vein. A blaeberry bruise soiled her linen-white flesh, but nothing entered the phial. The nurse tried again. Lilias breathed in sharply.

'Sorry, sweetheart.'

219

Her heart pumped blood into the syringe, a red so dark it was almost black. The same stuff that ran through my veins. Or half the same. I thought about *The Protectors*. Robert Vaughn like a photoshopped Jack Kennedy, my mother in seamed black stockings under a shortie lab coat. A third figure entered the reverie, a tall man in an undertaker's suit and brown brogues.

'This man Smith,' I said quietly, 'I know you know him.'

'What man Smith?'

'The man who applied for a job with me.'

Her eyes blinked open.

'Nearly finished, Missus,' the nurse said.

'If I've learned one thing from a career in the public eye, darling, it's that you have to ignore these people.'

'What people?'

'The sort of person you're talking about.'

The nurse removed the third phial of blood and pressed a scrap of cotton wool to the puncture mark. 'All done!'

'What "sort of person"?'

Lilias's eyes bored into mine. I knew this meant *not in front of the nurse*.

'The sort of person who goes to enormous trouble to apply for a job so he can drop your name in the interview, you mean?'

Nurse Grace wrapped a blood pressure cuff around Lilias's other arm.

'Lying about his age, concocting a fake CV—?'

Lilias's nostrils flared as if detecting her own bad smell.

'The sort of person who'd claim to have seen you in that episode of *The Protectors* even though you never made the cut—?'

The inflating rubber squeezed her scrawny arm. 'Try to relax, Missus,' the nurse said.

'And the next time I see him he's passing himself off as a farmer.'

'*He is a fucking farmer.*'

Nobody spoke. The air thrummed with expectation, like those first heightened seconds when the lights come up on an empty stage.

'It's not what you think,' she said.

'And what am I thinking?'

I could feel the words that would change everything waiting to be spoken.

In her most languid drawl, Lilias said, 'I'm sure I don't know, darling.'

The joke was, I hadn't been thinking anything. Not consciously. My father was an actor. My whole life had been built around this supposed fact. It explained Lilias's first sight of him, sprinting down the stalls in the middle of the first act (a fourth-wall-busting *coup de théâtre*). It explained how he fell in love with her. It even explained why he left. But it wouldn't be the first lie she had told me.

And then I said it. 'I'm thinking I'll never forgive you for this.'

She leaned towards me so abruptly that I jerked back in self-defence. In the jittery glare of the striplight her eyes were the colour of cold opals. I saw the runnel of saliva between her bared teeth and lower lip. The words came out cleanly, without any kid-on accent. 'You can be a real little bitch when you want to be.'

The nurse turned scarlet.

'Listen to me, darling, tomorrow they're going to cut off my breasts. After that, it's anyone's guess. I know you think you drew the short straw, getting me as a mother, but I've never asked anything of you. Until now. I want you to promise me – call it my dying wish, if you like – I want you to swear to me on the life of that thing inside you, you'll have nothing whatsoever to do with that man.'

1972

Five o'clock. Lili has been in her bedroom for at least an hour, listening to the rattle of saucepans downstairs. Another meal in preparation. They really should find out if sound travels as clearly the other way, but that would take organisation. Persuading him to listen when his mother goes out, unless baritone notes carry further and she should be the one in the kitchen while he fakes their amorous moans up here. Not the likeliest of prospects.

The yellow shade of the bedside lamp casts a softening light, kind to the bits of her body that make her wince in the mirror. She is tempted to undress, at least to her underwear, but the room is too cold for solitary nakedness, and what if Mrs S calls her downstairs? Besides, it would look presumptious. A formality governs their dealings out of bed. Her choice as much as his. They both know why he mentioned that he'd finish up when it got dark, but nothing more was said. It's bad enough that he can look up to see the expectant square of her lighted window.

Rolling onto her stomach, she returns to her book. The paragraph at the top of the page has the staleness of words read a dozen times. She flicks forward, waiting for a sentence to catch her eye so she can pick up the story further on. Ah yes, what about this: *I'm not angry with you, I'm in love with you*. After a page or two her spine starts to ache. She wonders how many more weeks she will be able to lie on her front. In the village the other day she saw a pregnant woman the size of a haystack shuffling along, swollen ankles crammed into fluffy slippers. That won't happen to her, she'll make sure of it, but there'll be no escaping the bump, and what happens then? Is that when this stops?

She hears the creak of the stairs, and still she jumps at his touch. His hand over her mouth. Machine oil and straw and that faint, persistent note of dung. She is used to hands that smell of soap in bed, but she would be wasting her breath asking him to wash. He hauls the jumper over his head, then his shirt. His hairless chest is still a novelty to her. Under her fingertip, the pale pancake of his nipple becomes a match-head. He catches her wrists, pressing them into the mattress. *What's the rush?* she would have said in the past, but time is the one thing they don't have. In half an hour, they'll be called down for tea. In five months, she'll give birth.

It's a kind of sex she has not had before: this rubbing and writhing, the straining erection chafing at its mark through two layers of clothing. *Practically a virgin*, she thinks when she's alone, was he unlucky enough to get the girl pregnant his very first time? When it's happening there's no space for thought, it's all grab and urgency. He pulls at her shirt. Even carapaced by a bra, her breasts make him gasp. A hesitation enters the air between them and she recognises the awkward moment when they must strip off, each mastering their own zips and fastenings. However guarded they remain with each other, undressing creates a punning sense of exposure. She kicks her clothes to the floor, flinching at the slippery chill of the taffeta bedcover. He spreads himself on top of her. Despite the cold, her pores open, nerves sparking. His limbs extend far beyond hers, but they are a perfect fit where it counts, and now she catches the tang of him beneath those farmyard scents.

Abruptly his head pulls back. Movement down on the first floor, his mother coming upstairs. They wait, frozen, listening to her lumbering tread and the shove she gives the

223

box room door directly below them. Something heavy is shifted. Then, ominously, silence. Filled, as the seconds pass, with the conviction that Mrs S is also listening.

Lili has a tickle in her throat. Any moment now she is going to cough. Or laugh. She takes a deep breath, but that just makes it worse. He puts a finger to her lips. Each of the lashes framing his black eyes, every whisker on his face, seems drawn by a fine-nibbed pen. His lips kink in a smile. He can always tell when he's being admired.

They're never less than careful, but today they're super-sensitive to every creak of the mattress, every pant of hot breath, every slap of flesh on flesh. No matter how pleasurable the action, if it's audible they desist. Hearing takes the lead over her other senses, registering the click of saliva, the whisper of the sheets, the sticky smack of his fingers between her legs. And now she, too, feels the urgency. Denied vocal expression, they resort to mime, teeth bared like snarling dogs, their whimpers and cries translated into widened eyes and funnelled lips. His grimace almost looks like pain. They both know the risk they're running. Any loss of control and they could be discovered, and neither wants that, though on balance, he wants it less, which adds a pinch of malicious provocation to the unstinting pleasure she gives him. In the end he has to stop her, holding her pinioned. She can tell he likes the way she struggles in his grip, her desperation as he brings his mouth to her most vulnerable places. She has never seen him so worked up. When he lets himself go, the headboard cannons against the wall. He withdraws from her, his face a mask of agony, his salt-slicked body gleaming in the yellow light. They wait, ears straining, sweat cooling on their skin. No sound from below. They should give it another five minutes – or, to be really safe, give up, but neither has the self-control for that.

He lies on his back, watching her above him. When she engulfs him he almost cries out, his eyes squeezed shut, lips

224

stretched tight. She repeats the trick, again and again, even when he tries to take over, their striving made more savage by the limited room for manoeuvre, their terror of rocking the bed. They're on the home stretch, neck and neck, when he overpowers her, pulling her down, rolling on top of her, his movements faster now, hurting her, not as he has hurt her in the past, heedlessly, or selfishly, taking his climax at her expense. She knows the ricochet pleasure gives his rhythm. This is different, a deliberation that makes each thrust discrete. Harder. Deeper. As if he wants to get to the core of her, the safe, dark place where the incubus is forming. And now she starts to panic, trying to throw him off her, to get him out, away from the baby, but it's too late. He screams air, his mouth a rictus, the tendons of his neck exposed as if flayed, while his loins grind through the waves of sensation, pushing for the place where life is made.

Cow

Paul was the first to notice me hovering in the doorway. The woman sitting at my desk shot him an enquiring glance. I didn't care for her snake-eyed smile when she realised I was watching. Then Dorothy saw me. Within seconds I was surrounded. Judith, Mary, Iain, Fiona, Maggie, Dymphna, Caroline. The new woman continued tapping at my keyboard for a minute or two, then lost her nerve and stood up, gesturing towards my old chair. I shook my head. She sat down again, and the full hopelessness of the situation was brought home to me. It wasn't unknown for staff to chase up the address of a sexy job applicant so they could engineer further contact. I'd given one repeat offender a verbal warning. And here I was, intent on a similar crime.

I sensed a low-level unease in the room. They all had work to do. Once upon a time I would have been reminding them of this.

I said to Paul, 'Remember that guy last summer, the one who faked his application form?'

Snake-eyes was watching, measuring everything she had been told about me against my presence in the flesh.

Paul grinned, assuming I had some gossip to pass on. 'Yeah.'

'Did you ever hear from him again?'

'Nup.'

I imagined saying it, *I think he's my father*. The nervous laughter that would follow. The embarrassment when it became clear I wasn't joking. The panic in their eyes at the half-craved, half-dreaded crumbling of my authority.

'You know Graham Mac didn't get the Justice job,' Caroline said.

And that was that. The conversation had moved on. It was almost noon. One of my organisational achievements had been the introduction of the staggered lunch break. The unit was never unstaffed. I thought of setting off the fire alarm, hiding in the lavatory, creeping back once they'd evacuated the floor in the hope that someone had left a terminal logged on. It wasn't going to happen.

We went to the canteen. They suspended the lunch rota in my honour. I ate spaghetti carbonara and they told me how difficult the spads were being these days. Dymphna wanted to know if the baby was kicking yet. When I shook my head, they went back to talking shop. Fiona asked if I missed the unit? I said no, and everybody laughed, certain the real answer was yes. I went back with them to collect my coat.

'Something came for you. I opened it by mistake.' Snake-eyes, not sounding particularly contrite. 'I-*ah*, didn't have your address in Perthshire.'

She slipped away to my desk – her desk now – and retrieved an envelope from one of the drawers. The postmark was five months old. Unfolded, the sheet of paper yielded a photo-copied snapshot. A young woman standing beside a cow. I turned it over. On the back, in pencil, was an address.

'Someone you'd lost touch with?' Caroline prompted.

'You could say.'

I reread the address just to make sure, in case my brain had scrambled the letters, but there was no mistake. All those years of fruitless searching, only to find him a stone's throw from the spot where chance had led me.

I studied the woman in the photograph, the sleekness of what was now skin and bone, the gentler gleam to her white-gold hair, the smiling overbite quite uncorrected. So unselfconscious in front of the camera. So obviously in love.

227

Sheep

Five miles past the Roman watchtower, the estate road forked. A wooden sign pointed the way to Shepherd's Cottage, a two-storey, corrugated-iron house with rust sores breaking through its white gloss paint. The five-mile drive over private land, the faint detonations of a shooting party on the far side of the estate, the loneliness of that tin house under the sodden sky, all of it conspired to put me in the wrong. *Call it my dying wish, if you like*. I knocked and waited, knocked again. The windows were too dirty to see much inside. Half a dozen hens scratched in the mud. I didn't know what I was waiting for until it came. A dog's bark puncturing the stillness, high on the hill above me.

I ran up that hillside, the heather like tripwire, black bog sucking at my boots under the straw-coloured grass. It was a filthy day, low cloud cloaking the summit, a northerly wind driving the drizzle into my face. I must have climbed a thousand feet before I heard the bleating, then more barking and that Biblical shout, much closer than the afternoon I'd heard it with Kit. A dozen sheep spilled down the hill, circled by a pair of Border collies. It seemed an unequal contest, the dogs' intelligence and speed against the flustered trotting of the ewes, but one tup managed to break away and, while the dogs were rounding her up, another made her escape. I stood awhile watching the chase before resuming my climb.

He manifested in front of me like an illusionist from a stage trapdoor. One moment I was alone, the next he was there.

A couple of minutes later I saw the dip in the landscape that had concealed him, but it was no less of a miracle: this sudden answer to four decades of longing.

'A bad day to leave the bunnet at home,' he said.

How many hundreds of times had I rehearsed this scene in my head, and now I was lost for words.

Standing so close, he seemed huge to me. Rangy, elemental, not to be judged. He had more hair than I remembered. Those overgrown eyebrows, the thicket in each nostril, the tangle of charcoal and steel wool the rain had half-plastered to his scalp.

He wrapped his creased palm around my hand as he had that day in Edinburgh. 'I'd given up on you.'

'I'd have been here quicker if you'd told me who you were.'

'Ach, well.'

'Why didn't you?'

He looked at me, his face full of things he couldn't say.

We stood like that for several seconds, my chilled fingers warming in his grip, my breath roiling in my chest.

He roused himself. 'Are you come to help with the gathering?'

'I don't know what that means.'

He smiled. 'Rounding up the lost sheep.'

One of the collies arrived, panting noisily, pink tongue at full stretch. It had the same spare build as its master. At a guttural command that was more snarl than syllable, the dog set off again, racing towards a patch of bracken. Two bleating ewes broke cover.

'Come on,' he said, 'there's work to be done.'

We followed the sheep down by a more oblique route than I had taken up the hill, over rubbery mats of cranberry and blaeberry, and blackened wastes where the heather had been burned leaving the twisted roots exposed like nests of snakes. We crossed a brown burn frothing with cream lace, waded through a bed of bracken down a slope so steep I had to grasp

229

the crumbling stems to steady myself. The dogs raced in front, heading off the wayward sheep, but always circling back to us, making a detour to pass in front of me before returning to their master. He was fitter than a man his age had any right to be, and set a punishing pace, using his crook to probe each footing, while I had to trust to momentum to save me from turning an ankle. I had no breath to speak, and he no spare attention, his gaze raking the hillside, snagging on those distant specks of fleece that I failed to spot time after time. Could he have recognised Kit and me that day? We'd laughed at my misapprehension, but now I wondered. If his voice could carry half a mile and still pack a punch, why shouldn't his eyes have a similar range?

He had brought me here, led me through the stations of acquaintance to this place of unmasking. I had no idea where we were going or what would happen next. It wasn't like me to be so passive – at least, not like the person I had been until then. Charging down the hill behind him, I felt the fatherless years lifting from my shoulders and the birth of another self: the fleet, sure-footed, cheerful child I should have been. When my wellington came off I didn't cry out, not even in those slow-motion seconds while I teetered on one leg before losing my balance and plunging knee-deep into the bog.

Looking up, I found him watching.

'All right?' he called.

I forced my muddy foot back into the boot and continued down the slope.

He was waiting for me on the next stretch of yellow grass.

'I could do with a drink,' I said.

Alcohol, I meant. It was a joke. He nodded at the ground. I looked down in dismay.

'It's spring water,' he said, 'cleaner than what's in the tap most places.'

'I'm OK.'

'It'll be the back of three before we're home.'

It was the word 'home' that did it. I hunkered down and cupped my hands in the icy cold. The water looked clear enough, between the fragments of leaf and root, but what if there was a dead sheep lying upstream?

'I've been drinking out of burns sixty years. It's done me no harm.'

His will was like a weight bearing down on me. The expectation of being obeyed.

'I thought you were thirsty.'

I was wearing my quilted coat. He couldn't have known what was at stake.

I stood up. 'I'd rather not.'

The words came like a smack. 'You'd best go back then. I'll see you at the house.'

The cottage was unlocked, though the door needed a shove over the offcut of carpet that served as a mat. The place was virtually a slum: a wing chair cauled by an ill-fitting stretch cover, a pile of newspapers in use as a side table, dirty plates. I could not imagine Lilias exchanging bodily fluids with a man who doused his cigarette ends in a teacup. Years of burned food enamelled the cooker, adding a meaty depth to the stink of damp and dog and chimney soot. There was more: a curling flypaper crusted with the summer's kill, a scorch-marked lampshade, a right-angle tear in the faded curtain, heaps of laundry (not all of it clean) on the Dralon two-seater. After a look at the cups in the washing-up rack, I slaked my thirst from the tap.

It took me seven minutes to search the place, and another ten to work up the resolution to do so. Before getting married, Frankie and I had agreed we would never empty each other's pockets before taking in the dry cleaning, never read a letter addressed to the other, and even now we held to this pact. But Mr Smith had given me this opportunity. It would have been insulting to refuse – insulting or spiritless, and I had

231

already failed one test. Anyway, there was nothing to find. No photographs (not even the snap he had photocopied and sent to me), no letters in a drawer, no chequebook to tell me his real name. My name, too, it occurred to me now.

I pictured his days. Rising in the dark to feed the dogs. Porridge and tea with the radio tuned to the farming prices. The daylight hours out on the hill. Back to the house at three for bread and cheese. A seven-mile drive to the Spar shop for a chat with the woman who weighed his corned beef, then home to peel the tatties for supper. Washing himself in the freezing bathroom (mildew spots on the shower curtain, perished rubber mat in the tub). Did anyone really live like this, without opening a can of beer and watching television, or reading a book, or filling in the crossword in that weekly paper? What did he do with his leisure? I pushed through the door into his bedroom and there it was. When I touched the space bar, it jolted into purring life. He hadn't bothered to exit the site. A satellite image of a Victorian rooftop. Chimneys. A cupola. My mother's leafy street.

I turned back the bedcovers and saw the yellowing bottom sheet, found the snot-stiffened handkerchief under his pillow, the matches and sweetie wrappers in the pockets of his only suit. I can't say what impulse led me to drag the chair from the computer table to the old wardrobe. Clambering up, I had a moment's unsteadiness, a watery feeling in my legs. The wardrobe had a detachable cornice, a feature useless except as a hiding place. The towel was less dusty than its surroundings, the shotgun wrapped inside not dusty at all.

I was downstairs when he got in. He touched the cold kettle, glanced at the newspaper still folded on the table, then went outside to check on the sheep he had penned behind the cottage. The whistling kettle brought him back. I watched him stoop to the fridge, saw the fussiness he brought to the pouring of hot water.

'Were you waiting long?'

I checked my watch. 'An hour and a half.'

'You'll have been bored.' He spooned sugar straight from the packet into a mug of tea.

'I've never been in a shepherd's cottage before.'

He stopped stirring. 'What do you make of it?'

'Lonely,' I said.

'There's worse things.' He handed me the mug.

'I don't take sugar.'

'It'll do you good.'

I took a sip. It was hot and strong and syrupy.

He busied himself at the grate with the same precision I'd observed in his tea-making. It might not sound like much, sitting amid his laundry, watching him take out the ashes and lay the fire, but I can't remember a time when I was happier. The failing light through the dirty window, the dogs snoring at my feet, steam from the mug condensing on my face. The only sounds were the rattle of the coal scuttle, the scratch of match on sandpaper, the low roar of catching flame behind the sheet of newsprint he held over the fireplace. I searched his profile as thoroughly as I had searched the house. It was difficult to see the young man in him, although it would be another ten years before he was really old. Would his chapped lips be mine one day? Those long ears and canopy eyebrows?

It might have been that the silence was another test, which I passed, or perhaps the accustomed task relaxed him. He sat in the cauled chair on the other side of the fire from me and we talked.

He looked after five hundred ewes on the estate. The price of a carcass had risen from the rock bottom hit a few years back, not enough to make anyone rich but, working for a family of millionaires, that wasn't a problem. He was a cattle man originally but his mother couldn't manage the farm without him. She'd sold up, and been ripped off. By the time he came back (*came back?* I wondered) there was nothing left. If you had to work for somebody else, hill herding was as good a trade as any. Leastways, on this estate, with the owners down in London during the week and plenty of excuses to make himself scarce at weekends. The laird didn't care, as long as the fences were kept up and the freezer well-stocked so he could tell his City pals they were eating his own meat. It was the keeper who had to show a straight face at the brand new tweeds and the twenty-thousand-pound gun.

'How long since you last saw her?' I asked.

'Aye, she used to change the subject like that when you weren't talking about her.' He moved to the table to pour himself more tea. 'Like mother like daughter.'

'Not really,' I said.

I wanted to tell him: *she's never loved me*. He was the one person I could trust not to reply *all mothers love their children*. He had known her well enough to leave her. I couldn't bear him thinking I was cut from the same cold cloth, but nor did I want him to see the aching need I brought to him.

'Must be twenty years,' he said, and it was a moment before I realised this was an answer to my question. 'She shut the door in my face. I wrote her a letter. It came back *not known at this address*.'

'Why?'

His eyes flickered. 'You'll need to ask her that.'

'I've done nothing but ask, all my life. Everything she ever told me was a lie – till the other day, when she let slip you were a farmer.'

'Farmhand was more like it.'

'Blimey,' I said.

It was eerie how smiling stripped the years from his face. 'I think she surprised herself.'

Suddenly there was a whiff of sex in the room. Good sex, and lots of it. Jealousy flared through me.

He put down his mug of tea. 'Will she see me, if you ask her?'

'Ask her yourself,' I said. 'You know where she is.'

234

His eyes turned hard as marbles behind those bifocal lenses. 'What else did you find up there?'

'What there was to be found.'

Those silent seconds we sat facing each other across the fire were as terrible to me as the preceding hour had been wonderful.

'I could ask her,' I said, 'but it wouldn't make any difference. She hates you.' I fortified myself with a mouthful of sugary tea. 'I thought you might tell me why.'

'Dinnae mess with me, lassie.'

I noted the strengthening of his accent, the extra layer it put between us.

'I'm not.' My voice shook. *I'm not.*

One of the dogs woke and looked at me.

The moment passed. He took off his glasses to rub his eyes. 'Are you hungry?'

I was, but I knew how little he had in the fridge. I could have eaten it all and still not been satisfied. I felt the same way about him. I was too old to call him Daddy, too old to be sat on his knee and tickled and tossed up in the air, but I needed *something*. I knelt on the fleece in front of the hearth and peeled off my Aran jumper, pulling the T-shirt underneath tight over my bump.

His shock jumped the air between us. If it wasn't exactly tenderness, I had no doubt that he was stirred.

'I thought you might want to see your grandchild,' I said.

Bandage

Every lunchtime now I visited Lilias in hospital. Frankie had sweet-talked the senior nurse into giving her a single room. It's possible she would have been put there anyway. Her presence wasn't great for patient morale. I had never seen her so inert, stranded without a role. Or rather, refusing to play the only role available to her. I was the actress by then, with my bedside equanimity, while my thoughts skipped ahead to the afternoon I would spend at Shepherd's Cottage.

The day after her operation I arrived to find her sleeping, that stink I'd noticed lately diluted to a top note in the animal fug of slumber. I had seen through her deceptions so long ago, spent so many years calibrating the shortfall between illusion and reality. I was so sure I had her measure, but I was wrong. In the merciless midday light I could see what she had concealed from me. She was an old woman. At temple and nape that white-gold hair was ashy. Her head was thrown back, exposing the lizardlike creases of her throat. How sparse her eyelashes were, their sore-looking roots in those swollen lids. Her mouth was open, her recessed gums, the metal rims of her crowns, the yellow nap on her tongue: all of it in full view. Her snoring was a percussive gurgle mid-throat. Swiftly as I pushed it away, the word 'rattle' came to me.

'Ma.'

I said it quite loudly but she did not wake.

I knew how to rouse a sleeper – the cooing voice, fingers smoothed along the forearm (never the face) – but even unconscious, she seemed to forbid my touch. I leaned closer until my head hung just above hers. I saw the mushroomy tint to her skin, the dried saliva at the corners of her mouth, the quiver in her nostrils as her breath came and went. All at once, I understood: I had entered the world from between her legs. I could have fitted two Liliases into me, and had room for more, but *she* had carried *me* in her long-vanished belly. I had been formed in the hot wet dark inside her as my daughter was now forming within me. What could have been more obvious? What more strange?

She stirred. The eyes that opened to mine were full of terror.

'It's all right, Ma. It's me, it's Freya.'

She looked up at me like a creature too young to be reached through reason.

'Ssshhh, Ma, it's OK.'

At last she recognised me.

And so the child becomes the parent. The channel from the outside world, sharer of funny things that happened on the way to the hospital. I filleted the newspapers for her, reading out reviews of the latest stage productions. She listened, but with a part of her mind elsewhere. Her wound? The pain? Or larger regrets? I didn't ask, keeping my questions anodyne. Was she sleeping through the night? What did she fancy for lunch? I had always been so hung up on talk as the only route to the heart of things. I knew better now. What mattered was being there day after day, the affirmation of a bond stronger than my feelings. Blood, I suppose.

As the days passed, I registered the changing faces in the ward. She should have been recovering at home. At the very least, sitting up in the green vinyl chair beside her hospital bed. I could have ambushed the consultant when she did her rounds, but my appetite for truth was much reduced by then. It was Lilias who breached the protocol between us, one day when I had exhausted the arts pages and the comic possibilities of the M8.

'It's true, you know, that thing about it all coming back at the end. People I haven't thought about for years.'

'Like Xavier?' He phoned me every evening asking if he could visit, but she wouldn't relent.

'Him too,' she said.

'Who else?'

She made a breathy sound that might have been amusement. 'Who do you think?'

Who else but my father? And yet it felt like a trick question: get it wrong and she'd return to her hundred-year sleep.

'You, for one,' she said.

'*Me?*' I couldn't have been more surprised.

She brought a hand up to her chest and began to dig at the dressing under her nightdress.

'Ma,' I cautioned.

Her hand dropped to the mattress. 'When I found out I was pregnant I thought my life was over. I was a very average actress then. I had my looks, but not much else. They weren't going to cast me with a baby in tow.'

'I was a burden,' I said. 'You've only told me ten thousand times.'

'I did something,' she corrected herself, '*tried* to do something I would have lived to regret. Or perhaps I wouldn't. How do you know, really? Anyway, I was glad later. But because I didn't do it, I did something else. Oh, I wasn't a saint, I knew I was setting the cat among the pigeons, but I had no idea it would end like that. How could I possibly have known?' Her voice rose as she became more agitated. 'I was young and stupid – it's not a crime. We all make mistakes. Most of us get older without...' She rubbed the heel of one hand across her mouth, removing a gluey strand of saliva and looking, just for a moment, as if she were trying to gag the flow of words. 'Is this making any sense?'

238

I groped for the gist of what she'd said. 'You were too young to know any better.'

'I should have known.' She wiped her hand on the sheet, her voice flat. 'After all, I had you, my little object lesson in consequences.'

Silently I absorbed this.

Her mood seemed to switch. 'But it taught me about life – about people. I had no idea they were so... all or nothing. It was the making of me, professionally.' She looked up to see how I was taking this. 'It's bad taste to say so, and I'm not saying it was worth the price, but I was a better actress afterwards.'

I had to ask, 'Are you talking about my father?'

She held my eye for a moment before her gaze slid away. 'You're not making this very easy, darling.'

'You're talking in riddles. If you want my best guess, you slept with somebody else, one or several, and he took it badly, and your pride was hurt because he cleared off, so you showed him the door when he came back.'

I knew that frozen expression of old.

'Or maybe I'm wrong.'

Her hand moved towards the dressing on her chest, then, anticipating my rebuke, fell back. 'It doesn't matter now.'

'It does to me,' I said.

I had never seen her look so bleak, on or off stage. 'Believe me, you're better off not knowing.'

Yes, she was ill, but I wasn't letting her away with this. 'You haven't the faintest idea what's best for me.'

'I'm *your mother*.'

The force she put into these words thrilled me, but the next moment she sank back against the pillows, exhausted. 'I did my best with you. I know it wasn't ideal, but it could have been a good deal worse. And you turned out all right.'

'You think so?'

'Of course.'

'In what way?'

'Oh, *darling*,' she said to the ceiling.

Then the nurses arrived to change her dressing and I had to go.

1972

It seems to Lili she has been carrying the incubus half her life, groaning with its hunger, gagging with its fastidious palate, despairing at the seal it draws across her throat the instant she sits down to eat. Every day it gets bigger. On what, God knows, unless it's sucking the marrow from her bones. She wonders if it is normal for pregnant women to see themselves as food. After all, that's what she is: meat and drink, and weatherproofing. She has spent years despising pillowy, thick-waisted women, and now she is one of them. She opens the jar of cold cream and moves her hands across her breasts, then down, smoothing her belly, skirting the protruding bolt of navel, telling herself she'll be glad she did this, afterwards. Not that she believes in *after* any more than she remembers *before*.

Footsteps in the corridor. Her heart skips a beat at the thought of someone the other side of the wall, inches from her nakedness, but there's no real risk. The office is out of bounds to the hired hands, Mrs S won't be back till late, and even if Lili were to be discovered, who could blame her? They've all noticed the sweaty sheen on her skin. It's like living in a different climate from the people around her. The office is cool as a cave, with its stone walls, and the metal shelves stacked with account ledgers and sheaves of receipts. The window is so high that, even on tiptoe, a peeping Tom would only see a stretch of the opposite wall. And as a bonus, there's the smell of desiccated paper to distract her from the odour that is never far away. Vaguely meaty, and yet fishy, with a hint of putrefaction. A symptom of her condition? Or have the sharpened senses of pregnancy finally made it possible to smell her essential self?

The door opens. Jake's eyes widen at the sprawl of her across the old oak desk. The damp tendrils of hair, the discarded towel, her marshmallow flesh. She gasps as the dollop of cream hits her belly, so much colder than a fingertip dab. The dirt on his palms turns it beige before it vanishes into her skin.

'I saw your girlfriend in the village,' she says, waiting to see if he corrects her. *Ex-girlfriend*.

He grunts, without looking up.

'She had a black eye.'

His fingers knead her flesh. She feels the mysterious world within her resisting the pressure of his touch.

'D'you know how she got it?'

It's strange, the connection she feels with the girl. A cowhand's daughter with a greasy face and vulgar, abundant body. Last night, undressing for bed, Lili glimpsed the same tumid breasts reflected in the darkened window.

'How am I going to know?' he says.

'I thought everyone round here knew everything about everybody else's business.'

He scoops more cream from the jar. 'Would it turn you on, if I'd done it?'

'Did you?' She sounds breathless.

'I asked first.' He presses harder, putting his body weight into the strokes.

'I think she's suffered enough, don't you?' Lili says.

His eyes give off their old hostile glitter.

He desires her, she has daily proof of that, but it's a matter-of-fact lust, no more or less than he might feel for any number of women. With Brod, lovemaking was as much verbal as physical. He took pride in his bedside manners, as he did in his silk ties and handmade shoes. Every inch of her was lavished with praise, from the thousand carats of gold in her hair to the elegant arch of her foot. With Jake, it's all so much less personal, a wordless pleasure that takes her by stealth, blurring her edges, reducing her to anonymous flesh.

When he takes the massage down to her pelvis, she releases an involuntary groan. His hands work her over, deep rhythmic strokes that would not have to be so very much deeper to hurt. She wonders if he feels the incubus through the taut shell of her belly, and if so, does the incubus feel him? Just how much does it intuit in its blindness? Can it sense her shameful thoughts? (If it died through no fault of her own, if she woke on sodden sheets in the middle of the night…?) No one wants it to be born. Not its father, or its grandparents (not that they've been told), certainly not herself. Would it not be the perfect solution: no straightened wire coat hanger, no gin, no scalding bath – the whole problem taken out of her hands?

She groans again. He bears down on her as if he would pierce through the skin. She pushes him away. 'No.'

'No?' he echoes mockingly as his hands return.

'No.'

This time, he takes her at her word.

He leans against the wall. 'What's that?'

She moves a hand to cover the brown line running down from her navel. 'Just something that happens.'

'How come?'

'I don't know.'

He pulls her hand away. 'Is it permanent?'

A question that has been troubling her. 'We'll have to wait and see.'

He seems more fascinated than repelled. 'Does it feel different?'

'Different?'

He nods at her pelvis. 'Inside.'

In bed, he means.

'Do I feel different to you?'

'Oh aye.'

'How?'

He grins. 'More desperate for it.'

'While you're not bothered one way or the other?'

'Have I ever said no?'

They laugh.

He asks her, 'Do you have forty quid?'

'For what?'

'The deposit on a cottage. I'm fed up with listening out for my mother every time I fancy it.'

'A bit extravagant, isn't it,' she says, 'renting a house for screwing in?'

He looks shifty. 'We'll be doing other things.'

'Such as?'

'Cooking, eating.' He shrugs, 'Sleeping.'

He wants to live with her! Is he crazy? Doesn't he know she's having a baby – a baby like the one he had aborted six months ago? They have sex, yes, but they're not *lovers*.

'I'm pregnant,' she says.

'You made your choice.' He reaches across and tweaks her nipple. 'There are compensations.'

'Will you still think that when I need a crane to get me out of bed in the mornings?'

'You'll need to bide somewhere. My mother's not going to share the house with a screaming bairn.'

'They take it away as soon as it's born.'

He clears his throat. 'Aye, well, we'll need to talk about that.'

'Are you going to make an honest woman of me?' she says mockingly.

'You don't want him thinking he's a wee bastard, do you?'

She stares at him, dumbfounded. He doesn't even like her, and now he's offering to be a father to her child. All her life she has feared the jeering girls on the street corner, walking on stage to feel the audience close ranks against her. No one knows what it cost her, keeping people sweet. The relentless eye contact, all that smiling. She only reckoned the cost herself when she stopped. When she came here. Who would have guessed that meeting the walking embodiment of her fears would prove so liberating? To know from the start that, whatever tricks she turned, he wouldn't applaud. To do precisely nothing and discover it was enough: he detested everything about her, and still he couldn't help himself.

'Have I gone deaf?' he says.

She can almost hear the laughter in the green room. A star-struck farm boy! *Did he tumble you in the hayloft, darling?* Flick might palp his bicep and Oliver appraise his codpiece, but neither would see him as anything more than a diverting hour on a rainy afternoon. Her ears burn as if she were already backstage gossip. *The big man didn't fancy becoming a daddy – surprise, surprise – and the silly cow took it to heart. Found herself a teuchter for some horny-handed houghmagandie.*

God, she misses the theatre. Catty laughter. Lightning repartee. Words are nothing to him. Anyone else would have taken a little trouble over this proposal. For a moment she imagines it: the leading lady turned farmer's wife, wiper of shitty bottoms and snottery noses.

'Why on earth would you want to live with me?'

'You've a lovely cunt.'

'What about the rest of me?'

'I can put up with it.'

'I'm not your penance,' she says.

This earns her another glittering look. 'Your man in Edinburgh doesn't want it – or you.'

A low blow, but he's right. Child or no child, Brod is never going to take her back. When did they last speak on the phone? Weeks ago now. There'll be plenty of girls only too glad to take her place. She's just another ex. Unless something should happen to reawaken his proprietary interest.

'I don't have the money,' she says, 'but there's someone I could tap for a loan.'

Bean

I sensed her first as an apple pip embedded in dark earth, putting out hair-like roots. Soon she was a butter bean, a fat white pod with a tentative pulsing heart. I swear I felt her climacteric, the face rising out of blankness, the loss of her primeval tail. Then the burgeoning: arms, hands, fingers reaching for the future. Her gills became ears, nudging into position either side of her swelling brain. Her sightless eyes made ready to look ahead. Next thing, she had eyelids, tooth buds, pursing lips, a wrinkling brow. On account of what? Was she having little hissy fits, practising for her terrible twos? Before I knew it she could grimace, too. She hiccupped. Her fingernails grew. Her retinae sensed light, her ears heard my song, her tongue woke to its lifelong love affair with taste. I saw none of this with my own eyes but it was as vivid to me as dreaming.

My little light bulb, my unhatched chick, *ma wee darlin*, my flesh and blood. My laggard heart was faint with love, even as the sturdy muscle pumped life through the coiling cord, giving, taking, from her to me, from me to her.

Lamb

'Hey!'

No answer.

'*Hey!*'

We still hadn't settled on what I should call him.

I turned to find him in the doorway. 'Where do you keep your bin bags?'

'If it's food it goes to the chickens, if it's...'

'...combustible, you burn it, I know.' I nodded at the bottles and tins I had piled on the table. 'But what happens to the rest?'

He gave me one of his inscrutable looks. 'I never asked you to tidy up.'

I decided to ignore this. 'So you've no black bags?'

'Never needed them.'

'Plastic carriers?'

'Go on the fire.'

I grimaced. 'God knows what that releases into the atmosphere.'

I knew what I was doing, the transgressive touch of role-reversal in the child wagging a finger at the parent. I'd seen Ruth's kids do it, stretching the elastic until it snapped back, so yes, I was pushing for a reaction. His face had given nothing away when I'd carried my suitcase in from the car. There had been no touch, no tender word, since he'd held my hand on the hill.

'And you've been pouring hot fat down the sink,' I said.

'What if I have?'

'It's taking for ever to drain.'

'I'm in no hurry.'

Perhaps it was for the best. When I considered the alternative, I wasn't sure I could have borne it. Being enfolded by loving arms, taken into his confidence, introduced to his friends. How could I not have been bitter, brooding on the upbringing I had missed, the little ray of sunshine I might have become?

I waved him back up to the computer. 'Never mind. I'll try flushing it out with boiling water.'

Some days we barely spoke, and even when he was chatty – by his standards – he told me nothing I wanted to know. How he'd met her, why he'd loved her, how he'd felt about becoming a father. So I wasn't there for the talk, and not for his cooking either. The porridgy broth he'd ladle into a chipped bowl, the blackened sausages served between slices of supermarket white slabbed with butter. Evidently tastebuds were not genetic. The olives I'd brought on my second visit were still mouldering at the back of the fridge. The seeded rolls stuck in his teeth (he'd never heard of dental floss). The bresaola I found floating in the lavatory pan two days running until I fished it out, wrapped it in newspaper and dropped it in a bin in Auchterarder.

I had come to hate the Travelodge: the endless hours with nothing to do but think about the life I had thrown away, how lucky I'd been to have Frankie, how far I'd had to push him to make him lose faith in us. I knew coming to stay with my father was a risk. He was a bachelor, set in his ways. I was bound to be an irritation. But there was something to be gained, a shared destination that drew a little closer every day. I was getting to know him. The ridges on his fingernails. His soundless laugh. The meticulous (or controlling) streak that had plotted to meet me. I knew he wasn't a happy man but I felt so alive in his company, and I thought – I still think – that in mine he found a taste of happiness. The world arranged itself around us so vividly. The smell of broken earth in the field behind the cottage, that hare we surprised and set racing across the hill, the first eagle I ever saw. One rainy afternoon I trimmed his hair, lopping a couple of centimetres off the back, pruning the wiry tangle of his sideburns, taking a pinch out of the thicket in each ear. It was a joy to me, holding his lobes clear of the snipping blades, turning his head between my hands, his scalp under my fingers like the surface of a new planet. The cut hair clung to his skin and the collar of his shirt, defeating all attempts to blow it away, so I fetched a tea towel and flicked at his neck as I'd seen barbers do in black-and-white movies. His deadpan expression gave me the giggles, and I flicked more recklessly, though once or twice I could see the contact stung. He bore it for another minute, then, without warning, snatched the cloth from my hands. I caught his eye, tasting metal under my tongue, the convergence we were moving towards suddenly more imminent. He got up and returned the towel to the kitchen.

So here I was, a house guest. Maybe, in the fullness of time, something more permanent. And maybe not. He had not offered me his bed. I told myself I was glad he wasn't constrained by courtesy, as families were not, but I was aware the situation could be read differently. I slept on cushions pulled off the armchair and the two-seater and arranged on the filthy carpet. It was comforting, lying there in the fire's dying glow, lulled by the snoring I could hear overhead, waking at five to his tread on the stair. He had just two questions. Did Frankie know where I was? And, when I said no, did Kit? Every morning he set a mug of tea on the floor by my head, released the dogs and left for the hill.

The first day I went grocery shopping in the nearest village, politely stonewalling the shopkeeper's questions. I thought about driving down to see Lilias in hospital, but one day off

250

couldn't hurt. The second day I cleaned the kitchen, making room for the food I had bought, promising myself I'd go to Edinburgh tomorrow. But tomorrow's weather was foul, a biting wind driving icy horizontal rain, so I kept the fire blazing all day and listened to the radio. By then my phone had died. I must have left the charger behind at the hotel. Who knows how much longer I'd have stayed away, had events unfolded differently? I might have driven down the next day to find Lilias hadn't noticed my absence.

Mid-afternoon on that third, icy day I heated the griddle I'd found at the back of the kitchen cupboard and whisked up a pancake batter. When he returned the room was fugged with the smell of wood smoke and dropped scones and stewed tea. He shed his wet coat and slumped in the fireside chair while I fed the dogs. Looking up, I noticed he had something inside his sweater.

'I found her up by the black crag,' he said. 'The yowe's dead.'

It was a newborn lamb, a scrap of shivering life, treacly with afterbirth.

'Lucky I saw her. They're not due for another week.'

The dogs caught my excitement. He made a harsh noise and they dropped to a crouch, ears flattened.

'Get a towel.'

I did as I was told and he rubbed at the stickiness, revealing the concave flanks covered in tight-curled fleece. It was trembling uncontrollably. I had seen lambs before, of course, from the car, exclaiming over their cute little ears, the vertical lift-off in their gambolling. But I had never been close enough to notice the baggy skin and delicately etched nose, the restless movement of the lips, like an old man whose dentures were slipping. He pinched them apart to reveal a mouth that was astonishingly clean and pink. 'See the teeth?' he said, and I saw the top set, their shape quite clear under the plastic-looking gum and, just behind, the pristine pink tongue. He took several newspapers from the pile, making a platform on the sheepskin rug and setting the lamb on top, nearer the warmth of the fire. When he put her down she made a high-pitched creaking sound.

I found the feeding bottle in the shed and fetched the whisky he'd requested but, instead of lacing the warmed milk, he poured a nip into our mugs of tea. The first sip seemed to bring home how tired he was. He took off his glasses and rubbed his eyes.

His face. I couldn't get enough of it. Those flaccid earlobes, the cracks in his chapped lips, the platinum glint of whisker in the slack flesh under his jaw. I stared as I'd stared at the Mona Lisa as a teenager in the Louvre, my eyeballs raw with staring, trying to find the trick of light or love that would show me what she had seen in him. He opened his eyes. They were darker without the magnifying lenses.

I glanced at the lamb on the bed of newsprint, her shuddering ribcage and twitching haunches. She seemed to be straining for something.

'Pick her up,' he said.

'I'd better not.' But he was right: there was nothing I wanted more. 'Toxoplasmosis is all I need.'

That faint glassiness in his look whenever I baulked him.

'How old is she?' I asked.

'A couple of hours.'

The tail lifted to reveal a patch of flesh as shockingly pink as her mouth. A glistening olive of shit squeezed out.

'Will she be all right?'

'If there's a stillbirth. Once lambing starts I'll not have time to footer about hand-rearing her. I'll flay the corpse, tie its skin on.' His mouth formed a pessimistic line. 'Even if the yowe accepts it, after a week on the bottle they don't always fancy the real McKay.'

'And then?'

He looked at me.

'I'll feed her,' I said.

'What about toxoplasmosis?'

'I'll wear gloves.'

He laughed his soundless laugh, reaching for the whisky to pour us both another nip. I knew I should refuse because of the baby, but I didn't want to say no to him again.

I touched the dusty neck of the whisky bottle. 'How long have you had this?'

It was just something to say, not a real question, but he replied with a snippet of real information. 'It only comes out at Hogmanay. For twenty years I didn't touch it at all.'

'Was there a high you liked better?'

'Drugs, you mean?'

'You lived through the Summer of Love.'

'The sixties was the fifties round here.'

'So the seventies was the sixties?'

His eyes reflected the firelight. 'Not where I was.'

I leaned back against the settee. 'If I'm supposed to guess, you'll have to make the clues less cryptic.'

He lifted the mug and drank. I could see I wasn't going to get anything more out of him. The lamb yawned, showing the bubblegum-pink inside of her mouth. I touched her hoof. It was smooth and faintly warm. Outside, the daylight was ebbing. Neither of us rose to switch on the lamp.

I said, 'How did you know about Kit and me?'

'I saw you at the bull sale.'

'We weren't together then.'

'Any gowk could see what way the wind was blowing.'

My memory of the day was changed, the crowd turned away with a smirk. 'Do you think badly of me?'

He looked up from the fire. 'Do you think badly of yourself?'

'Apparently I do.'

'How'd you do it then?'

'I wanted a child.'

'Ah.' It was barely a syllable, a breath.

253

'The joke is, it's not his.'

He was staring into the flames again. 'It might be your idea of a joke, Lil, it's not mine.'

The awful silence came from him, I merely complied. The fire spat a glowing spark onto the rug, leaving a stink of singed wool before it died. I took a nervous swig of tea, forgetting it was spiked. The whisky's heat blazed a trail through my veins.

He picked up the poker and goaded the fire. 'You're nothing like her.'

'I know.'

It's just...'

I held my breath.

His eyes slid across my bump. '...it brings it all back.'

She had told me so many lies, and still this surprised me.

'She said you didn't stick around for the pregnancy.'

There was no mistaking the smile of a man whose appetites are roused. 'She had me up all night many a night, even with a belly full of arms and legs.'

I looked down at my own belly, my own arms and legs. 'Were you there when I was born?'

'When she went into labour.'

'In the audience?'

He looked at me blankly.

'The King's Theatre.' But already I knew I was wasting my breath. Her waters breaking over the red surcoat, the ginger understudy: all a fiction. Who was I, if not the daughter of Lady Macbeth?

'I suppose I wasn't born in Edinburgh, either?'

'The hospital at Crieff,' he said.

'But you saw me, you held me, after?'

'No.'

There was too much feeling in the eyes I raised to his.

'Dinnae ask.'

They had been lovers late into the pregnancy. He was with

254

her when she went into labour. Then it was all over. The only shred of comfort I could find was that he had tried to see her later. She was the one who had slammed the door.

The lamb stirred on its bed of newsprint, struggling to stand on quivering legs. The bottle of milk was still on the floor by his chair.

'You should feed her,' I said.

He picked her up and dropped her in my lap. She was lighter than a cat, her fleece surprisingly harsh to the touch. I expected her to struggle, but she settled trustingly against my bump. The arc of milk I squirted across the back of my hand seemed fine – not too hot, not too cold – but what did I know? The dainty nostrils sniffed at the rubber teat, but she would not take it in her mouth.

He got up from his chair and sat beside me on the arm of the settee. 'Like this.' He wetted his pinkie with the milk and insinuated it between her lips. She resisted for a moment, then began to suckle, pulling at his finger, her tail whisking against my thigh. His head was very close to mine. I could smell the whisky on his breath, the fusty-leathery blend of skin and sheep and coal smoke that was his characteristic scent. I nudged the teat into position, replacing his finger the instant he withdrew. The lamb accepted the substitution. I ran my palm over the scratchy fleece. My nipples were hard, with that same tight tug in my breasts I got when Ruth fed the baby. I could feel him leaning over me, the bony shelter of his body, its heat detectable even in the charmed semicircle of the fire.

His hand settled on the back of my neck. His palm was hot and dry, his voice hoarse. 'You should ca' canny with folk.'

'I do,' I said, 'with everyone else.'

His calloused fingers caressed my cheek. 'You should ca' canny with me.'

I held still, hardly breathing.

The dogs began to bark before the knock came at the door.

My heart leapt at the sound of Frankie's voice, then shrivelled when he walked in with Kit, who seemed younger to me, though that might have been his deferential manner around my husband. Frankie looked sick, something deadened about the way the skin hung on his bones, a sorrowing heaviness in his movements. He stood in front of the settee. I looked up, still holding the lamb.

'Is it Lilias?'

He nodded.

'Is she OK?'

He shook his head.

Lily

Frankie arranged the funeral, put the notice in the papers, booked a bar at the Criterion Theatre for the funeral tea. I let him do it, the good Catholic boy in him rising to the occasion, while I went back to the Travelodge. I knew I should find myself a flat, but it was too much to think about. I used to be galvanised by bad news, never more efficient than with a crisis to be managed. Now I couldn't be fagged. Nothing I or he or anyone did was going to change the central fact.

She left it too late to get treatment. The mastectomies were irrelevant, an indignity she could have been spared. The secondaries had already seeded in her liver. It wasn't worth taking the overdose. Within a month, two at the most, the cancer would have done the job. But she could never bear to be upstaged, so she discharged herself from hospital, went home, locked the door, glammed herself up, put on some Rachmaninoff, opened a bottle of champagne, and sat down to write her last note.

Except she didn't. She was found in that white *djellaba* of hers, which hadn't been washed for weeks. No make-up, her hair lank. Frankie tried to talk me through it, telling me everyone owns their own death. However upsetting I found it, she had the right to choose. I recognised this as the healthy view, but it meant nothing to me. Suicide as dramatic gesture I could have accepted. It would, after all, have been the logical consummation of the life. But she had slipped out through the back door, indifferent to those who lived on.

I couldn't shake the suspicion that she knew. Rationally, there was no way she could have found out. Frankie had no idea until he phoned the farm, and even Kit was taking a wild guess on the back of a half-rumour that had made it across the strath. Still I tortured myself. She had left me in no doubt: I could have him or her, not both. What if she thought I'd made my choice? *I want you to swear on the body of that thing inside you…* Her last words to me of any significance. Terrible, but no more terrible than the words I'd said. *I'm thinking I'll never forgive you.* These were the thoughts that looped through my head, chased by scenes from my childhood. The day she sent me back to Uncle Nellaney because I'd caught the mumps. The day I waited two hours for her outside the school gates. The day she told me I'd never be a heartbreaker so I'd better learn to cook. All my memories were tinged with blame: my blame of her, the counterpart to my lifelong conviction that she blamed me. For being insufficiently graceful, or charming, or playful, or lovable. For fetishising the real over the ideal. And for some other crime too, some failure of mine I never understood. Or maybe I'd just wished there were something else: the broken part that could be fixed, making everything all right. How I longed to make a clean cut through the knot of grievance that bound us. Or rather, to *have made* such a cut, to turn back the clock and have what had happened unhappen, to make her un-die, not only for my sake (but yes, for my sake too), to snatch her from that locked room and save her from the unimaginable moment when she was no one but herself.

I once caught her eye on-stage. I was ten, or maybe eleven, and living most of the year with Uncle Nellaney, which would make it Easter, or summer in one of the more bourgeois resorts. It was an accident, yet I'd seen a performance earlier in the week, I was familiar with the blocking. I chose that particular seat in the first row of the stalls, knowing that just before the interval she would walk to the front of the stage, stand on the very brink of the eleven-foot drop to the orchestra pit, and look down at where I was sitting. I can't remember the play, whether she was in contemporary or period dress, but I remember that terrible shared glance. The audience noticed nothing, she didn't miss a beat, but I knew I had breached the ultimate taboo. A tremendous wave of heat passed through my skinny frame. My cotton vest was soaked, my cheeks ablaze, while my consciousness (my soul, Frankie would say) left my body to share the space behind my mother's panstick mask. For a split-second I felt what it was to be Lilias, acting over that vertiginous drop, her nerves strung so tight that the stale air of the auditorium tasted thin and sharp and the actors' words reached her ears through a high-pitched whine. This was what she called being alive. Afterwards, in her dressing room, she insisted she hadn't seen me and I didn't press the point because I knew I'd been privileged to experience it, even as I prayed with all my skinny girl's soul for it never to happen again.

Was that who she was: that tightrope walker across the void? There were times in the years that followed when I'd hoped so, because it would serve her right, and now the thought of it tore me apart.

I decided not to go to the funeral. For a moment I thought Frankie was going to drag me out of my hotel bed and fling my clothes at me, but he walked away and looked out of the window until the impulse passed. I felt sorry for him then. I knew he was struggling with troubles of his own. He was no longer the face of Scottish football. The bloggers had turned against him. Scott had won. His marriage was over. It wasn't just that I had slept with someone else, was carrying someone else's child (but whose?). I had been reunited with the father I had been seeking my whole life and I hadn't thought to tell him. He'd had to ask the boy who cuckolded him to find me.

Whatever my shortcomings as a wife, I had always turned to him as my best friend. Now that too was in the past.

He walked to the door. 'I'd better get home. The car's coming at ten.'

A stretch Jag. The undertaker would walk ahead of it to the end of the road. A theatrical touch, but not nearly hammy enough. Lilias would have wanted the mahogany casket drawn by black-plumed horses, weeping men lining the streets, a showreel of her greatest scenes playing simultaneously on giant screens in George Square and Princes Street gardens. Or would the Lilias who'd swallowed eighty amobarbital not have wanted any of this?

He hesitated, then had one last try. 'You'll regret it if you don't go.'

I looked at him, letting him see how little this mattered in the grand scheme of all the things I had to regret.

I lay under the duvet watching the clock, working out when Frankie would arrive at the funeral home, and how long it would take to get the coffin into the hearse. At five to eleven they pulled up at the church. I didn't need to be there, I saw it all in my head. A short wait for the last of the mourners to arrive, then she was wheeled up the aisle, followed by Frankie and Andro, her agent, while something suitable played over the PA. I'd suggested Sondheim's 'Comedy Tonight', earning a disgusted look from my husband. He couldn't see that, far from a jibe, it was a tribute to the woman I thought she'd been, the woman I never appreciated until she turned out to be someone else. At ten past eleven, they finished the first hymn and Andro got up to read the passage from Luke. At twenty past, the minister read out a list of her roles and the starry names she'd worked with. At twenty-five to, they sang her out of church with her favourite hymn (*My song is love unknown/my savour's love to me/love to the loveless shown/ that they might lovely be*). At quarter to twelve, Frankie and Andro tossed their fistfuls of earth into the grave. By midday

I could stand it no longer. I rolled out of bed, climbed into the clothes I had been wearing four days earlier, and called a cab.

The Criterion was Lilias's favourite Glasgow venue. A *proper theatre*, she used to say, meaning a proscenium arch with gilded cherubs, and opera glasses clipped to the backs of the seats, and grand and upper circles still in use. In the mirrored bars on the half-landings, boys in polyester shirts and dickie bows did not blink when asked for a Gin and It.

No one noticed my entrance, though I was by far the worst-dressed of the forty-odd people there. (Frankie had persuaded the MacKewon clan to stay away.) The noise in the bar was startling: all those roundly enunciated conversations with their rhythms of soliloquy and repartee. Lilias's friends. So they did exist. I was grateful to them for turning up in their spotted veils and velvet capes and vintage cocktail dresses, their frock coats and breast pocket silk handkerchiefs. Of course, they were getting something out of it too. An excuse to dress up and scintillate on a dull afternoon, with free food and drink. Already the silver trays were almost emptied of their smoked salmon blinis and coin-sized chard-and-cheddar tarts. The staff were mixing Kir royales with proper champagne, though Prosecco would have done the job. Was Frankie making this grand gesture to compensate for my failings as a daughter or for reasons of his own?

At one end of the counter sat a huge glass vase of lilies, their wax-white trumpets streaked with orange pollen. Beside them was propped a black-and-white photograph of Lilias in the early seventies, looking like Julie Christie. Frankie had had it enlarged and mounted on black-bordered card to go with the purple drinks and the Piaf CD playing behind the bar. The sight of that white-lipsticked pout caught me off guard, tripping me into a memory. She was always smiling back then, the golden smile of mothers who want their children to know the world is full of wonders. And it was. The twinkling of the star-cloth. The hazy dazzle of the gels. The secret kingdom

261

up in the flies, the tinny susurrus of the spotlight barn doors when a stagehand prowled along the gantry. Three decades of disenchantment, and still I felt the sadness of exile from the garden. Around the age most children stop believing in Santa, or the Tooth Fairy, I had stopped believing in theatre. In Lilias.

I felt a touch on my arm and turned to find Xavier, in a casual but clearly expensive black moleskin suit. His silver hair had been cut so short the pink of his scalp showed through. Otherwise he was as handsome as ever.

'How are you, Freya?'

'Oh, you know.' I saw us from the outside: his solicitous enquiry, my dignified evasion. We were playing to a script. Revolted, I said, 'If she wasn't dead I'd kill her.'

He chose not to react to this, which raised him in my estimation. His glance took in the room. 'Who are they all?'

'I thought you could tell me. They look like they were famous forty years ago and they're still waiting to make a comeback.'

I realised how rude this sounded and started to apologise, but he cut across me, smiling. 'All the thesps I know these days are French.'

I must have moved slightly.

His glance sharpened. 'Do that again.'

'Do what?'

He gestured. 'With your head.'

I didn't know what he wanted, but I seemed to do it anyway.

'I can't believe I didn't see it before. The way you carry yourself – you're very like her.'

'I'm starting to think it was the other way round: she was like me. She just made a better fist of hiding it, till the end.'

There was a moment's dead air, made more awkward by the babble around us, before he opened his arms.

He smelled of garlic and expensive aftershave and something bodily that was faint enough to be intimate rather than

262

disgusting. I pressed my face into his shoulder, trying to blot out the grief I hadn't known I felt until I saw the compassion in his eyes. I could have stood like that for ever, lost in the forgiving pressure of the cloth and the bright-black patterns on the backs of my eyelids, but I sensed his attention pulled away by something behind me.

I turned round to find my father in his interview suit. Lilias would have told him to get out, but she had forfeited her rights over the living when she swallowed those pills. It was our wishes that counted now, his and mine.

'Xavier, I'd like you to meet my...' I couldn't say it. 'John Smith.'

Against all the odds, that really was his name.

Xavier put out his hand. 'How're you doing, John Smith?'

'Jake,' he said, ignoring the hand.

'Weren't you ASM at the Everyman?'

My father was studying the photograph of Lilias propped on the bar. After longer than was polite, he said, 'You're thinking of somebody else.'

'Or the Crucible, under Clare Venables—?'

This time there was no reply.

'I know I know you from somewhere.'

Against my will, I found myself comparing them. Moleskin and polyester. The chef's rumpled charm. The shepherd's weather-beaten hide and swimmy specs. Every man is an alpha male to his daughter but, objectively, Xavier had the stronger claim.

'Xavier acted with Lilias in Manchester,' I said.

'And when would that have been?'

There was something obscurely insulting in this phrasing.

Xavier looked him in the eye, and I knew he'd managed to place him. 'About five months after you went away.'

'It didn't take her long to go back to tarting herself about on stage, then.'

'She had a child to support.'

'And she loved it,' I butted in, not sure whether I was accusing or defending her. 'Acting was what she lived for.'

'Not when she was with me,' my father said. His eyes glittered behind the distorting lenses.

Xavier's voice dropped. 'Oh, that's right, you gave her a taste of real life.'

A flush spread across my father's cheeks.

Xavier pressed his advantage. 'Nothing fake about what happened to *him*.'

They both turned to look at me.

Across the room a woman started to sing a quavery ballad.

'Oh Christ,' Xavier muttered.

The gathering became a recital. We had to stand and listen as mourner after mourner took their turn. We heard 'My Love Is Like a Red Red Rose' and 'She Moved Through the Fair' and 'Somewhere Over the Rainbow' and even – from a dapper old queen whose dentures, like his jacket, were a size too big for him – a vibrato-rich 'Something in the Way She Moves'. A couple of the singers closed their eyes, the better to concentrate on the notes, while the listeners wore that effortlessly inward look actors assume when forced into the role of audience. There was a poignancy in those stilled faces lit by the iridescent lozenges of the 1950s chandelier. The softness of ageing skin, the wrinkles and thread veins and extra chins. *I'm thinking I'll never forgive you.* Why had I said it? Because it was true. And so I had done something equally unforgivable. Though she was beyond all that now. Beyond our lifelong disappointment with each other, beyond the brief, blessed truce we declared in our moments of gallows humour, beyond the sardonic eyebrow she might have lifted at this singalong, even as her vanity lapped it up.

When the songs petered out, Andro tapped his Mont Blanc pen against his glass and made a speech about how he was sure Lilias was looking down on us. My father made a tutting

264

sound, shouldering his way to the door. Glasses were lifted in a toast. One of the barmen restarted the CD.

'How long have you known him?' Xavier asked.

Here was the chance to satisfy my curiosity. Without a doubt Xavier wanted to tell. There might never be another opportunity. I remembered the safety of being held in his arms, the soft nap of moleskin against my eyelids, his barrel chest taking my weight. It would be so easy to ask, what did you mean when you said you gave her a taste of real life? But the next time I met my father, he would see at a glance that I knew.

How long had I known him? The six months since our first meeting? The three weeks since I'd found him on the hill? Or was the question immaterial, since I didn't really know him even now?

I leaned in to take my leave with a kiss on his cheek. 'Since before I was born,' I said.

1973

In the last weeks of pregnancy Lili is overtaken by an unexpected euphoria. After months of distracting awareness, she learns to live with her engorged breasts. Her queasiness is now appetite, her super-sensitive nostrils a gift. Her weariness has become a voluptuary's languor. She is amazed by the furnace heat she generates just lying here, the industry beneath her drum-tight flesh as her body tends the incubus. Once this thought repelled her, now it stirs her like a stranger's glance. Her nervousness about the birth is gone. They say some women rise above the pain: why not her? Her old infallible luck has returned. The week she travels to Edinburgh to ask Julian for a loan, he inherits seven thousand pounds from his detested father and, utterly compromised by the bequest, is only too glad to part with a hundred. Distracted by Jake's increasingly skilful touch in bed, she forgets her ulterior motive in approaching her least-discreet friend. Or, if she does not quite forget, it suits her not to dwell on the matter.

The cottage secured with Julian's cash is little more than a bothy. The factor doesn't care what they do inside its walls, so long as they continue to pay the rent and keep no dog to molest the pheasant poults in the adjacent wood. She spends Monday painting the table and chairs, Tuesday wheedling one of the farmhands into staining the floorboards black, and Wednesday cutting down a pair of curtains bought at a jumble sale in Blairgowrie. (She had hoped for curtains from the farm, but Mrs S takes a dim view of her son's new

266

ménage.) By the weekend she has created a rustic approxima-
tion of those London mews flats featured in the *Sunday Times*
colour magazine. Jake makes no comment, but she can tell he
approves. It's strange, washing his clothes, cooking his tea,
waking in the night to find his thigh pinning hers. Sometimes
he slides down the mattress to sleep with his face pressed to
her bump.

They don't talk much, even now. What is there to say that
their bodies don't communicate more eloquently? She can't
imagine a lifetime of this – or even, if she's honest, a year – but
minute by minute it is everything she needs. Food, shelter, the
wind's music in the wood next door, the aromatic heat of the
logs he saws off the storm-felled pine, the pulse-quickening
thought of the night to come. The only shadow on this life is
the hours after their lovemaking, the images that disturb her
fitful sleep.

That winter she has a recurring dream, her first since those
nightmares of standing naked on stage before some vast auditorium, or inching along a crumbling ledge a thousand feet
above ground. In this dream, too, she is up high, but indoors,
in an attic room she knows to be hers although nothing about
it is recogniseable. She looks out over what might once have
been a pleasant garden suburb. The surrounding buildings
have been reduced to rubble. The devastation stretches for
miles, forming mountains of stone and brick and splintered
wood. In the distance what remains of a house is on fire. She
watches the flickering, blue-tinged flames in excitement, until
she notices that they are crossing the rubble towards her.
Then she is afraid. She turns from the window. In a corner,
by the painted skirtingboard, burns a tiny blue-and-yellow
flame. The room is empty apart from a cot. Inside sleeps a
newborn baby. A girl, she knows, without knowing how,
the loose skin mottled, the spine still tending to a foetal curl.
The existence of this infant is always a surprise, no matter
how many times the dream recurs. Lili is worried about her

267

catching fire and so, in a pre-emptive measure that makes perfect dream-sense, she carries her to the sink and turns on the cold tap. As she holds the baby in the running water, the force of the jet flays the skin from her body. Underneath, she is still an embryo, a clot of translucent jelly threaded with blood. Lili watches, feeling a cool horror, her dreaming self detached from the woman in the dream, as the water blasts this layer of jelly away, leaving a fistful of slime and, when that too is gone, some looser protein, like albumen. And still she stands there, incapable of turning off the tap or pulling her hand out of the column of water, as the albumen, too, is washed down the drain, until all that remains is a single eye, runny in her palm, looking up at her.

Gun

There was the land and the sky. Squares of red earth broken by the plough, bleached fields of wintry grass and, from horizon to horizon, the milky blue. Shading my eyes against the sun, I could see his silhouette on the ridge, the dogs at his heels. He lifted the shotgun, training the barrels across the strath to find me in the sights. I stood perfectly still until he lowered the gun and set off down the slope.

'What was that about?' I asked.

Sometimes he answered, sometimes he didn't. I was learning not to take it personally.

'Here's where I was born,' he said.

This strath, he meant, amid these potato fields and grazing cattle.

'This was your farm?'

'It would have been, if I'd stayed.'

We were standing on a fraying ribbon of asphalt barely wide enough for a tractor, lined on one side by a beech hedge, on the other by wind-stunted thorns. The lichen covering their branches was the same colour as one of the dresses I had inherited from Lilias. Antique silk crêpe de Chine, reeking of mothballs and far too small, but I couldn't bring myself to throw it away. I touched a pale green frond, and there it was: the sadness. She had been with me all my life, more often in my thoughts than in the flesh. In a way, nothing had changed. I took a deep breath to clear my throat of the tears I couldn't shed. A hint of leaf mould carried from the coppice below us, mingling with the promissory scent of earth. Sun reflected white from the metalled road, a faint warmth on my face snatched away by the wind.

'It doesn't seem like Lilias's sort of place,' I said.

'She was wound tight as a fiddle string when she first came here, but she settled.'

I gazed across the landscape, wondering how different it was from the view she had known. That uPVC conservatory tacked onto the farmhouse. The wind turbines just visible on the horizon. Nothing too dramatic. *She settled.* Had she stayed, I would have been that fleet, sure-footed child with the wind in her hair and dirt under her nails, and maybe a sister or brother to run wild with across the fields. But even as I conjured this fantasy girlhood, I found myself listing everything I would have missed. Uncle Nellaney, the house of ticking clocks, every school holiday in a different theatrical digs. Not much to mourn there, but the thought of a wholly other Lilias gave me pause. And never meeting Frankie.

I turned from the view and followed my father through the gate into the field. He broke the gun and took two cartridges from his coat pocket, his face gaining that narrowed look it wore when he was absorbed in any task. When he offered me the gun I took it, raising it to my shoulder, nestling in to the cheek-plate as I'd seen him do, noting the movement of the barrels between my inward and outward breaths. He had taught Lilias to shoot. Apparently she was a natural. Odd that she'd never boasted of it. A pearl-handled revolver tucked in a black-lace garter would have been just her style.

I gave back the shotgun and he squinted down the sights, aiming at nothing I could make out. Only when I saw his finger on the trigger did it occur to me he might actually fire it with me beside him, six months pregnant.

'Not while I'm standing next to you.'

'*Wheesht*,' he hissed.

A fox was trotting along the bottom of the field. I put my

hand on his arm. He lowered the gun and turned to me with a look on his face I can only describe as spooked.

'What's the matter?'

Sunlight glinted off the metal legs of his glasses. The wind teased his hair. I was close enough to see the odd wiry strand still grew jet-black.

'I was here with your mother,' he said.

'When?'

He looked at me as if I knew. 'The day you were born.'

I was touched that he had brought me here, that he cared enough to sense I'd want to come.

'What happened?'

A pointless question, I thought, even as I asked it. Her waters broke, he took her to hospital. What always happens.

'He comes down off the ridge, city shoes and his fancy coat. I ken who he is as soon as I see him—'

I had no idea what he was talking about.

'He's wanting a fight. He doesn't care about her, but he's not going to have a teuchter have one over him. A shortarse, big head, older than I thought, not as fit as he thinks he is. He's peched from the walk. He stops up there, looking down on us.'

I got the picture. It was pretty much as I'd surmised: Lilias up to her old tricks, a shouting match, a punch or two thrown.

His glance dropped to the gun.

'It was my mother's,' he said. 'She got it back. After.'

It was then I asked the question that had been at the back of my mind ever since I first visited Shepherd's Cottage.

'Is it usual to keep a shotgun on top of the wardrobe?'

'It's out of the way. If the police call in.'

'And if they find it?'

A wagtail landed on the ground nearby.

'I go back to jail.'

The world slipped its axis, the ground tipping beneath me. He released a long, audible breath. 'Now you know.'

'Who was he?'

He jerked his head dismissively. 'He was a cunt. He grabs a loaded gun, my finger's stuck in the trigger guard...' His mouth worked soundlessly. 'He could have killed both of you—'

I didn't doubt his account. It was the corollary I could hardly believe. My mother, the *femme fatale*, the drama queen, had rewritten history to deny herself the most sensational role of her life. Small wonder she had treated herself to a consolatory fable. I realised then I had underestimated her, thinking she was oblivious to the irony of Lady Macbeth. A coded admission? Or just a gallows joke?

'The shock kicked off her contractions. I had to get her to Crieff in the back of the Land Rover. She was hysterical, I couldnae manage them both.' His eyes glittered. 'By the time I got back he was dead.'

'And she blamed you.'

'She blamed me, aye, but she couldnae forgive herself.'

'It didn't stop her sleeping around,' I said.

'I'm not talking about *sex*. It was love she had the problem with. She couldnae trust herself to be loved, you know that—'

I did, but I had never put the knowledge into words.

'And a man died for it. Two men, maybe – the man I was then, anyroad.' His eyes showed a sudden suspicion. 'This is the first you've heard of it?'

'Yes.'

'She never said?'

'No.'

She must have been tempted. *Your father killed a man.* There was a handy finality to it. A bad dad, nothing more to be said. Was she protecting me with her silence all those years, making sure I had someone to love? I might not have needed him so much if she'd let me love her. But she didn't believe in the kind of love that was there day in, day out, through bad reviews and three-quarters-empty houses, through boredom,

272

and getting old, and cancer. *I'll never forgive you.* I'd meant it when I said it. It seemed so long ago now. I could remember being angry with her, but the feeling itself was gone.

'So you went to see her when you got out of jail?'

'She was in a play in Aberdeen. My mother saw it in the paper. I'd not had a word from her in twenty years, but I thought if she saw me, if I could talk to her and…' *and hold her,* he meant. 'I thought I could convince her.'

'Maybe you could have,' I said, 'maybe that's why she wouldn't let you in.'

He broke the gun and put the cartridges back in his pocket. He was ready to move on, but there was something else I wanted to ask. He'd spent twenty years in prison, which meant he'd been out for another twenty.

'Why didn't you get in touch with me?'

His smile was sheepish. 'I couldn't find you. I've only just got on the Internet.'

He had found the means to track us down just as the cancer had dragged her out of reach.

'I should have tried to persuade her to see you,' I said.

He shook his head.

'I'm not saying I could have swung it, but I should have *tried.*'

'Ach,' his eyes connected with mine, 'I got more than I bargained for, anyroad.'

That was when it happened.

I gasped and clutched my belly. He stared at me with the same spooked expression he'd worn when he saw the fox.

I laughed and took him by the wrist, placing his hand over the spot so he, too, felt it. A fluttering deep inside me, the swimmer in her viscid pool.

'It's OK, Dad.'

His smile was shaky. 'She used to…' he had to swallow to get the words out '…I used to do this with you.'

Lanterns

It was one of those nights when sirens shriek along Great Western Road and tomcats yowl in tenement back courts. I hadn't been home since the funeral (if Glasgow was still my home), but it made sense to see out the last weeks of pregnancy ten minutes from a hospital. I locked the car and walked to the gate. Frankie hadn't drawn the blind. Under the protection of a broken street lamp, I stood and watched the scene inside.

Ruth was at the sink, washing utensils as soon as the cooks put them down. Torcuil, tied into my blue-and-white striped apron, was stirring something in a pan. Under Frankie's supervision, Meaghan was feeding oranges into the juicer. Kenny was chopping syboes at alarming speed with the cleaver I liked to keep out of harm's way in the bottom drawer. Every so often he crossed to the stove, knocking his head on the Mexican lampshade. The third time, he turned it into a gag, ducking the shade on the ouward journey, only to blunder into it on his way back. For a few seconds Ruth disappeared from view, returning with her red-faced baby daughter. Frankie took her. Surprise showed on everyone's faces. Evidently the crying had stopped. Ruth bowed to him. The baby in my belly did her little flip. Kenny looked up and waved through the window.

The children were marginally less like themselves once I'd entered the house, barely smiling at my lame joke about them teaching their dad and Frankie to cook. Although Ruth and

Kenny hid it better, they too seemed uneasy. Coded glances passed across the table. I gathered a surprise would be sprung after dinner. A kitten to find sitting on my daughter's face? A nippy little dog to sever a couple of fingers? I heard my mother's voice in my inner ear. *Wait and see, darling.*

We ate spaghetti with artichoke pesto, and a salad of bitter greens, lemon and capers zinging with folic acid, and *affogato* with goat's milk ice cream. At school Torcuil was learning to skip. He had tripped on the rope. He rolled up his trouser leg to show us the graze. This led to Kenny's broken nose (playing rugby), the snooker cue that had just missed Frankie's eye, Meaghan's broken toe and Ruth having the top of her finger sewn back on. My turn. The kids were fascinated by the laparoscopy scar. Kenny was appalled. 'Jaysus, yer man off the street would have done a neater job.'

Frankie made no comment.

When he got up to fetch the brandy I followed, intercepting him in the hall. 'Can I have a quick word?'

He looked me in the eye for a long couple of seconds before his wary nod.

We climbed the stairs and sat side by side on the bed.

I had phoned him five days earlier. It had all been very terse. He was busy at work, but could manage Friday night. Kenny and Ruth were coming round to dinner. I noted his need for chaperones, but maybe he wasn't fending me off, maybe we'd be more natural in the company of old friends, and by the end of the evening he'd realise how much poorer his life was without me. From the minute I arrived, I had been losing faith in this scenario.

I told myself he knew what I was going to say, but still it was hard.

'I want you to give me another chance—'

He exhaled in a long sigh.

'I am so sorry.'

'Are you? For what?'

I supposed I should have anticipated this.

'For sleeping with somebody else. Quitting the clinic and not telling you. Finding my dad and not telling you. Not telling you anything really. It's all such a mess.' I stopped, defeated by my own indictment.

'But I didn't help, staying in Glasgow every weekend?'

'I never expected Saturdays, I knew you had to work.'

'You could have come home.'

'I felt I was doing enough, stuck on the farm, being injected with God knows what. It's only an hour's drive. I thought you owed me that much.'

'So you shagged somebody else to square the balance sheet?' I looked down. 'I suppose.'

He said nothing. I wondered if he was censoring some inflammatory remark, or was he just embarrassed by my grovelling now it was too late? *You could have come home.* Would he have said that if we were finished? Wasn't the impulse to quarrel a hopeful sign?

'It might not be my baby either.'

He squinted as if I'd said something unbelievably crass.

'Read the newspapers,' I said. 'It happens. And we know they're not exactly careful.'

For the past month I'd thought about little else. A clearly Sinhalese baby. Being sued by the genetic parents and forced to take a test. Red-top reporters camped outside the door. Even with Frankie's fame dimmed by three months on radio, his wife would be news. Or his ex-wife. I might get lucky with the genetic lottery, her colouring might suggest she was mine, but there would always be a doubt. Was it *right* to keep somebody else's baby, even if I had carried her to term? How would I feel about a child with my DNA somewhere out there in the world? Then there was the ticking bomb of the child herself, her sense of identity, her right to know – and to reject her substitute mother, if she got that far. If I kept her safe from asthma attacks and nut allergies and speeding cars.

276

I said some of this.

'You've got it all worked out, haven't you?'

There were angry words I could have said then, but they weren't going to help, so I shrugged. 'You know me, always planning ahead.'

'Aye,' under his breath, 'I know you.'

I had a burning feeling around the eyes I remembered from childhood. 'Don't be cruel, Frankie. Tell me yes or no.' Was it a mistake, admitting the possibility of refusal? 'It doesn't have to be for ever. Even if you just put up with me till she's born. I want her to hear your voice in the womb.'

'Why?'

'So she can find you one day.'

In the silence I could hear the ticking of the bedside clock.

His voice was so low he might have been talking to himself. 'All I wanted was a wee Freya—'

I stared at him.

'But I've been thinking: I guess the nipper was always going to be himself.'

'Herself.'

'Whatever—'

I waited, hardly daring to hope.

'A wean needs two parents.'

'She might have two parents,' I said. 'There might be a couple out there childless because of us.'

'There might be. We don't know.'

'We could find out.'

'But we won't.'

'And you're OK with that?'

His eyes held mine for a moment. I knew the question should never have been asked, that I'd left him no choice but to lie, and that when he lied I would choose to believe him.

'I'm going to be a father. OK, my sperm count's twenty-three and a half, but I don't know one of the plucky wee bastards didn't score the goal.' He stood up, as if everything

277

were settled now he'd decided to co-parent. As if our getting back together were too self-evident, or too self-evidently impossible, to discuss. 'Kenny and Ruth'll be wondering what's happened to us.'

I looked up at him. 'And me?'

'What about you?'

'Have you been thinking about me?'

A mordant breath. 'A forty-year habit's hard to break.'

Again I heard my mother's voice, that sing-song phrase. *Wait and see.* But I couldn't wait, I had to be sure.

'And?'

He sat down again. 'OK, I didn't drive up there to see you. It's not an hour, it's three hours, ninety minutes there and ninety minutes back, and even when we were in the same room it was like you were on the other side of the world. Aye, maybe I did work too hard, but it wasnae just me. You were so mad about being signed off. I knew what was going to happen when you heard about the second count – it was one more way I'd taken a loan of you. So I kept shtum. Then I find out you're pregnant. I was going to call Doctor Ross, ask her if there was any way they could have cocked the test up twice. *I dialled the fucking clinic.* I knew, but. There's this thing you do when you're not being straight with me.' He made his voice clipped and efficient. *'Hi, I'm going to have a baby.* It's like talking to the speaking clock. You're playing away from home, I had Scott taking me for a mug at work – fuck's sake, what am I, some sort of patsy? I thought, who's to blame here, how'm I turning it on myself? How'm I no—'

'Blaming me,' I said.

He didn't deny it.

'Next thing, I've got the police at the door. I thought something had happened to you. When they said it was your mother, you know what I said? *Thank God.* "You'll tell your wife?" Aye, of course, officer. I'd nae fucking idea where you were. Phoning him was bad enough – I had to drive halfway across the fucking country with him. I saw that place, like something out of a Stephen King novel, and I thought, we're barking up the wrong tree here. I couldn't see you spending five minutes in a dump like that. The old feller lets us in. You're sitting there quite joco. You've put me through hell. So then I tell you about Lilias, and the look on your face, the way you just...' he clenched his fist, his voice dropping away, '...*crumpled*. It killed me.'

He gave another long sigh.

'So I can stay?'

'Just for tonight.'

I looked at him.

'It's a *joke*, Freya.'

But it would be a long time before we could laugh about this.

I glanced down at the bed, made up with our best sheets, crisp from the airing cupboard. On top of the kist was a vase of roses with the refrigerated look of blooms flown in from another season. The room was dressed for romance, like his bachelor flat all those years ago.

And then it came to me, what he needed to hear, the words I'd said so many times, though never with so much feeling.

'I love you.'

He lifted his head. 'You think I'd still be here if you didn't?'

When we got downstairs the baby was alert and vocal in her mother's arms. Ruth pulled a smiling, desperate face that said she'd get no sleep that night. Kenny was busy in the garden. Torcuil and Meaghan were hopping from foot to foot. They made me close my eyes as they led me outside.

I stood on the path, the children's hands hot in mine, the night air pleasantly cool on my skin after the centrally heated house. I could smell the damp mulch on the flower beds and diesel from the buses on Hyndland Road. The breeze dashed a few spots of rain against my eyelids, and with them a sense of benison, like the feeling I'd had lifting my face to Frankie's to be kissed.

'You can open your eyes now,' Torcuil said.

They were rudimentary contraptions: a pad soaked with meths, a wire frame and a tissue-paper sack. Kenny lit the wicks. I wasn't sure they'd leave the ground but, after bobbing on the lawn for a minute or so, each floated into the air.

'They're a present for your mummy,' Meaghan said, 'because she's dead.'

Ruth caught my eye. We managed not to laugh.

Our seven upturned faces watched the sky. The lanterns were slow to gain height. For a long time I thought the flames might blow out or the paper catch fire. Five hundred feet up, they met the wind and started to drift. Higher they rose, growing smaller, but still visible to the naked eye. Like stars, pure and white. Minutes passed, and they were still there, impossibly high. The children were getting restless. Part of me wanted to say *Thank you, that was lovely, shall we go back inside?* But I held still, my eyes following those pinpricks of light as they floated ever higher, ever further away.

Acknowledgements

Many people helped with the writing of this novel. Thank you, Jim Carruthers, Mark Clements, Geraldine Doherty, Charlotte Fleming, Sandy Ingram, Iain Mackintosh, Siobhan O'Tierney, Heather Reid, Graham Spiers, David Sutton, Fiona Thackeray, Bill Walker and Alice Walsh. An early draft was written while I was the William Soutar Fellow in Perth, in time funded by the former Scottish Arts Council. I am especially indebted to my agent, Judy Moir, and my editor, Moira Forsyth, for helping to sort the wheat from the chaff, and to Jim Melvin for keeping me company in all those farm B&Bs.

www.sandstonepress.com

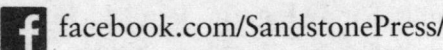 facebook.com/SandstonePress/

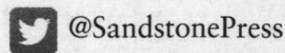 @SandstonePress